"It Takes . . . Every Bit of Strength I Have To Let You Go . . ."

Bryce drew back into his own seat, his breathing still ragged. "I don't know what happens to me when I kiss you, Katie!"

His words sounded so plaintive and their surprise so equaled her own that Katie gave a short cry. "Oh, Bryce, I don't know what happens to me, either!"

His abashed eyes met hers, their dark concern beginning to lighten with relief. Their hands linked again, naturally yet loosely, and after a moment they laughed together, no self-consciousness in the sound.

"The next time I try to give you a brotherly kiss," Bryce said, "you mustn't part your lips so invitingly or hold me so tight."

"That's right, blame the woman," she accused, but already her tingling body welcomed his promise of a "next time."

ANNE LACEY

began writing as a child in the small Arkansas town where she was born. She currently lives and works in Texas, though she considers southern Louisiana her spiritual home and would love to return. She is an exercise and health food nut who also loves to travel.

Dear Reader:

Romance readers have been enthusiastic about Silhouette Special Editions for years. And that's not by accident: Special Editions were the first of their kind and continue to feature realistic stories with heightened romantic tension.

The longer stories, sophisticated style, greater sensual detail and variety that made Special Editions popular are the same elements that will make you want to read book after book.

We hope that you enjoy this Special Edition today, and will enjoy many more.

The Editors at Silhouette Books

ANNE LACEY
A Song in the Night

Silhouette Special Edition

Published by Silhouette Books New York

America's Publisher of Contemporary Romance

Silhouette Books by Anne Lacey

Love Feud (SE #93)
Softly at Sunset (SE #155)
A Song in the Night (SE #188)

SILHOUETTE BOOKS, a Division of Simon & Schuster, Inc.
1230 Avenue of the Americas, New York, N.Y. 10020

ISBN: 0-671-53688-5

First Silhouette Books printing September, 1984

10 9 8 7 6 5 4 3 2 1

Map by Ray Lundgren

America's Publisher of Contemporary Romance

Printed in the U.S.A.

BC91

A Song
in the Night

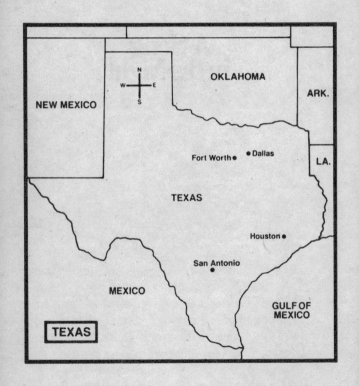

Chapter One

Eighty-nine days and counting!

Pleasure and anticipation ran through the fabric of Katie Brentwood's busy evening, providing a ground swell of inner excitement as she stepped off the hospital elevator. In just eighty-nine days her life would change dramatically and irrevocably. It was all a little scary but was thrilling at the same time.

Meanwhile there was business as usual and an irate patient awaited her in Room 627. Katie's heels tapped their way briskly down the tiled corridor. A small cluster of nurses with head nurse Sheila Rigley in the forefront stood outside the room. Katie nodded to them pleasantly and they parted to either side of the door, giving her a straight path within.

Katie stepped inside the open door, looked up—way up—and knew she had trouble. It was stamped on the disgusted face of Sheik Ali Ben Hassim, written in his flaring nostrils and disapproving black eyes, and Katie read his message clearly.

The sheik had no intention of dealing with a *woman* even if this American hospital had been misguided enough to hire her!

Nevertheless, Katie plunged in gamely. "What is the trouble, sir?" she said in her most courteous voice.

Angrily, the sheik swung away from her to regard the huddled group of nurses standing just beyond his door. "I wish to speak with the hospital administrator," he announced coldly in Oxford-accented English.

"Mr. Ben Hassim, I am the administrator," Katie replied and drew herself up to her full five-foot-five height. "My name is Kathryn Brentwood."

The sheik turned back to her, his expression now one of infuriating male amusement. "I have already met the administrator," he said coolly.

"Yes, you met Mr. Harvey, another administrator," Katie said, keeping her voice carefully level. "I am the evening administrator. Now, do you care to tell me what is wrong?"

She saw his look on her sharpen incredulously. Could this woman possibly be serious? Could she be running this immense teaching hospital and shocktrauma center in Dallas, Texas? Katie saw his dark eyes narrowing on the beeper clipped to the waist of her smart black suit, the hospital badge pinned to her jacket collar, the clipboard and pen she held.

The wide nostrils of his sharply beaked nose flared once again. "I will speak with the day administrator," he announced loftily.

"Sir, you will speak with me or with no one," Katie

replied, her voice as implacable as his. "I am the administrator on call."

Outraged, the sheik turned with a swirl of his long, white robes. A click of his brown fingers summoned the dainty Arab girl from her perch on the sofa in the VIP suite. Katie had heard from Darrell Harvey that the sheik had a young wife less than half his age. She was a delicate little thing, with frightened doe eyes.

Katie turned away, too. If the sheik wished to act like this, so be it! She had plenty of other things to do. It was eight o'clock and she still hadn't made her rounds.

She had almost reached the hall when the sheik's imperious voice stopped her. "You will call my doctor!" he commanded ominously.

Katie swung back to regard him once again. His little wife whom rumor had it, he usually called "my Flower," had already scurried into the adjoining hospital room.

"Mr. Ben Hassim, your doctor left written orders," Katie said, choosing her words with care. "There is no reason for him to be disturbed—certainly when I don't even know what is wrong here. Unless you tell me, he will *not* be called."

The angry Arab stared at her again. Katie had spoken with firmness and authority. To the sheik she might be just a weak, silly female, but within the walls of this institution she had strength and clout. Slowly, the realization of her power dawned on him.

Katie watched the sheik's demeanor change. "Do you wish to tell me what is wrong?" she offered again.

"I have had nothing to eat!" Apparently, the aggrieved sheik had decided that of the two evils—

speaking to a woman as though she actually had sense or starving through the rest of the night—addressing Katie was the lesser.

Katie drew a breath. This was frequently a source of trouble. She glanced over her shoulder at head nurse Rigley. "Ms. Brentwood, we served him a light dinner at six—" the nurse began.

"Pah!" The sheik exploded in a torrent of rage. What sort of *food* was that thin broth, the quivering Jello, the tiny carton of milk and a cup of lukewarm tea? He was a sick man who needed to keep up his strength! Furthermore, his Flower had not found her guest tray to her liking either. The food was tasteless and bland. It was all quite terrible!

Quietly, Katie expressed her regrets. She was sorry the sheik was hungry, but a liquid diet was exactly what his doctor had ordered. It was standard fare for patients, such as himself, who must undergo rigorous tests tomorrow morning. Now, as for the Blossom . . .

"She's 'the Flower,' Katie," hissed Sheila Rigley, and Katie could almost feel the inaudible ripple of mirth running through the listening nurses. They were probably holding their sides to keep from laughing out loud.

Very well. Katie expressed her profound sorrow that the Flower had not found her tray delectable. Unfortunately, the kitchen for special orders was now closed, but the hospital's cafeteria remained open twenty-four hours a day. If the Flower wished to go to the cafeteria . . .

The sheik's black eyes widened in horror. Allow his Little Jewel to go to a public cafeteria where strange, foreign men would stare at her? It was unthinkable!

Furthermore, the sheik had need of his Jewel. The abomination growing within his skull, which had brought him to this tragic pass, making his head ache so constantly and relentlessly, was eased only when his Little Jewel massaged his temples with her soft, pale hands.

"Well then," said Katie heartlessly, "the Pearl will just have to go hungry, too."

"She's his 'Little Jewel,' Katie." When Sheila whispered the second correction it was too much for the nurses. Guffaws escaped them, then swelled, until the mirth in the hallway resembled the laugh track of a TV sitcom.

Outraged, the sheik spun about and stormed into the safety of his hospital room. He slammed the door with such a resounding boom that Katie winced, hoping it hadn't disturbed Mrs. Sarabeth Winslow, the occupant of the adjoining suite. Mrs. Winslow, wife of the renowned senator, had been admitted as another possible candidate for neurosurgery, but extensive tests had recently ruled out any abnormalities. It was now thought that Mrs. Winslow's persistent headaches stemmed from depression—a likely possibility, Katie thought, for she had met the senator last night. In his folksy, homespun way he was every bit as chauvinistic as the sheik.

Sighing, Katie picked up the pen attached to her clipboard and made an entry on the Night Administrator's Report that the sheik and his Blossom—correction, his Flower—had been dissatisfied with the food.

By the time she returned to the hall, the nurses were all back at their station. Only Sheila Rigley stood waiting for Katie, a question in her blue eyes.

"Go ahead and call the sheik's doctor," Katie directed as she and Sheila began walking down the corridor. "If he checks out of here in a towering rage, we could get some adverse publicity, and we don't need that! Who is his doctor, by the way?"

"He has the two biggest guns: Blakely and that new man, Dr. Emerson."

Katie's heart jumped at mention of the second name. "I see." For a moment she stared blindly at a spot on the wall. "I hope you can track down one of them, Sheila."

"That's easy. They're downstairs," Sheila announced.

Katie held on to her clipboard. "You mean Dr. Emerson—and Dr. Blakely, of course, are both here tonight?"

Sheila nodded. "All available neurosurgeons have been called in. I heard about it on my dinner break. Life Copter has flown in two auto wrecks, one gunshot and one motorcycle," she said, describing the victims in hospital shorthand. "They all have head and/or spinal injuries."

Katie groaned. She had known about the flights but not the specific injuries. "The next thing I know, Dr. Blakely will be screaming to shut down the helicopters."

Sheila nodded again. "He panics. Fortunately, Emerson seems to have a cool head."

Cool and calculating, no doubt, Katie thought to herself.

"Hang in there," Sheila advised.

"You, too!"

They smiled at each other, then Sheila reached for the telephone and Katie headed toward the elevator. They were both competent, professional women who understood each other and, if once their personal lives had crossed, it hadn't affected their working relationship.

While Katie waited for the elevator to arrive, she wondered if Sheila was still dating Doug Sears. He was one of the dashing helicopter pilots who at thirty, with his tousled brown hair, reckless eyes and disarming grin seemed still to be the essence of youth.

Katie had dated Doug last year when she was still relatively new to Harwick Memorial Hospital and before she had learned that he was the longtime boyfriend of the head nurse. As soon as Katie heard of their relationship, she had quietly refused all future dates with Doug. Although he was handsome and fun and Katie had missed him for a time, she had no intention of participating in a triangle.

Men! she thought now, stabbing the elevator button again. Why did so many of the exasperating creatures want a harem? She felt quite sure that Senator Winslow's young blond secretary performed more than clerical duties. Undoubtedly, that secretary was a contributing cause of Mrs. Winslow's headaches and depression.

I'd rather never marry, Katie thought, than to wind up with an American sheik!

She was twenty-eight, and love and marriage seemed quite remote, especially since she'd made the career decision that kept her counting the days. Not that Katie was averse to marriage. When younger, she had confidently assumed that one day the right man would come along. She had spun daydreams about him, envisioning a mature man who would understand and appreciate what Katie had achieved and be supportive of her career. But for the last year or two she had begun to wonder if such a paragon existed.

Tonight, for some reason, her mind flew again to Dr. James Bryce Emerson. He had arrived at the Harwick-Harding Medical School, which adjoined the hospital, just a week or two before. Professionally, Katie knew a good deal about him since his excellent reputation had preceded him. He'd been lured away from Stanford to Harwick-Harding on the strength of Dr. Ash Blakely's promise to retire at the end of the year. At that time Dr. Emerson would assume chairmanship of the troubled Neurosurgery department. And she also had memories of Bryce Emerson from ten years before.

She'd had one glimpse of Bryce the week before. She and Steve Wills, the night administrator, had been standing outside their office when Dr. Blakely and a tall, black-haired man with rather hawklike features came out of Flight Operations.

Surprised, Katie had stared. Was *that* . . . ? Oh, could it be . . . ? Unconsciously, she touched Steve's elbow. Since she worked from 4:00 P.M. to midnight, when Steve took over for the rest of the night, they'd grown to be friends. "Steve, is that who I think it is?" she had said softly.

"That's the California hotshot." Steve had nodded. "You can tell 'cause he's got that Pacific tan. Supposedly, he's gonna overhaul Neurosurgery."

For a moment Katie had stared, wondering why her heart insisted on racing so. "He's changed," she had murmured.

"Changed? You mean you knew him?" Steve had asked, surprised.

"We met ages ago in Seattle. He was a resident. I was a kid." Katie's voice had slid downward as she had repeated, "He's really changed!"

"No wonder, the hours those guys work! Don't you want to say hello to him?" Steve had asked.

The two neurosurgeons had already turned and were walking briskly down the hall. "No!" Katie had breathed as her eyes followed the green scrub suit that outlined Dr. Emerson's broad strong back revealingly. He towered several inches over the shorter, wiry Dr. Blakely.

Steve had looked at Katie questioningly. She knew she'd aroused his curiosity, but she felt in no mood to explain further. What could she say? *I was once a one-night stand for Bryce Emerson.* That would certainly open Steve's eyes wide.

Katie was surprised and discomfited by the memories that came rushing back. She could still see the blue shadows gathered in the call room where they'd been. She could still hear the patter of rain on the windowpane and remember the glow in Bryce's gray eyes.

Katie had not seen Bryce since the week before, but just knowing that he was at the hospital tonight made her heart lift a little.

What's wrong with me? she thought irritably as she waited for the elevator to arrive. When its doors finally clanked open, she stepped inside and pushed the down button. She had little use for surgeons with their inflated egos and omniscient airs. Heart surgeons and neurosurgeons, the elites of the medical profession, were usually gods to their patients and, all too often, to themselves as well.

Of course, in fairness, Katie had to admit that her opinion was jaundiced. Physicians and hospital administrators were natural antagonists, mixing about as well as oil and water did. Both cared about the fate of patients; beyond that their special areas of concern inevitably brought them into abrupt conflicts. Doctors complained about the state' of operating rooms and the nature of nurses. They badgered Administration for the latest, expensive medical equipment. Administrators, by contrast, fought for the hospital's employees and its overall reputation. They were charged with holding the budget in line and showing a satisfactory amount of revenue at the end of each fiscal year.

Katie's musings ended when the beeper clipped to her waist began its shrill pulsing alarm. She reached down and clicked it on. "Ms. Brentwood, come to the Emergency Center STAT," a male voice implored. STAT was medical jargon for immediately.

What now? Katie thought grimly. Ordinarily, Monday nights were quiet but tonight, the night of a full moon, was running her ragged. When the elevator reached the ground she hurried off to answer the latest summons, aware of the overhead clatter of an incoming helicopter. Administrators agreed with astrologists that a full moon increased human violence. Tonight there would be more "knife and gun business" than usual.

Katie, braced for the worst, was relieved to find that the trouble in the Emergency Center was only Bessie.

Bessie was a huge woman of mixed race and indeterminate age. Toothless and cunning, she was one of a group of transients who lived in the large, danger-ridden park just two blocks south of the hospital.

The transients were mostly alcoholics, drug addicts and prostitutes. They invaded Harwick Memorial Hospital regularly, and the staff had to be vigilant to keep ahead of them. Sometimes the transients came to get food from the vending machines, using slugs or well-aimed kicks for payment. Sometimes they sought safe naps on waiting-room benches. If these unfortunates, the outcasts of society, weren't evicted quickly they were likely to pass out in stairwells or to panhandle in halls.

Bessie came over periodically for showers. She had discovered the gleaming, inviting shower stall in the call room next to the Emergency Center. Whenever she could evade detection by Security or other hospital personnel, she slipped in, undressed and availed herself of the free soap and hot, running water.

Katie found a distraught young intern, half-dead on his feet from putting in long hours on call. He had stumbled into the bathroom only to be confronted by the grinning Bessie, who waved at him from beneath a cascade of water. Katie could appreciate that Bessie in her birthday suit, must have been quite a startling sight.

She waited until Bessie had finished her leisurely shower then phoned Security. Elliot Wainwright, the guard who arrived, was familiar with Bessie and her foibles.

"Last time I escorted her off the grounds she propositioned me," he said in an aggrieved voice to Katie.

"Maybe you'll get lucky again tonight, Elliot," Katie replied.

Elliot threw her a disgusted look as he got a hold on Bessie's arm.

At 9:45 a fire alarm in the basement went off, and

Katie sped down to check it out. Every hospital's greatest fear was fire. Mercifully, this was a false alarm. The sensitive smoke detector had probably been triggered by an employee smoking a cigarette. Katie turned off the alarm and hurried away to answer her next call. This was an anguished patient who had found a column of ants marching across the floor of her room. Katie arranged to have the patient transferred to another room and noted on her Night Administrator's Report that Maintenance should come in tomorrow and spray for insects.

Eighty-nine days and counting, Katie reminded herself wearily.

At 10:00 she was notified that Life Copter was flying out to pick up a gunshot victim. At 10:10 the predictable summons she had been dreading finally arrived. Grimly, she walked down the deserted corridors to meet Dr. Blakely outside the Shocktrauma Unit.

While she walked, Katie's mind hummed busily. Shock was the inevitable result of every traumatic accident—car wreck, gunshot, stabbing and so forth. It wasn't the broken limbs, the crushed chest, the bullet in the abdomen or even the blood clot on the brain that killed a critically injured patient; it was shock. Whenever heavy bleeding caused an extreme loss of blood pressure, shock followed immediately. It triggered a number of insidious bodily processes that led, quite remorselessly and inevitably, to the patient's death.

Yes, shock was the killer if it wasn't halted quickly, before a patient's brain cells began to wink out, so time—precious *time,* measured in fleeting minutes—was of the essence. Only in recent years had the medical profession discovered this. Now special shocktrauma units, such as the one at Harwick Memorial, were the result. Critically injured patients were flown there by helicopter where the Shocktrauma Unit stayed in a state of constant readiness, always prepared to take heroic measures. First, the trauma team had to snatch the patient back from death by stabilizing his heartbeat and breathing. If they could stop the bleeding and restore the patient's blood pressure within an hour of the accident, they could probably save his life. After that, the patient could be turned over to the specialty surgeons such as the orthopedic, thoracic or neuro.

It was at this point at Harwick Memorial that the beautifully functioning, lifesaving system occasionally threatened to slip a cog. If a number of patients with head and/or spinal injuries requiring neurosurgery were all admitted within a relatively short period of time, Dr. Blakely would panic—and Katie Brentwood would soon hear about it.

As soon as Katie entered the Shocktrauma waiting room she saw that Bryce Emerson was also with Dr. Blakely. Immediately, her heart reacted by producing a series of bumps and knocks. The younger neurosurgeon, clad in a green hospital scrub suit, leaned back against the wall. Katie's eyes flickered over him in her best attempt to be impersonal, and the grayish eyes that gazed back at her were equally impersonal. His silent, deferential attitude reminded her that Dr. Blakely was still in charge, so Katie turned to confront the older man.

Dr. Blakely greeted Katie with his customary fire. "Ms. Brentwood, two patients are presently being stabilized by the trauma team and will be prepped for neurosurgery. That should tie up both Dr. Emerson and myself for the rest of the evening. We have now been informed that Life Copter is bringing in a gunshot victim with a bullet in his brain. Dr. Weaver is coming in to take over that case. I *insist* that any further patients for neurosurgery be diverted to other hospitals. We simply don't have enough staff to handle them!''

"You're asking me to shut down Life Copter?'' Katie asked bluntly. Again her eyes flew to the tall figure in greens who was leaning against the wall, listening to them. His eyes met hers briefly, and Katie's heart speeded up again.

"I am indeed,'' Dr. Blakely said, his voice equally blunt. "Either shut down the helicopters or transport neuro patients to the shocktrauma unit in Ft. Worth.''

"Dr. Blakely, you know I can't do that,'' Katie said firmly. "This matter has been discussed fully by our operations council. It was agreed that we can't ground three helicopters and decline to treat patients just on the chance that neurosurgery will get overloaded.''

" 'Just on the *chance'?''* Dr. Blakely repeated Katie's words, his tone incredulous. "Ms. Brentwood, what is the point of having Life Copters if a patient then has to lie on a gurney and wait for a surgeon? Why, he might as well come in by ambulance or mule train!''

"No, not really—'' Katie started, but Dr. Blakely was just warming to his subject and was in no frame of mind to be interrupted.

She listened patiently while he explained the obvious to her once again: that trauma patients frequently suffered multiple injuries; that while certain injuries, such as broken bones, could and did wait, what often could *not* wait were injuries to skull and spine. Dr. Blakely then itemized the patients who would receive neurosurgery tonight and estimated the long hours required for each operation. Now, did she understand why he didn't want the helicopters bringing in any more such patients?

"Of course, I understand," Katie said, determined to keep her voice level and reasonable. "But Life Copter also flies in medical patients. We transport premature infants, heart attacks, burn victims and high-risk pregnancies who *don't* require neurosurgery. My point is, of course, that we never know from one night to the next what type of emergencies will arise. We simply do the best we can with a given set of circumstances."

Dr. Blakely slapped an angry hand down on an empty Life Copter stretcher. "One night—possibly this very night!—you'll get more neuro patients than we can possibly handle," he warned. "If they stack up, there will be hell to pay. I can promise you that, Ms. Brentwood!"

"It's never happened before," Katie said hopefully.

"The responsibility will be on *your* head if it does!" Dr. Blakely blustered.

Oh, no, it won't! Katie longed to shoot back. You're the chairman of neurosurgery, why don't *you* rectify the situation? Providing adequate staff coverage to meet emergencies is your responsibility, not mine!

She didn't say the words trembling on her tongue because she realized they would be unfair. It wasn't Dr. Blakely's fault that neurosurgeries lasted for hours, tying up both surgeon and operating room. It wasn't his fault that one of his staff had drowned recently in a boating accident or that another had accepted a job at an East Coast hospital and resigned.

Nor was it Dr. Blakely's fault that he was a weary old man looking forward to retirement and that the new pace of trauma medicine was too fast and furious for him. Still, something had to be done by the Neurosurgery department and quickly!

Perhaps Bryce Emerson would know what to do, Katie thought as she reached for the pen attached to her clipboard. "I will note your request," she told Dr. Blakely.

"See that you do!"

"Keep me posted," Katie added, implying that if circumstances changed, she might be persuaded to change her mind.

"You can be assured I will!" Dr. Blakely snapped. He turned and stormed out.

Dr. Emerson, who had said not a word, stood away from the wall and cast an appraising glance at Katie.

For a moment, she wondered: Doesn't he recognize me at all?

No, he obviously did not. Well, what did she expect? she thought with chagrin. It had been ten years and all their meetings then had been brief, even the final and intimate one. He'd probably had dozens—no, *hundreds* —of women in his bed both before and after her.

Perhaps it was better that he didn't remember. Would she prefer a leer, a wink or a suggestive remark? Yet glancing again at the strangely silent man, she could not imagine him doing anything so crude. How changed Bryce was! His once jet-black hair was now threaded at the temples with gray. Katie had remembered his having quite a solid build and an unlined, youthful face. The decade since then had whittled him to the bone until his craggy features held a Lincolnesque cast.

"Oh, Miss Brentwood—" Dr. Emerson said.

His voice had a musical quality. It lilted melodiously, stopping Katie as she turned to leave. "Yes?" she said, stirred by a tone she had never forgotten.

"I spoke with Sheik Ali Ben Hassim a short time ago and think I've calmed him down. Asking the nurse to call me was a wise decision. If I hadn't talked with him, I think he might have checked out."

"Good. I'm glad you approve." Katie nodded. "And this decision?"

He hesitated for a moment. "You're taking a calculated risk."

"I realize that," she said a trifle stiffly.

"Of course you do." His voice implied that he didn't make the mistake of underestimating her as Ash Blakely did. But that grateful realization was tempered by the dismay of knowing that he didn't remember her. Otherwise, why wouldn't he say something?

Bryce Emerson threw her a courteous departing smile and memory chimed again. Katie remembered that curve of his mouth and flash of even, gleaming-white teeth. His eyes were still the same, she realized, clear, gray blue and lustrous.

Before he had not been so deeply tanned, but early spring in Seattle had not provided any warm, sunny beaches. Now his bronzed skin was faintly lined at the outer corners of his eyes and his mouth, and across his forehead.

He was still a very attractive man and radiated masculine virility. In the V of his green scrub suit she could see the patch of thick dark chest hair. How tall was he? Katie wondered, and her interested gaze measured him as at least six feet two. He had long, sinewy arms lightly covered with the same dark hair and long, lean thighs. The wide-shouldered, trim-waisted body outlined revealingly by his green scrub suit was entirely, almost blatantly, male.

Katie turned again to go, rather disturbingly aware that his gaze had been assessing her as thoroughly as she had eyed him. A little sensation of alarm tightened her throat as she walked away, her heels clicking softly on the tile floor.

At 10:20 things finally quieted down enough for Katie to take her belated dinner break. This was probably the lull before the storm, she thought, relishing the hospital hush that was presently unbroken by the clatter of helicopter rotors. When the bars closed, the night would likely explode again. There would be shoot-outs in parking lots. Accidents on freeways. Rapes . . . batterings . . . child abuse. The number of human disasters seen regularly at a hospital such as Harwick Memorial was incredible. At least, anything that happened after midnight was Steve Wills's to deal with. By 12:20 A.M. Katie was usually home in her apartment near the medical center and, ten minutes later, abed and asleep.

In the cafeteria, there was only the subdued rattle of dishes and clink of silverware. Katie took a tray and inspected the offerings on the large revolving carousel. She selected a plate with sliced roast beef and two vegetables, then succumbed to a piece of chocolate pie.

She filled a mug with coffee, paid the yawning cashier and took a table against the wall.

There were very few people in the cafeteria at this late hour. She could identify several hollow-eyed people brooding over coffee cups and well-filled ashtrays as relatives of patients. The rest of the occupants of the huge room were either in whites or scrubs.

Eighty-nine days, Katie thought again with a tingle of anticipation. In less than three months, she would be through forever with all of this—with the murder and mayhem, violence and viciousness, emergencies and alarms. She would be back in the cool, green, rainy country of her childhood, away from sweltering cities and mean, hard streets. She would be high in the mountains where the clean, sweet air carried the fragrance of spruce and pine. Just a few miles away was the Pacific Ocean, its waves crashing over great boulders, its beaches gray from volcanic ash. She could walk a few miles through a rain forest to reach the beach, then sit and watch the foamy surf roll in, its endless rhythm refreshing her mind and heart.

In eighty-nine days she would be with children, too. Bright, clear-eyed children who would need her concern and support. Oh, how wonderful it was all going to be when she was back in that magical world of forests and sea!

A shadow dropped over her table, ending her reverie.

"May I join you, Katie?" asked Bryce Emerson.

Chapter Two

K atie! He had called her by her familiar nickname, so he did remember her after all. She looked up the long length of greens, now topped by a white lab coat, and was so startled, surprised and happy that she couldn't even muster a reply. She nodded instead.

So she had not been as forgettable as she had feared!

Bryce slid into the chair opposite hers, holding his mug of coffee. Again he smiled—that curving, flashing smile that lit up his eyes and did erratic things to Katie's heartbeat. She finally found her voice and realized that it would be immature of her not to acknowledge the past.

"It's been a long time since Seattle, Bryce."

Nothing Katie had imagined prepared her for the way his eyes blazed. "So you do remember me!" he exclaimed in amazement.

"I wasn't likely to ever forget," she said dryly. After

all, he had been the first man in her life. Before he could respond, she rushed on hastily, "I'm more surprised that you remember me."

"You were very young—barely eighteen, wasn't it?—but you were beautiful even then, Katie."

She felt a flash of color sting her cheeks. She was both embarrassed by his compliment and strangely, deliciously pleased. Yet she had no wish to discuss the past further. "How could you have finished operating so soon?" she said curiously, returning them to the present.

"My patient died before we could get him on the operating table," Bryce replied regretfully. "We weren't able to resuscitate him. So I decided to grab a break while I could."

"That's wise of you," Katie approved. Her next thought followed automatically. There was a neurosurgeon available now. So much for Dr. Blakely and his unnecessary panic.

Bryce's eyes went to the chocolate pie on her tray. "Hey, that pie looks good."

"It's chocolate bavarian," she informed him. "One of the few things our cafeteria does really well."

"I think I'll try a piece. Be right back," he said and rose.

He needed to rest and eat while he could, for neurosurgery was often quite lengthy. Operations of four, five and more hours were commonplace. The surgeons had to be a hardy breed with plenty of stamina as well as patience and meticulousness to do delicate cranial or spinal exploration.

Unfortunately, the exacting, time-consuming surgery took its toll on them in other ways. The neurosurgeon, who had to exercise such inhuman patience in the OR, often had to live with results that were less than ideal. Sometimes, as the old hospital adage went, the operation was a success but the patient died. Or the neurosurgeon might manage to save the patient's life but a human vegetable would be left, requiring a lifetime of specialized care.

The frustrations of such experiences often left its practitioner explosive from tension. Away from the OR, an immature man might take out his tension on his subordinates, his family or anyone else within range.

Oh, yes, Katie Brentwood knew all about the personality quirks of neurosurgeons.

Bryce returned with his pie. By then Katie was nibbling at hers. "You didn't eat much of your dinner," he chided softly, regarding her barely touched plate.

"Hospital food!" she said wryly.

He nodded knowingly, his gray blue eyes in agreement as he cut a neat piece of pie. "I was sorry to hear about your father," Bryce said to Katie after he'd swallowed his bite.

"It was a shock," Katie said briefly.

When she saw his face tighten at her curt remark, Katie felt she had to say something further. "You know what my first reaction was? Relief!"

Bryce looked neither shocked nor aghast as most people would have. But, of course, he had once known Dr. Max Brentwood very well. "Still and all, Max was a genius in neurosurgery," he reminded Katie.

"Oh, I know," she said automatically. "I realize medical centers all over the world use the Brentwood shunt. I'm glad he devised it—glad he helped save so many lives. But the fact remains, Bryce, that my father was something of a monster.''

"He wasn't an easy man," Bryce acknowledged honestly. "I used to alternate calling him a despot and a tyrant—but always under my breath.''

"You were right on both counts," she said and drew a deep breath.

"Had he been sick long? Or was it sudden? Forgive the questions but—''

"He died very suddenly," Katie related. "He was screaming at an intern when he had a massive stroke.''

"And you were relieved." Bryce baldly restated the fact.

"Yes. It meant he could no longer make trouble for either me or my brothers." Finished with her pie, Katie pushed it aside and took a sip of coffee.

"Brothers?" Bryce asked her curiously. "I thought you had only one brother. Wade—wasn't that his name?''

"Yes. But I have a half brother now. Dad remarried after my mother died. Eric is seven." Rapidly, Katie rushed on, wishing to get the entire subject out of the way as quickly as possible. "My stepmother was a neuro nurse he worked with.''

"Which one?" His gaze was sharp, his eyes filled with interest.

"Celia Holland.''

"Max married Cee? My God!" Bryce exclaimed, clearly shocked.

"Yes. She can't say she didn't know what she was

getting into. But the man at home in his great stone castle even shook Cee." Katie pushed at a piece of pie crust with her fork.

"Do I detect a note of fondness for Cee?" he quizzed.

"Oh, yes, we're quite good friends." Katie drew another deep breath. "She left Dad two years ago. She said she wouldn't allow him to wreck Eric's young life the way he had Wade's. Since Cee was from Texas originally, she moved back here. She works special duty at Presbyterian Hospital, and I see her and Eric regularly. He's a bright boy, undoubtedly the brightest of Dad's children. He says he wants to be a doctor but, of course, that may change."

"How is Wade?" Bryce asked the question cautiously, as though he feared hearing the answer.

"After he recovered from his breakdown, things finally worked out for him. He's married. His wife, Janet, is a calm, practical sort and has quite a good job as a banker. They have a small daughter. Janet works, and Wade stays home to write and look after Jessica. My father, of course, was horrified by Wade's 'unmanliness.' "

Bryce's broad, white-clad shoulders gave a negligent shrug. "I say whatever works to make people happy is what's right. Apparently, your brother was much more like your mother than Max."

"Yes, although Wade has never written poetry as she did. Fiction is his forte. His first novel was published last year. It didn't sell a lot of copies, but it got excellent reviews."

"What was the book about?" Bryce asked over the rim of his coffee cup.

"Oh, it was the typical first novel," Katie said, feeling suddenly weary. "An autobiographical tale of a sensitive young man with a brutal, unfeeling father who tried to mold the son in his own image. At the big climactic scene the son leaves the old man's castle never to return—which, incidentally, is exactly what Wade finally did."

Bryce Emerson's eyes ranged slowly over Katie's face and hair. "I should keep you around," he said softly, "to remind me of the sort of father I *never* wish to become!"

For a moment Katie allowed herself to remember the tenderness he'd shown her once. Across the years she could still recall the rough texture of Bryce's sports coat when he'd first caught her close and its contrast with his smoothly shaven cheek resting against hers. "I don't think you could ever be quite like my father," she said generously. At least Katie hoped he couldn't. Quickly, she rushed on. "How many children do you have?"

"None." When Bryce saw her start of surprise, he smiled. "I know I'm getting rather old for kids, but I still have hopes."

He must be thirty-nine or forty, Katie calculated. "Your wife . . . ?" she started and let her inquiry trail off.

"Melinda and I were divorced a few weeks after you left Seattle. I've never remarried. You see, I really wasn't lying to you when I said we were separated and that the situation was irreconcilable."

"Oh!" Katie exclaimed, stunned, but the small, inadequate word didn't describe how she felt. Unaccountably, her heart took wing. It lifted, soared and skimmed exhilaratingly across the sky—or, rather, the prosaic hospital ceiling. He wasn't married now!

For years she had clung to the thought that Bryce Emerson was a married man. That had been her defense against the memories of her melting, yielding flesh warm against his and the taste of his hot, desirous mouth. She had tried with all her might to forget the small call room where rain dashed against the windowpane while they made love.

"I—I didn't know," Katie floundered.

"How could you?" Bryce's hands moved in an expressive gesture of understanding. " 'My wife and I are getting a divorce' is one of the classic clichés, isn't it? Actually, when I thought about it later, Katie, I was proud of you. Pleased that you had such strength and character—"

"Don't!" she murmured, aghast at his admiration.

But words were torn from Bryce as though they'd been bottled up for too long. "I'll admit I didn't feel like that when I stood in the rain in Victoria, watching the last car drive off the last ferry from Seattle. When I realized you weren't going to meet me, I've rarely felt sadder or more depressed. Yet even then I understood. What a brave little girl you were!"

She couldn't allow him to go on praising her nobility. "Bryce, I *did* go to Victoria," Katie said rapidly. "I went on the first ferry of the day."

She watched his face go still, as stunned as she'd been earlier by the revelation of his divorce. Then questions flared in his eyes.

She answered before they could reach his lips. "I

walked up to that big front door at the Empress Hotel. Then . . . well, I couldn't go in. My world had crashed down around my ears with Mother . . . Wade . . . you. I suddenly realized very clearly that the next thing to crash would be me, if—if I went upstairs to your hotel room.''

A slow smile curved his lips. His eyes had, if anything, only grown more admiring—and oddly relieved. ''So you actually came to Victoria!'' he marveled.

''Oh, yes. I did want to be with you . . . *then*,'' Katie stressed. She wanted to make certain he understood that the moment she described lay years back in the past.

''I always felt that I had taken rather cruel advantage of you,'' Bryce went on after a moment. ''I've been afraid that you held only bad memories and bitter regrets.''

''In a way, I did . . . I do,'' Katie said candidly. ''But you didn't take advantage of me, Bryce.''

''For what it's worth, I could never do such a thing again,'' he said, his voice quite low. ''At least, with the years, I've learned self-control.''

There was such dogged honesty in his voice that Katie looked at him more closely, seeing Bryce exactly as he was now, tonight, instead of a physician or a figure from the past. The features she'd earlier branded craggy really weren't when viewed up close. Staring at him, as she was now, she could see how warm were his deep-set eyes, like the first day of spring before the sunshine had quite broken through the sky. His nose was straight and nicely proportioned and his chin firm.

Thick black eyebrows cut a startling arch against the pleasant tan of his face. He had the high forehead associated with intelligence. The hollowed cheeks and slight indentations at his temples revealed the discipline of his work. He was a striking-looking man now, she realized, instead of the merely handsome one she remembered. Katie was surprised that some eager woman hadn't snapped him up!

Then she clamped down on her feelings and speculations. What was the matter with her? Why was she eyeing Bryce as though he were a prospective husband? Long ago she had vowed to never be involved again with a surgeon.

Bryce's eyes went to the large clock on the wall, and he drained the rest of his coffee quickly. "I'd better get back," he said.

"Yes, I should go, too," said Katie in brisk agreement.

But, for a long moment, neither of them moved. They simply sat looking at each other. Oh, how warm Bryce's eyes were!

"I can't believe that we've found each other again," he said, almost wonderingly.

Katie's wayward heart gave a sharp knock in response, but her brain said, "Whoa!" She framed her reply carefully and formally. "I'll look forward to seeing you and working with you occasionally, Bryce."

He appeared not to have heard her words. His right hand, warm from his coffee cup, slid across the table and lightly covered one of hers. The feeling of his fingertips and skin on hers was electric, and Katie's heart suffered an abrupt second jolt. Something about Bryce still stirred her to vibrant awakening. He'd always had that effect, she thought, as her hand prickled with response.

"You may not appreciate my saying it," Bryce remarked quietly, "but I'll bet your old man was very proud of you."

That did it, snapping the spell that held Katie in thrall. Just the mere mention of Dr. Max Brentwood was like a dash of cold water. "If he was, he was quite successful at concealing it," she said coolly.

Bryce's eyes lingered caressingly on her lips, then ranged upward to encompass the whole of Katie's face. "Max was always a fool in certain ways," he said. Then, slowly, his hand retreated from hers, leaving Katie with a sudden feeling of loss. He pushed back his chair and stood up.

"I'll see you, Katie," he said.

Was that just a casual farewell or did his words hold an implied promise? she wondered and was glad, at that moment, not to know the answer.

Abruptly, Bryce Emerson bent down. His lips, even warmer than his hands, grazed her cheek momentarily.

He had kissed her like that once before. Despite all the years and events that had intervened since then, nothing in her response had changed. Such strong, fierce emotions assailed Katie that she felt herself quaking inwardly. Bryce's touch threatened the whole correct, professional demeanor she'd cultivated and learned to sustain. His radiant eyes saw a woman, not a hospital administrator, and his brief kiss told her so.

Stunned, Katie watched the tall, lean figure leave the cafeteria, then she raised a trembling finger to the place on her cheek that still throbbed and tingled pleasantly.

For once in her life her busy mind was completely still, without a single thought to interrupt its quiet savoring of joy.

Katie's sensible heels clicked rhythmically on the tile corridor as she hurried back toward the administrative suite. When she neared the ladies' room, she turned and went inside.

She stopped before the large, clear mirror and looked at her reflection, trying to see herself as Bryce Emerson had.

The cool woman looking back at her gave no hint of the emotional havoc he had just wrought. Her mask—the name she gave to her working image—lay firmly in place. A modest amount of makeup, a trace of blush and a touch of lip gloss brightened the clear translucence of her skin. Blessed with a perfect complexion, Katie wisely left it alone, only washing and moisturizing it.

Her thick, chestnut brown hair had a natural healthy sheen. That was particularly evident when she let it spill down over her shoulders, but, of course, she never wore it that way at the hospital. Instead her hair was pulled away from her face and fastened firmly into a knot at the back of her head.

Whenever she wore eyeshadow and mascara, her brown eyes were transformed into twin pools, beckoning and seductive. Over the years a few men had declared extravagantly to Katie that they could get lost looking into those deep brown depths. For that reason she never wore eye makeup to work. Her presently unadorned eyes gave a direct and businesslike impression.

I don't look very pretty tonight, she thought, surveying her dark suit critically. Only the white silk bow of her blouse softened its severe effect. But so what? She wasn't supposed to look pretty at work. She was supposed to look competent and efficient, and in that she had succeeded very well.

Still, Katie continued to feel dissatisfied by her appearance. Quickly, she washed and dried her hands, throwing the discarded paper towel into a nearby bin. She wished she could discard the mask as well. Then she berated herself for entertaining flighty feminine fantasies. What sort of sorcery had Bryce Emerson worked on her to arouse such contradictory feelings? At any rate, their lives could only touch briefly once again, for she would soon be gone.

Abruptly, her pager came to life and Katie heard herself being summoned to the Intensive Care Unit.

Three members of a Korean family awaited her there. The man wore a business suit, but the two weeping women were clad less formally in slacks and pullovers.

A nurse on duty supplied Katie with the details. A patient in ICU was the husband of one woman and the brother of the other two. Until yesterday he had worked as a night clerk at one of the local convenience stores. In the course of a robbery, he had been brutally stabbed. An off-duty policeman had discovered his body and called for Life Copter.

Clinically, the man was dead. Only a humming respirator maintained his life. The doctor in charge of the case had recommended that the respirator be disconnected and the tearful family had agreed.

Pity squeezed at Katie's heart as her eyes ran compassionately over the small, grieving group. "Before the respirator is turned off, they want to phone Korea and inform the patient's parents," the nurse whispered to Katie.

"I'll arrange for them to do that," Katie replied. "But any plans to disconnect a respirator must be discussed in our attorney's office by all involved parties." With a tragedy such as this, the hospital had to protect itself against possible future lawsuits.

"The doctor told them that would have to be done tomorrow," the nurse added. "They understand, but they'd like to place the call now."

"I'll take them to a conference room where they'll have privacy for an overseas call," Katie decided.

First, though, she took the hand of each family member in turn, pressing it between her two, with a wordless sympathy they all seemed to appreciate. Then she motioned them to follow her down the hall.

While the family placed their call, Katie waited in the anteroom. After they had finished she led them back to the waiting room. When she saw the three of them huddled together in grief, Katie's mind ranged back across the span of ten years. She remembered when she had been one of a similarly grief-stricken threesome. It had happened during the spring of her eighteenth year, the spring when she had first met Bryce Emerson.

She had come home from school on a blustery afternoon in April. She stopped briefly in the garden to watch a cool wind whipping the yellow daffodils about. Then she went inside. The huge, gray house was quiet. Her brother's door was shut, but Katie suspected that

Wade was inside, his head buried in a book. Already he had begun to retreat from the rest of the family.

Her mother's door stood invitingly ajar. Katie tiptoed in, wondering as she had at least a dozen times before: What's wrong with Mom?

It was nothing but nerves and hypochondria, Max Brentwood had said impatiently. When he finally grew tired of looking at his wife's wan face and hearing her tearful complaints, he had sent her to a psychiatrist of his acquaintance. Privately, Katie couldn't see that the shrink was doing her mother any good, but no one ever quarreled with Dr. Brentwood's diagnosis in that household. He was always so confident and emphatic that he could cause Katie to doubt the evidence before her eyes.

That afternoon she found her mother asleep. Sandra Brentwood slept so much lately, and she had stopped writing the poetry that had previously occupied many of her hours. Katie tiptoed back out of the room, then sped down to the kitchen to make sure that dinner was in the final stages of preparation. If Dr. Brentwood came home from the hospital and his dinner wasn't ready, his fiery temper would explode on all their heads.

Minn, their Chinese housekeeper, had the meal well in hand. Satisfied with the preparations, Katie went back to her room to do her homework.

Before she had gotten very far in writing a theme, Katie realized she needed to check a couple of references. A set of encyclopedias were among the many books crowding the floor-to-ceiling bookshelves in her father's study. Katie and Wade had permission to avail themselves of those volumes.

Katie had opened the study door and stepped inside before she noticed that her father was there and that he wasn't alone. He must have come in through his side entrance while Katie was still upstairs.

"Oh!" she exclaimed in dismay and skidded to a stop. Her father sat behind his desk. Before him, sitting in a leather chair, was a very attractive young man whom Katie had never seen before.

"Ah, Katie. Come in," her father said pleasantly. He was always courteous to his family when visitors were present. "Did you need something?"

"Just an encyclopedia," she mumbled.

"Help yourself," Max Brentwood said and waved graciously toward the bookcase.

That would have probably ended the exchange except that the young man had leaped up politely. It left Dr. Brentwood with no alternative but to introduce his daughter to Dr. Bryce Emerson, a neurosurgery resident.

How tall he is! Katie thought first. How handsome he is! was her second thought. He had thick wavy black hair, mesmerizing eyes and a healthy color to his face. He smiled at her, revealing a gleaming flash of perfect white teeth.

Although it was rare for Dr. Brentwood to invite residents to his home, it had happened once or twice before when he was particularly impressed by a resident. The young men were never invited to stay for dinner or even offered a drink or a cup of coffee. They were there, for a special hour or two, to confer with the master of neurosurgery. This did not include squandering valuable time in what Dr. Brentwood considered "pointless social frivolities."

Something about this young man was, indeed, impressive. To Katie, easing out a heavy volume from between two equally heavy ones, it was the way his eyes lingered on her rather than returning respectfully to her father. He wore such a kindly expression and pleasant, attentive smile that she tingled all over.

Then she felt her father watching her impatiently, clearly eager to resume his discourse, so Katie retreated hastily with her book. She returned to her room and soon the memory of the striking young doctor faded as she buried herself in homework once again.

She did not see Dr. Emerson again for almost a month. Then, in mid-May, she came home from school one afternoon and instead of finding the house quiet, with Wade sequestered in his room and Minn stirring something on the stove, they were huddled together, standing just outside her mother's bedroom.

Two pairs of alarmed eyes met Katie's. Minn's face was darkened by concern while Wade's looked white and pinched.

"What is it?" Katie said, setting her books down on the hall table while her heart accelerated in sudden alarm.

"Your mother hasn't gotten up all day," Minn said, her voice deadpan in contrast to the worry on her face. "When I called her, she'd just whisper, roll over and sleep some more."

"Katie, I can't awaken her at all!" Wade said, twisting his hands together in a gesture of hopelessness.

"I called your pa about two o'clock," Minn went on, her black eyes beginning to smolder. He said, 'Oh, let her sleep. When she's sick and tired of sulking in her room, she'll get up.' "

He would, Katie thought, hurrying to join them.

"I think something really bad is wrong with her, Katie," Minn concluded.

Her heart pounding even more, Katie stepped inside her mother's darkened bedroom. With the drapes drawn against the bright afternoon sun, Sandra Brentwood looked as though she were peacefully asleep, her light brown hair fanned across her pillow.

"Mom?" Katie said, her voice apprehensive.

Sandra had always awakened whenever one of her children called to her. That day, when she didn't, when she neither spoke nor stirred, Katie flew into action.

She had always been more decisive than Wade, who still stood in the doorway wringing his hands. Swiftly, Katie rushed across the room and drew the drapes, then she dashed back to her mother's side.

With the added light streaming in the room, Katie saw Sandra's parted lips and her blank, half-closed eyes. Her shaking hand went to her mother's bare arm, which felt cold and clammy. For a moment a child's scream of terror rose to Katie's throat. She bit her lip just in time to stifle it and grabbed for the bedside phone. Even through her panic, Katie still remembered the emergency number to call.

Her voice was shaking as much as her hands were when she told the police dispatcher the address and cause for alarm. She remembered to ask for an ambulance.

No sooner had Katie replaced the receiver when she

heard the front doorbell ring. Perhaps it was someone who could help!

She ran back out to the hall and pushed past the two frightened, motionless figures. She hurled herself down the staircase and flung open the heavy front door.

Dr. Bryce Emerson stood there. "Hello, Katie," he said cordially. "Your father asked me to stop by, but I think I've arrived before him. I don't see his car—"

His voice halted, and his smile faded when he saw how distraught she was. "Is something wrong?" he asked.

Katie's mind focused on the single thought that he was a doctor. Frantically, she seized his arm. "My mother! Upstairs! Oh, come quickly!"

Bryce didn't waste a moment. Following the direction of her pointing finger, he plunged up the stairs.

Katie followed just a little less swiftly. By the time she reached the door, Bryce was already bent over the lifeless figure of her mother. Katie stopped, reaching for the doorjamb for support. In her heart, she already knew.

Bryce stayed in the room only two or three minutes, but to Katie, waiting, those minutes seemed an eternity.

When he came out at last to face the frightened, little group, she saw the somberness of his gray eyes and the grim set to his mouth. "I'm so sorry," he said quietly. "She's dead."

Wade turned his face to the wall and began to cry. Minn went to console him, but Katie stood as though she'd been carved of stone. In that devastating moment she could not imagine life without her mother.

Bryce took them all in hand. He led the way to Dr.

Brentwood's study, his arm around Katie's shoulder. It was an unfortunate choice of rooms, but, of course, it was the only one with which the young doctor was really familiar.

Katie sat down and stared numbly at her folded hands until the doorknob to the side entrance rattled and Dr. Brentwood stepped inside.

He arrived, scowling, and the sight of four stricken people in his sanctuary did nothing to improve his mood. "What the hell's going on?" he demanded.

His voice quiet and subdued, Bryce informed Max Brentwood that his wife was dead.

"Oh, my God, she's killed herself!" Dr. Brentwood blustered. Then, because he related every happening to its effect on his own life, he raised stormy eyes. "Sandra's done this to embarrass me! Committed suicide to cause a scandal that the newspapers will pounce on—"

"Hush!" Dr. Emerson commanded in such an angry, ringing tone that all eyes flew to him. When he regained his composure, he informed Dr. Brentwood that he had examined Sandra and felt certain that she had died of natural causes.

Dr. Brentwood blinked. "I don't believe it!" he cried.

Later, events proved Bryce right. To Dr. Brentwood's embarrassment and discredit, an autopsy revealed that Sandra Brentwood had suffered from a progressive heart disease. Eventually, her overburdened heart had simply stopped beating.

In the wake of his wife's death, Dr. Brentwood suffered considerable loss of prestige. That Sandra's physician-husband had paid so little attention to her symptoms that she had died without ever having been diagnosed was a week-long scandal at all the major cocktail parties.

Gossip would dog Dr. Brentwood for years, and Katie could never feel very sorry for him. At the time, though, her thoughts were too much of a muddle to comprehend any further ramifications of the tragedy. Although Wade and Minn both wept and even Dr. Brentwood blew his nose resoundingly, Katie's own grief had left her numb.

Only when the ambulance arrived to take her mother away did she stir from her chair. She walked outside and into the garden. The daffodils her mother had planted during a happier time had lost their blooms, but Sandra's prized rosebushes were still covered with tight green buds in promise of summer.

Bryce Emerson followed Katie into the garden. He watched as she bent down mechanically and pulled up a few weeds.

"That can wait," he said to her gently as they stood in the glow of a waning sunset.

"My mother was always very careful of her garden. Now it's gotten out of hand," Katie said in a stranger's shrill voice.

Abruptly, Bryce pulled her into his arms. He was so tall that all Katie felt at first was the nubby fabric of his jacket scratching her cheek. Then the realization struck her that her adored mother was gone forever, and wrenching sobs began to shake her.

Bryce drew her closer still, bending his long frame down to her smaller one and offering her shelter. His smooth cheek rested against her wet one, and his hands stroked her back, moving up and down from her waist to her shoulders.

For a long time Katie simply cried, comforted by the hard strength of his arms holding her, his hands tracing meaningless patterns on her back and his soft, wordless murmurings. Finally, when her grief was spent, she realized that Bryce's lips were moving across her cheek. They stopped there and kissed her briefly.

Suddenly, a wave of primitive feeling surged through her and, for the first time in her life, Katie Brentwood knew just what it meant to be a woman. To feel a woman's emotions—to cherish the feel of a man's tight embrace and his warm lips on her face.

She was too young then to know that grief was often transmuted into desire, rage or even laughter. That they were all natural human reactions to the realization of still being alive although a loved one was dead.

Instead, when Katie comprehended that what she felt in that moment was raw, hungry passion, she was appalled and ashamed. She struggled against Bryce's arms until he freed her and led her gently back into the house. But from that moment on she had always felt a special awareness of him.

That unique attraction resurfaced at her mother's funeral two days later. To Katie's surprise, Bryce attended the service. Several times she glanced up, as though compelled, to see Bryce watching her, and each time she felt strengthened by his concern and obvious caring.

She knew then that she would never forget him.

Chapter Three

$\mathcal{N}$ow Katie jerked back to an awareness of the present. To Harwick Memorial Hospital where a helicopter roared as it landed on the rooftop helistop nearby. She had been staring blindly at the darkened window, as though expecting to hear the dash of raindrops there.

She realized that she sat at the desk she and Steve Wills shared in the administrative suite, having walked back there automatically. No sooner had she noted the time, which was almost midnight, than Steve came through the door.

Katie stood up, reached for the Night Administrator's Report, and began briefing Steve on the evening's events. Steve nodded and agreed with her decisions as he usually did, then Katie handed him the pocket pager and she was free to go home.

"Hey!" Steve's voice stopped her before she reached

the door. "I didn't see any of the Security guys around to walk you to your car."

"Oh, Steve, I don't need a security guard," Katie protested. "I'm parked on Three, quite close to the elevator."

Steve's jaw took on its square, stubborn set. "You know there was an incident in the parking garage last month, Katie," he reminded her.

"I know, but—"

"No buts!" Steve said, cutting forcefully through Katie's protests. "I'm on call now, and I don't want you mugged or raped." He reached for the phone and paged Security.

While she waited for her escort, Katie shifted from one foot to the other. She felt tired from her busy night. The emotional turmoil of seeing Bryce and the trip to the past had taken its toll. She wanted only to go home and sleep.

Five minutes later, Elliot Wainwright arrived. He took Katie's arm protectively, as he usually did, and they made their customary trek out of the hospital and into the huge parking garage.

In every respect but this one, Katie knew herself the equal of a male administrator and she relished the knowledge. But equality ended here. Now she was just a woman, like any other woman in the world, and because she was open to attack she had to be walked to her car every night by an armed escort. It was infuriating, but it was just the way things were.

Katie's apartment complex utilized such strict security measures that she never feared returning home alone at night. A gate card was required to open the heavy main gate, and guards patrolled the grounds all night. Of course, Katie paid dearly for the privilege of living here, but at least the security system allayed the fears of her stepmother, co-workers and she had to admit, herself.

Wearily, Katie climbed the outside stairs to her second-floor apartment, unlocked the door and walked inside to switch on lights and kick off her shoes. Her apartment was her quiet refuge from the rush and stress of her job, and she had hired a decorator to assure that it was furnished in quiet, good taste. Green plants flourished near the window that caught the morning sun. Muted paintings and traditional furniture in a blend of earth tones completed her haven of serenity.

Tonight serenity escaped her. Even her soothing bedtime routine of a warm bath, a glass of milk and a few pages read from a dull book failed to lull her into slumber. Although Katie switched off her bedside light and curled on her side in the posture she found most restful, her mind still whirled from the impact of her earlier encounter with Bryce.

Unbidden, the memories swirled around her again, memories of that wind-whipped spring in Seattle when dark clouds scuttled in to dash down brief torrents of rain then glided away, the rain easing only temporarily until the next dark clouds appeared.

The stormy day when Wade had been committed to the Adolescent Psychiatric Unit at the hospital where Dr. Brentwood practiced returned again to Katie's mind.

It had happened a week after her mother's death, a nightmarish week that found Wade utterly withdrawn and unresponsive. At first, he would not talk. Then he would not eat. He did not appear to hear his father's command to "snap out of this" or to feel his stinging slap. When at last Wade had curled up into a ball of human despair even Dr. Brentwood had been appalled.

So the ambulance had been summoned again. Wade had been strapped to a stretcher, and Dr. Brentwood had followed the ambulance to the medical center, informing Katie and Minn tersely that he would let them know.

Katie feared that Wade had also been lost to her forever. She had cried until she was exhausted and drained of tears. Then, as the hours passed without word from her father, she began to grow angry. Shortly before dusk she sent Minn home and then, taking the keys to her mother's car, she drove herself to the medical center.

Katie was not allowed to enter the barred unit where Wade was being held, but a psychiatric social worker emerged to talk with her gently. She was a lovely young woman of Oriental descent, and her brown eyes were compassionate as she explained that Wade had been sedated and was now asleep.

"Why can't I see my brother?" Katie demanded, while frightening images of straitjackets and electric shock flashed through her mind.

"No family member will be allowed to see your brother for the first several days he is here," the social worker explained. "We want your brother to feel safe, to grow to trust us, and be spared the pressures of home and family that have prompted his breakdown."

"You mean my father can't see Wade either?" Katie said, amazed.

The social worker confirmed it with a nod, and her

rueful smile admitted that she had already encountered the formidable Dr. Brentwood.

Katie relaxed. That made it all right. To know that Wade was being sheltered from his unsympathetic father more than made up for her own longing to see him.

"We'll take very good care of your brother," the social worker told Katie reassuringly and, with a nod of thanks, Katie accepted her dismissal.

She had stepped back into the corridor when anger at her father swelled anew. Determinedly, Katie marched off in the direction of his office. She was going to have it out with him at last, she vowed. She would tell Max Brentwood to his face just what an abominable, contemptible human being she thought he was. She would tell him she hated him and hoped never to see him again! Then she would go home, pack her clothes and move out of his house forever.

Until that night, all Katie's future plans had centered around college. She had already applied to and been accepted by Ashwood College, an exclusive women's college outside of St. Louis, Missouri, and she had been looking forward to the opportunity of being essentially on her own and pursuing higher studies.

That night she was ready to toss her future aside. I can get a job, I suppose, she thought vaguely, as she neared the neurosurgery wing of the hospital where her father's office was located. Then, when Wade is discharged, I'll make a home for us both.

Her thoughts had no roots in practicality. That she was untrained for anything except the most menial work did not even impinge on her consciousness.

The nurse on duty in Neurosurgery dashed Katie's

brave but thoughtless plans by informing her that her father was in surgery.

He was *operating?* On the very day that his only son had been admitted to a psychiatric unit! For a moment Katie was shocked into complete immobility. God help his patient! she thought silently.

Then, her mind clearing, she realized that the patient would probably be fine. Any other doctor would have been too distraught to set foot in an operating room, but Max Brentwood had always had ice water in his veins.

"It was an emergency," the nurse explained to Katie solicitously. Her father was supervising a resident who would implant the famous Brentwood shunt. "Is there anything *I* can do for you, Miss Brentwood?"

"No," said Katie, then a name flashed into her mind. "Yes. Is—is Dr. Emerson here?"

It was a ridiculous question, she thought the moment she asked. By now it was seven o'clock and the chance of Bryce's still being at the hospital were remote, but the nurse's face lighted with relief.

"Why, yes, he's on call tonight. I'll let him know you're here."

Before Katie even had time to wonder why she'd asked for Bryce, he was walking down the hall toward her, his handsome figure clad in clean, snow-white scrubs. At that moment he looked like a god to her.

"I know about your brother," he said gently, taking Katie's hands between his two strong ones. "I'm so sorry, my dear."

She looked up into his face with its chiseled, near perfect features and the healthy sheen of color on his high cheekbones, and felt her lips quivering wordlessly. Perhaps she hadn't cried all of her tears over Wade, after all.

One arm went firmly about her shoulder as Bryce led her down the hall. "How about a cup of coffee?" he offered, and Katie gave a wordless nod.

"The staff room is here." He stopped and pushed at a half-ajar door where a number of other white-clad figures had congregated.

Sighting them, Katie shrank back against Bryce. Immediately, he understood that she didn't feel up to facing a crowd of her father's co-workers.

"Down here," he said swiftly and drew Katie with him along a narrow corridor. By then she was crying helplessly.

Almost before she knew it, she was seated on the edge of a single bed in a small, quiet room, and Bryce had closed and locked the door. Then he sat beside her, one arm around her shoulders while the other thrust a large man's handkerchief into her hands.

"Where are we?" Katie whispered when she had successfully quelled her sobs.

He took the handkerchief from her hand and gently dried her tears. "This is my call room," he explained.

"Oh," she said, realizing that Bryce would sleep here tonight if there were no further emergencies. The bed and a nightstand with a lamp and telephone were the room's only furnishings. To her right she could see a tiny bathroom with a shower stall.

"Tell me about it," Bryce urged, and the words poured out of Katie in a rush. Her concern and grief for

Wade, her anger at her father and all the harsh, bitter things she longed to tell him.

"It won't do any good, you know," Bryce said to her, his voice reflective. "Max won't understand. You'll just anger and alienate him. No, Katie, you must think about yourself now. Don't throw your future away . . ."

His calm, reasonable, reassuring words gradually dissipated Katie's rage and hurt, while his arms, linked loosely about her, felt as comforting as her mother's embrace. "Thank you," she whispered at last and turned to kiss Bryce's cheek gratefully.

Instead she found his lips poised over hers. After a moment's hesitation, their mouths came together instinctively in a fiery kiss of such stunning sweetness that Katie felt her head begin to reel. Her heart pounded, and there was no thought of resistance. She had never known a man's lips could be so delicious.

She heard the single, surprised gasp that escaped from Bryce, then their mouths crushed together even more hungrily, almost bruisingly. A dark, hot flame sprang to life within Katie, a mindless and welcome release from all the emotions that had wracked her. The flame licked through her veins, speeding her breath and activating anew those strange feelings of passion and desire that she'd already experienced once with this man.

His mouth took hers more gently, as though he couldn't seem to resist tracing the outline of her lips with his tongue. The kiss tantalized and delighted her. At the same time her limbs began to feel weak, as though her bones had turned to liquid. She melted against the strength of his chest and arms. Then her breasts began to tingle, their nipples tightening, and below her waist another hot, dark fire awoke to arouse a new and unfamiliar clamoring.

Almost painfully, Bryce wrenched his mouth from hers. "I—I never intended . . . I'm sorry, Katie," he said, drawing a ragged breath.

"Don't be sorry," Katie whispered, closing her eyes against the doubt and chagrin she saw in his. "Oh, Bryce, you make me feel alive again!"

"My poor little girl!" He moved abruptly, and Katie felt him stretch his long length out on the bed. Gently, he drew her down beside him, and she relished this closer, nearer contact with him. She could feel his heart pounding against her own and the muscles of his legs contracting against the soft warmth of hers.

He buried his face in her neck, his hands caressing the softness of her tumbled hair. His tenderness pleased Katie and yet the clamoring of her body pressed for more. "Please," she whispered as the hunger inside her deepened. "Please kiss me again, Bryce!"

His lips rose to claim hers, and she could only marvel at the magic they evoked. Dizzily, she drank in the clean scent of his skin and hair. No smell of hospital antiseptic clung to Bryce, and his natural male aroma was an aphrodisiac to Katie's already swimming senses.

One of his hands moved to switch off the dim light on the nightstand, and then there was only the darkness and his delicious lips, and Katie's own hungry, almost greedy excitement to know and feel and taste more—so much more of him.

His tongue darted inside her receptive mouth as their bodies strained together even more closely. She felt his fingertips gliding over one of her breasts. They touched her tentatively, then moved away. In a sudden frenzy of desire, Katie caught Bryce's hand and brought it back to her soft, tingling roundness.

"We've got to stop this," he said half-despairingly.

Her mind said he was right, but her arms locked around his neck and drew his face back down to hers for another burning kiss.

Bryce's hand rotated over the nipple of one eagerly arching breast, and the motion was so exciting that Katie's body came totally alive, awash with sensations. She sought even more sensory input by caressing his face with her lips, teasing his tongue with her own and moving her body insinuatingly against his. Instinct guided Katie's movements, for she had never gone so far with any man before, but tonight she simply didn't care. Bryce aroused her, excited her, made her feel more alive than she had ever felt in her life. Her fingers found the hem of his scrub suit's loose top, and she slipped her hands beneath the cotton fabric to explore, touch and caress the warm springy hairs there and his small, hard nipples half-hidden in the hairy forest.

"God, Katie, you inflame me!" He groaned. "You're driving me wild!"

She was wild, too. Wild and heedless of the consequences, unconcerned about right and wrong, driven only to quench the fire that had ignited them. Her body writhed against his with her desire.

Bryce's hands, shaking with eagerness, slid Katie's sweater up and over her head until it dropped beside them on the bed. Expertly, his hands unclasped her bra hook, and then her bra, too, was gone as his mouth moved to her breast.

He sucked gently yet passionately on the soft mound, his tongue teasing the nipple while his fingertips stroked her other breast. After a moment his mouth moved to it, too, and that sweet, moist tugging on her nipple left Katie almost faint, she was so breathless with desire.

While he continued to touch and taste her breasts, her legs rubbed insinuatingly against his and parted invitingly as she felt the unmistakable evidence of his own powerful desire for her. Then Bryce tore his mouth away. "We have to stop this!" he gasped. "It's madness!"

Katie made no reply, but her hands slipped down to glide beneath the drawstring on the bottoms of his scrub suit. She felt the briefs he wore and sent her hands below them. She didn't know exactly what she was doing, but some ancient wisdom guided her eager, curious fingers. From his sudden intake of breath she knew he found her touch as exciting as she found his.

Then, his breathing gone harsh and hoarse, Bryce turned her hastily until Katie lay beneath him. Quickly, he removed her remaining garments—her shoes, slacks and panties—and she arched her body to help him. Then his lips and hands were on her bare skin evoking sensations she had never even imagined, powerful sensations that sent her tumbling off the brink of control. She was mindless, unable to think, only to feel the primitive, driving excitement racing between them.

His hot tongue flashing, his fingertips delicately probing, Bryce explored Katie with such thorough, arousing intimacy that gasps tore from her throat. Her head thrashed from side to side on his pillow as her unbearably excited body quivered with spasms and begged for release. In a swift, almost fluid motion, Bryce stripped away his scrub suit, and his naked body covered hers. His heated skin encompassed every inch of hers.

"You're sure you really want this?" he whispered as his fingertips cupped the soft fullness of her buttocks.

"Yes!" Katie cried, only aware of the fiercely aching void inside of her that their frantic excitement had created. "I want *you!*"

"Then take me!" he gasped. In one powerful thrust he merged their bodies, and Katie left girlhood behind her forever.

Although she was a virgin, his entry caused her no pain. She'd been roused to such a pitch of sensual excitement that his throbbing body filling hers brought only welcome relief. Bryce's lips captured Katie's, and his hands feverishly caressed her breasts while his own desire drove him forward relentlessly.

She met his desire as though she'd been born for this, for him. She moved with Bryce and let their avid movements rocket her away, far away, from the narrow bed in the small call room and the two hungry bodies in motion there. Katie rose on to a sublime, other-earthly plane where there was only the perfection of pleasure and total satisfaction of passion. At its peak she felt rather than heard the ecstatic cry that escaped her. At the same time, she was aware of the shudders wracking Bryce's body and his own fierce pleasure.

Slowly, Katie came back to reality. To her pants for breath and Bryce's, to their limp but still linked bodies and to the sudden cheery splatter of rain on the windowpane.

Gradually, as her awed mind began to function again,

Katie realized the full import of what had happened to her. Tragedy had plunged her into the depths of grief, and rapture had introduced her to adult joy. In one week she had crossed two important boundaries and could never be a child again.

Gratefully, she snuggled against Bryce, unable to feel either shame or regret in the quiet, contented afterglow. Then he moved away, and they became two separate beings once again. Another shudder rippled through him, and she sensed an ominous difference.

"Oh, Katie, you should have told me you were a virgin!"

His voice held a tremor of utter despair, and her heart lurched at the sound. "It's all right, Bryce," she assured him softly.

He groaned and sat up on the edge of the bed, reaching automatically for his clothes. "It's *not* all right," he said fiercely, dressing himself with jerky motions that contrasted painfully with his earlier fluid ones.

"Yes, it is!" Katie insisted, propping herself up on her elbow and covering her breasts with the crisp hospital sheet. "We both wanted each other. Wasn't it beautiful for you, too?"

He gave a despairing moan of assent.

"If you think I'd *ever* tell my father . . ." Katie began, then realized that this wasn't Bryce's fear at all.

"It just seemed to happen . . . naturally, inevitably," Bryce murmured as though trying to explain to himself the unexplainable. "Once I started kissing you, it was like something else took over. But I thought you knew the score. By the time I realized you didn't, I—I couldn't stop! Oh, Katie, you're just a kid!"

"I'm eighteen," she whispered, stricken by his piercing remorse.

Bryce switched on the bedside lamp, and she saw his visible relief that she was, at least, of legal age. Then, as a new fear struck him, he buried his face in his hands. "I didn't even think to protect you! I didn't think at all!"

"I won't have a baby," Katie promised. "It's too soon after . . . well, you know . . ."

She saw another brief moment of relief cross his flushed, handsome face.

"Oh, Bryce, please don't be sorry!" Katie cried, her hands going out to stroke his hunched shoulders. "It spoils everything if . . . if all you feel is sorry!"

"That's not all I feel!" Swiftly, he turned and caught her to him, pressing Katie's face over his still-racing heart. "You wouldn't believe what I really feel at this moment."

Relief seeped back along her veins. "Try me," she said with a little laugh.

"I knew you were special from the moment I first saw you, Katie. Now I want you with me day and night. I want to watch you, know you, talk to you. I want to learn what you like to eat and what you enjoy reading and every single little wrinkle in this pretty head of yours!" Fiercely, he pressed a fervent kiss on her forehead.

"I feel the same about you, Bryce! Why—why can't that come true?" she asked.

She felt rather than saw the stiffening of his body. "The timing is so bad, Katie!" His voice trailed off into awkward silence.

In her naiveté she thought he was referring to her mother's death and what had happened to Wade.

"That doesn't affect you and me," Katie protested with the confident assurance of youth. "We'll make the timing right!" Surely with the glorious way they made each other feel, they could work out anything, she thought.

Bryce turned to look down at her, cradled against him, and she saw the flare of impulsive hope that sprang into his gray blue eyes. "Yes, maybe we can," he muttered. Then he held Katie off to look at her while he spoke swiftly. "Could you spend this weekend with me? I'll be at a medical convention in Canada—Victoria, actually. You could catch the ferry and meet me there."

Katie let herself get caught up in his plans even as she wondered curiously why she couldn't accompany Bryce to Victoria instead of arriving separately.

She didn't ask because she was so relieved by his changed frame of mind. She knew her father wouldn't attend the convention because he considered most such meetings a waste of his valuable time. She also knew that he would not question her very closely if she invented a weekend trip to Victoria with a girl friend.

But fellow physicians of Dr. Brentwood's acquaintance might well be at the medical meeting. That's why Bryce was being so careful, she decided as she listened to the strategems he swiftly devised. She would take a room at the Empress Hotel on a different floor from his. She would produce some plausible reason—sightseeing? shopping?—to explain her presence there.

Suddenly, the telephone in the call room jangled, and

they both jumped at the intrusion. Before it could ring again, Bryce reached for it.

"Dr. Emerson," he answered.

Because Katie still lay against his heart, she could hear every word. "This is Pauline, Dr. Emerson. I just came on duty and found a message for you to call your wife. Have you received it?"

"No," said Bryce, his face growing troubled once again. Fleetingly and apologetically, his eyes met Katie's shocked ones. Then he turned his attention back to the phone. "Thanks, Pauline. I'll call Melinda in a bit."

His wife? Shock waves rippled up from Katie's feet while horror completely immobilized her. Meanwhile, Bryce had replaced the receiver.

Slowly, Katie drew her tongue across her dry lips. They still held the taste of him. "You're *married?*" she managed at last.

"Why, yes," said Bryce as though it were the most commonplace reply in the world. Then seeing Katie's cataclysmic shock, the troubled look returned to his face. "I thought surely you knew."

She hadn't known, but she should have. Most residents were married; it was the exceptional one who was not. Of course, Bryce hadn't worn a wedding ring, but that was no explanation either. Many surgeons didn't, including her father.

Katie knew all of that. She, of all people, knew that! But she simply hadn't wanted to know or to think. Bryce had appeared in her life like a storybook hero or prince come to rescue her, and Katie had wanted to remain in a magical, movielike dream.

But this—*this* was real life. A jangling phone, a

tumbled bed, a married man. Still, the shocks continued to ripple through her even as Bryce began to explain earnestly.

Katie heard him out in a daze. He and Melinda had been college sweethearts who had married on Bryce's twenty-first birthday. For about a year they had played house. Then the demands of their separate careers had grown like a wedge between them. They had drifted apart until their differences were now quite irreconcilable.

"We've been separated for a number of months," Bryce explained, his eyes earnest, his voice imploring Katie to believe him. "I'm certain Melinda's call tonight has something to do with the divorce."

Katie wanted to trust him, to believe him. She tried to. After Bryce had finished his painful explanations, she even agreed to meet him in Victoria on the coming weekend, but it was a promise made in shock.

She put on her clothes, allowed Bryce to walk her to her car and kiss her good-bye. Then she drove herself home. For the next couple of days she argued with herself, torn between the knowledge that married men were *always* going to get a divorce but rarely did and the remembered rapture that she and Bryce had shared.

By the weekend she was aching for him all over again. In her healthy body a new hunger and thirst clamored. She wanted to lie in his arms, drink in his kisses and merge herself with him again and again. Because she felt so weak, so human, she boarded the ferry from Seattle to Victoria.

But then, because Katie was also stronger than she knew, she reached the huge door to the Empress, a massive British colonial hotel in the heart of Victoria, and stopped still. Desperately, she looked around for a means of escape.

A sightseeing bus stood at the curb loading tourists for a trip to Butchart Gardens. Impulsively, Katie ran back down the steps and jumped onto the bus. As it pulled away from the curb, rain began to fall.

She spent the afternoon in the fabulous gardens, viewing them through a fog of rain and tears. Finally, she sat on a cold stone bench.

The riot of flowers reminded her poignantly of her mother. "Poetry and posies, they're more than just hobbies to me," Sandra Brentwood had once told Katie whimsically. "They're something of my very own. I think every woman needs something of her own, whether she's married or not."

That day in Butchart Gardens in Victoria, British Columbia, Katie vowed that she was going to have something of her very own, too.

The sightseeing bus was continuing on to Vancouver on the mainland and so, at the appointed time, Katie clambered back aboard it.

She took a lengthy, circuitous route back to Seattle, staring numbly out of the bus window at the beautiful Canadian countryside until gradually the spectacle of mountains and sea, forests and islands, calmed her turbulent emotions.

A week after Katie's return, Wade was released from the Adolescent Psychiatric Unit and he departed immediately to live at a residential home for troubled adolescents that was miles away in Spokane. Wade was still partially withdrawn, pale and unwell, but he was obviously relieved to escape from his father.

Katie drove Wade to the plane and kissed her brother good-bye. Then she went back home and informed her father that she saw no reason to spend her summer in Seattle. She would like to leave for St. Louis as soon as possible and enroll for the summer session at Ashwood College.

Dr. Brentwood could find no fault with her plan, so Katie departed on the last day of May. Mercifully, she had neither heard from nor seen Bryce Emerson in that time.

In the outlying suburb of St. Louis, she plunged immediately into classes and studies, schedules and plans. Once again Kathryn Brentwood took charge of herself and her life. Fiercely, she strove to expunge all thoughts and memories of Bryce, often playing tennis until she was exhausted, or riding a spirited horse down wooded riding paths when memories of him crowded her too closely.

For the most part Katie succeeded in her goal. But there were still nights when she could not sleep, nights when she was tortured by all the new desires Bryce had aroused in her. Sometimes, asleep at last, she saw his lustrous, gray blue eyes again in her dreams.

And the dash of rain on a windowpane was always, always, a trigger to her memories.

Chapter Four

Eighty-eight days . . .

Katie came slowly awake to a morning bright with Texas sunshine. She had finally fallen asleep last night, and now she wondered why she had felt compelled to relive the past in such precise and time-consuming detail. She was not the sort of woman who spent a lot of time looking back over her shoulder, but the meeting with Bryce had apparently affected her more than she knew at the time.

Well, all of that was over and done with, she thought briskly. Even though Bryce Emerson was still quite an attractive man, with more charm than the law allowed, they were—once again—like ships passing in the night. He had arrived in Texas just as Katie was making preparations to leave.

While she still lay sleepily in bed, Katie thought again

of her future plans. In a way, her course had been set at the time she'd first visited a children's hospital.

That had been years ago, but Katie still remembered the poignancy of those small cribs with their tiny inmates. She would never forget the little boy with curly brown hair who had smiled beguilingly and reached for her with his one good arm. The other, a pitiful mass of bandages, had hung helplessly at his side, and one tiny, brown eye had been covered with an eyepatch. By a miracle the child had survived the reckless driving of his teenaged mother. Why had a child so greviously hurt looked with such trust and love at any adult? Katie had wondered even as she smiled back and bent to drop a kiss on the little boy's cheek.

Yet so many of the children, like that boy, had smiled. . . .

Later, she had seen many others. One, so tragically burned in a house fire that he wore a face mask, had haunted her thoughts for weeks.

In a cruel world where innocent children too often suffered, Katie Brentwood longed to be their champion. At last she had found that one special something that she wanted for herself, the one thing her mother had counseled her to find.

Yawning, Katie rose to face another day that would bring her one step closer to achieving her dream. In the kitchen she switched on her coffee-maker and waited for the liquid to brew.

She had taken only two sips of coffee when her telephone rang. Who could it be this early in the day? she thought warily, then set down her cup and scooped up the receiver. "Hello?" she said.

"Hi, dear. I hope I didn't wake you up!"

"Cee! Oh, hi." Katie recognized her stepmother's voice with relief. "No, you didn't wake me. Is anything wrong? Eric . . . ?"

"Oh, no, everything's fine. Eric just leapt on the school bus so full of energy and questions that I pity his poor teacher!"

"You're not working this week?" Katie asked Cee.

"No, I decided to take off," she replied.

There was no financial need for Cee to work. Although she and Dr. Brentwood had been separated at the time of his death, he had left her and their son amply provided for. With Katie and Wade he had been considerably less generous since he had disapproved of both his daughter's career and his son's life-style. Presently, Cee worked as a special-duty nurse, mostly to keep Eric from driving her bonkers, she had explained.

"I'm so excited I just had to call you!" Cee rushed on. "Guess who phoned me last night?"

"I have no idea," Katie replied a trifle impatiently. Then all the air seemed to seep from her lungs. Did Cee mean she'd talked with Bryce?

"He said he'd had dinner with you," Celia went on archly.

"Oh. Dr. James Bryce Emerson," said Katie. Good heavens, Bryce had certainly wasted no time in calling Cee. Does this have anything to do with *me?* she wondered.

No, that was a conceited assumption, indeed. Sternly, Katie reproved herself. Why, Cee and Bryce were old friends.

Cee, meanwhile, had kept right on talking. ". . . so

glad to hear from him! I didn't dream Bryce was in Dallas. Goodness, Katie, why didn't you tell me?''

"I really never thought about it," Katie said truthfully.

"Why, Bryce was always the nicest neurosurgeon in Seattle and all the nurses adored him," Cee said enthusiastically. "I can't imagine why he's never remarried."

A warning chime rang in Katie's mind. Was Cee really interested in Bryce as a former colleague or as a potential suitor?

"Even Max liked him," Cee went on, "and you know how critical your father was!"

"Uh-huh," said Katie noncommittally.

Of course, there was no reason for Cee *not* to be interested in Bryce, Katie realized, and wondered why the thought gave her a sharp pang. Celia was still a relatively young woman, attractive and wealthy. She was near Bryce's age and she could certainly be a help and support to him in his work. Katie knew she had no right to disapprove. Still, a certain leaden feeling crept around her heart.

"I've invited him for dinner tomorrow night," Cee went on, "and I certainly want you to come, too, Katie."

"Tomorrow? Oh, but—" For a moment Katie floundered.

"Don't tell me you can't make it!" her stepmother wailed. "Didn't you work a shift last Saturday, covering for the weekend administrator?"

"Why, yes," Katie said grudgingly, recalling too late that Cee had a memory like a steel trap.

"And didn't you tell me that the weekend administrator, Darrell-what's-his-name, said he'd relieve you on Wednesday? Of course, if I've got it wrong, then I'll call Bryce back.''

"No, I am off duty tomorrow night. I'd simply forgotten.'' Still Katie hesitated, unwilling to commit herself to an entire evening in Bryce Emerson's company. That strange little feeling of wariness and alarm tightened her throat all over again.

Cee waited expectantly while Katie debated. Oh, heavens, she was making too big a deal out of this! Why shouldn't she see Bryce socially? It wasn't like accepting a date with him. She would simply be one of the dinner guests.

Also, she needed to spend more time with Eric, Katie reminded herself. The events of the past two years—the separation from his father, the move to Texas and then Max Brentwood's death—had affected the intelligent child. It was partially on Eric's account that Katie had accepted her present job in Dallas two years ago. Now that Eric was adjusted and coping well with his new life, Katie felt free to move on.

"All right, I'll be there,'' she agreed.

"Good! Come at seven for drinks, and we'll eat about eight.''

"Fine. I'll see you then.''

After Katie hung up the phone, she warmed up her coffee and carried it back into her bedroom. Then she sat down on the edge of her unmade bed.

Despite her acceptance of Cee's invitation, Katie still felt troubled. Her mind insisted on dwelling on all the reasons why she should *not* get her life entangled again with Bryce's and none of her reasons were unsound.

For starters, she still had eighty-eight nights to work at Harwick Memorial Hospital. The new children's rehabilitation center in Port Angeles, Washington, would not be opened until then. In eighty-eight nights at the same hospital where Bryce practiced, some contact between them would be inevitable. Since those contacts were likely to involve problems, it would be far wiser to keep their relationship strictly professional. When a neurosurgeon and an administrator bumped heads, it was important to make a judgment on the facts, not the personalities. Grimly, Katie reflected that in his role as Dr. Emerson, Bryce would eventually come screaming because a scanner was down, because he wanted a new piece of medical equipment that the hospital's budget didn't provide for, or because some nurse hadn't jumped quickly enough to please him.

Medical folklore said you could always tell a surgeon by his arrogance. Although last night Bryce had appeared quite pleasant, even subdued, Katie did not believe for one minute that he was totally immune from his occupation's hazards. Her earlier experience with Bryce, when added to what she already knew of her father, had not exactly increased her faith in surgeons, and working out of the administrative suite for two years had not been particularly reassuring either. Surgeons were as temperamental as they were talented. Katie had heard—and sometimes seen firsthand—the temper tantrums, the locker doors bent off their hinges from fury and the sarcastic and occasionally profane comments they scribbled on official memos posted by Administration.

No, Katie did not like dealing with surgeons, although, through the years, she had acquired a deeper understanding of them. Surgeons had to live with their split-second decisions. If the decision proved right and the patient recovered, then all was well. If the decision was wrong and the patient died . . . well, for the surgeon it must *still* be right. He had to believe he had done the right thing because he could not afford to be uncertain, to hesitate, to be nagged by self-doubts and feelings of inadequacy.

Then, from deep inside of her, Katie acknowledged the most pressing and imperative reason why she could not allow herself personal involvement with Bryce. As a teenager she had been willing, even eager, to experience the hot fires of desire and passion. Now, as a successful, mature woman she was not. That fire had burned her once—and badly. Now, even when she dreamily contemplated marriage, Katie did not envision the sort of love that included such blinding, consuming, earthshaking passion. She thought instead of mutual trust, closeness and respect. She imagined a warm, healthy physical relationship but not a devastating one.

Bryce, with his enormous physical appeal, threatened her hard-won equanimity. Even the brief touch of his lips last night had done wacky things to Katie's heart. He had set her emotions askew, shaken her demeanor thoroughly and caused her to experience a restless, troubled night. No, she certainly did not wish to get involved with that man again!

And yet, perversely, she did! Some awkward, contradictory part of her had never forgotten the brand of his arms and the taste of his lips, or the irresistible, primitive feelings they had wrought within one another. Therein lay her conflict.

Oh, enough of this brooding! She was making a damned dinner party into an epic, colossal production, blowing it up entirely out of proportion. Decisively, Katie stood up, set down her coffee cup and began swiftly to make her bed. She had a dozen errands to run today and the sooner she got on with them the better!

She dressed in jeans and pullover shirt to go shopping, ate a quick breakfast and then was off to do her chores. The day was glorious, she thought, rolling down her car windows to enjoy the sunshine and fresh air. It was early April, already warm, but too soon as yet for the blinding Texas summer heat.

When Katie returned to her apartment a couple of hours later, her telephone was jangling again. She dropped her sack of groceries on the kitchen counter and reached for the receiver. "Hello?" she said breathlessly.

"Katie?" A lighthearted male voice spoke her name. "I've been ringing your phone off the wall. I thought you'd moved and sent everyone but me your forwarding address!"

It was Doug Sears. Even if Katie hadn't recognized his voice, she would have identified him by his banter. "Oh, hi, Doug." She sighed. "I was out shopping."

"You could sound more enthusiastic," he complained. "Like 'Wow, it's Doug! The best-looking and most skillful helicopter pilot at Harwick Memorial Hospital! You know that Pilot Sears always brings 'em back alive!' "

"Doug, you're still much too modest," Katie retorted.

"Yeah, I'm just naturally the strong, silent type. Listen, how about a date tonight?"

"I'm working tonight," she replied.

"I have nothing against late dates! Matter of fact, I prefer 'em," he responded.

"I'll bet," she said sardonically. "No, Doug. Sorry."

"You don't sound sorry one bit!" he went on plaintively.

"I guess I was merely being polite," Katie admitted. She swung her purse off her shoulder and dropped it down by her grocery sack. "Now, if you don't mind, my ice cream is starting to melt—"

"Wait a minute, Katie." His voice lower and more serious, Doug pressed her to stay on the line. "There's something you should know. Look, I've really missed you."

"I'm flattered. But isn't there someone else? A tall, blond, efficient head nurse? Does that ring any bells?"

"Sheila and I have split. It's over. Kaput. Dead and finished. I moved out last weekend."

"Oh," said Katie noncommittally. She had not known that Sheila and Doug were actually living together, but, of course, it was the modern way.

"'Tis true. I'm sitting here in a small, furnished apartment looking at a stack of unwashed dishes and a pile of dirty clothes."

"Doug, there's something I never told you. I'm not exactly the domestic type."

"I never meant *that!*" He laughed. "All I meant was that I'm lonely and a bit depressed and I couldn't help remembering that you and I used to have a lot of fun. We did, didn't we, Katie?''

"Well, yes," she admitted. "But I didn't know about Sheila then—or of any others you have on the string."

"There's no string anymore. It's busted. I really mean that, Katie. Now I'm just looking for one good woman."

Although Doug sounded sincere, Katie wasn't buying any of it. "Have you thought about going home to your mother, Doug?" she suggested.

He gave a shout of laughter. "No, and I'm not about to either! She's heartless, just like you, and she'd kick my butt right out of the house. So how about tomorrow night, Katie? Aren't you off duty then?"

"Good lord, other people seem to know my work schedule a lot better than I do!" she exclaimed.

"You mean some other guy has already called you?" Doug said, a trace of jealousy in his voice.

"My stepmother called me. I'm having dinner at her house tomorrow night. Now, Doug, my ice cream really is melting. I'll see you around," Katie said in firm dismissal.

"I'm not going to give up," he warned.

"Oh, shoot!"

Doug chuckled, and the phone clicked off.

For a moment Katie stood still, musing. With Doug, life had been uncomplicated and fun. He was not by nature a very complex or serious-minded person and yet he was not quite as shallow as his teasing banter would indicate. He was an excellent helicopter pilot who could, it was said, set his chopper down between two parked cars. Despite the exaggeration, Katie knew the compliment to his flying had been genuine. Especially at night, the most treacherous time for emergency medical flights, Doug seemed to have an instinctive radar for all the treetops and high wires, or perhaps he just had a very good memory. The doctors and nurses who flew with Doug trusted him, and he'd had enough medical training that he could pitch in and help when such assistance was needed.

Yes, Doug Sears had the reputation of having a cool head and calm, steady hands. If only he wasn't such an incorrigible flirt and ladies' man! Still, Katie did not totally dismiss Doug from all consideration as she put away her groceries. Although she rather doubted that he had gotten very serious about life, she couldn't help a small feeling of pleasure that he'd phoned her today, and she wondered if his pursuit of her would continue. A few dates with him might help to speed the passage of her next eighty-eight days.

And, at least, where their work was concerned, Doug's area of authority and Katie's did not overlap. He controlled the aircraft. Period. He, not the administrator, decided whether weather conditions allowed him to fly or not. So Katie's working world and Doug's had never collided.

At four that afternoon she went back on duty and soon her mind focused again on business. There were things to check, employees to counsel, beeper pages to answer. Katie kept her mind firmly off neurosurgeons and all matters of that sort.

But lying in bed late that night, just before sleep beckoned, her subconscious mind was freed from its restraints. For just a moment as she drowsed, Katie couldn't help but remember that hot rush of passion and pleasure that still lingered in her memory, vivid and unchanged, across the expanse of ten years.

Eighty-seven days . . .

"Katie?" The male voice was warm and low. "It's Bryce Emerson."

This time, late on the following afternoon, Bryce caught her with her defenses down. Katie's heart leaped and soared at the sound of his voice on the telephone. She had just returned from lying in the sunshine by the swimming pool after enjoying a leisurely, restful day.

"Yes, Bryce?" she replied, while her pulse raced. Even her voice held a strange, breathy note.

"I wanted to offer you a ride to Cee's house tonight. I thought you probably lived close to the medical center like I do. If your address in the phone book is correct, I'm just a few blocks away."

"Yes, the address is correct," Katie said automatically.

"Good! Why don't we go together and you can show me the way?" His soft, smooth tone practically caressed Katie's exposed nerve endings. "I'll pick you up at six-thirty—OK?"

"Yes, thank you. That will be fine." Her own voice emerged again like that of a wilful stranger's.

"Fine. See you then," Bryce said.

Oh God, what am I doing now? Katie thought as all of her earlier resolutions were dashed. Why hadn't she contrived some small excuse—"I'm stopping to see a friend first''—or some such line? Oh, why couldn't she handle Bryce Emerson with the same facility with which she handled Doug?

The trouble was, whenever she heard his voice she ceased to think. A strange shock set in. She could only feel, respond, agree.

What is it about that man? she thought irritably as she hurried into her bedroom to strip off her swimsuit.

By the time her shower was running, Katie's string of excuses to herself began to emerge. Well, of course, he's only being polite to offer me a ride. I'm making too big a deal of it. Why shouldn't I agree when I dislike driving alone at night? It's not like my life is really getting mixed up with his again!

But as she stood beneath the shower, sudsing her long, chestnut hair, Katie grew painfully aware of liquid, languid fire licking at her veins. Apparently, even the sound of Bryce's bedroom voice could activate it. She turned the shower down, and the slower drops striking the glass door reminded her of the dash of rain against a windowpane.

She was *afraid* of Bryce Emerson, she realized with a sudden flash of insight. She was afraid, deeply afraid, that if he made a move toward her she might be as powerless to resist him as she'd been once before.

She scoffed at her fears. She was a grown woman now and she never had trouble holding off other men. Doug Sears could certainly attest to that!

Still, the fear remained curled like a cold knot in the pit of her stomach, at war with her desire.

Katie dressed carefully, wanting to look casual without also looking abandoned. She would send signals with her attire and appearance, and she wanted these to be noncommittal.

She selected a pair of tailored, wheat-colored slacks and an emerald-green silk shirt. She used a light hand with her makeup but did succumb to applying a bit of eyeshadow, liner and mascara. Not a lot, just a touch, she warned herself. Then she reached for her heavy mass of hair.

She could, of course, wrench it back into her familiar knot but that would be a shame when it looked so nice lying loose and wind-blown. Small, curly tendrils crept about her face while the rest of it fell in soft waves. Anyway, Eric didn't like her hair pulled back severely. . . .

She topped her clothes with a beige blazer, then fastened a single strand of gold around her neck. Small gold earrings went into her ears, then Katie slid her feet into a pair of frivolous, high-heeled sandals. That's because Bryce is so tall, she argued with herself. I don't want to strain my neck looking up at him all night.

Her finished image, reflected back to her in the mirror, was not quite what she'd intended. She looked rather . . . well, *pretty*. The sun had brought an attractive flush to her cheekbones; the emerald blouse darkened her brown eyes; and her rippling hair was definitely softening to the contours of her face.

I should have skipped the eye makeup, Katie thought critically, but by now it was too late to go and wash it off. There was nothing to do but look more alluring than she had planned to.

Nervously, she rearranged the contents of her purse, discarding a couple of crumpled tissues. He'll probably be late, she warned herself when she stood at last in her tidy living room. Doctors often had a poor sense of time.

Her doorbell rang exactly on the stroke of six-thirty.

Katie drew a deep breath and went to answer the door, squaring her shoulders against the expected impact. Bryce was *not* going to bowl her over tonight or any night!

He met her with a radiant smile, that curving, flashing smile that lit up his whole face. How happy he looks! Katie thought irrelevantly. How attractively masculine he is!

Bryce towered over her, casually yet neatly dressed in an expensive, tan sports jacket, a pale yellow shirt open at his throat and trim, dark brown slacks that outlined the length and strength of his long legs. He looked so appealing that Katie found it hard to keep breathing normally.

She became uncomfortably aware that neither of them had said a single word yet. Bryce simply continued to stare at her and smile.

Katie drew another breath. She needed it because her lungs felt suddenly empty. "Hello, Bryce," she said, in the most casual voice she could manage.

"Katie." Bryce's wide shoulders moved as he seemed to shake himself loose from a spell. "How lovely you are! How elegant!" His voice was hushed and low.

That voice carried a reminder of their shared past. Oh, this would never do! Katie thought. Furthermore, Bryce took a step forward as though he might touch or even embrace her. Swiftly, Katie turned away. She crossed the room to pick up her purse and switch off one of the table lamps. She left one glowing as she always did when she went out at night.

"Shall we go?" she said to Bryce, her voice terse.

"Sure." But he didn't move for a moment. His eyes went around the living room slowly, admiring the tasteful decorations, the thriving green plants and the large painting over the sofa that dominated the room. "I like your place," he said in a conversational tone. His gaze lingered on the painting for a moment longer. "I'm fond of the Impressionists myself."

"Oh? Do you collect paintings?" Katie inquired, swinging her purse strap up and over her shoulder.

"No, I'm not a collector." Courteously, Bryce held the door open for her.

Katie slanted a sidelong look at him. She knew that many doctors were collectors: some enjoyed paintings; others acquired chess sets or, like her own father, books that were first editions. More than a few doctors collected women although, of course, they never admitted to that. Perhaps Bryce, with his devastating smile, fell into the latter category.

They went down the outside stairs, then Bryce touched Katie's elbow to guide her to the right. "I've parked over here."

He's certainly not a collector of cars, she mused as he opened the door to his dark blue sedan. Oh, the car was quite nice with leather seats and padded dashboard, and it had the usual complement of features and gadgets, but it was not the raffishly spectacular auto so many single doctors favored. Katie wondered at her disappointment that Bryce so steadfastly refused to fit the image into which she yearned to cast him. Why did she *want* him to be a playboy physician?

Katie did notice, as she started to slide inside, that Bryce's car had been freshly washed and waxed. Its interior was gleaming. Was that simply part of a scheduled maintenance by him, or had he spruced it up for her?

Oh, quit trying to make such a big deal out of the little things, Katie warned herself as Bryce dropped down into the seat beside her.

When they neared the main gate leading out of the apartment complex, Bryce gave her a whimsical look. "May I use your gate card or shall I talk my way through once again?"

"Oh!" Katie cried, chagrin seizing her. "I forgot to phone the gate and tell the guard you were expected! Oh, Bryce, I'm so sorry!" Rapidly, Katie unzipped her purse and fumbled for the card she kept handily in her billfold. "I've never done such a thing before! How did you get in?"

"Oh, it wasn't hard," he said, making light of Katie's impolite omission. "The caduceus on the back of my car and the black bag in the trunk, which I keep for emergencies, turned the trick—or opened the gate, in this particular case."

"You doctors do have a way of getting what you want," Katie said brightly, although she was still chagrined and amazed at herself for having forgotten.

"Not always!" Bryce shot back. He turned serious, gray blue eyes on her. "Right now, I'm asking myself why I frighten you, Katie."

She felt a pulse jump to life in her throat—felt her eyes dilating in surprise. She hadn't thought Bryce would notice, but, of course, he'd always read her so easily. Now denial seemed her safest recourse. She heard herself give an awkward little laugh while she gazed through the windshield to avoid meeting his penetrating gaze. "Frighten me? You don't frighten me, Bryce," she lied.

"No?" They had reached the gate. Deftly, he wound down the window and inserted Katie's card, and the steel barrier rose. "A surgeon often sees fear in the eyes of his patients—their relatives as well. By now I can identify it quite readily, Katie. Several times since we've met again I've seen fear in your eyes, too. I've also had enough psychology to wonder why you tried, at least symbolically, to lock me out of your life tonight."

"Oh, Bryce, don't be ridiculous—" Katie stopped because his large, warm hand, returning her gate card, was suddenly over hers.

"I'm sorry. You're right," she admitted stiffly and used the card as an excuse to withdraw her hand from the energizing warmth of his. But she still couldn't admit the actual truth, nor could she meet his eyes. "I don't know why you frighten me."

"Katie, look at me—please!"

Bryce's voice held such urgency that Katie had no recourse but to look; it was as though she were mesmerized. To her surprise, his eyes had a twinkle in them. "What do you think I'm going to do to you?" he asked gently. "Besmirch your reputation? Wink at the fellows in the locker room and boast that beneath your professional façade lies a real femme fatale? Or blackmail you?'' His voice became a movie villain's hiss: ''Help me get a new CAT scanner, Katie Brentwood, or I will tell all!''

She burst out laughing at Bryce's foolishness.

His voice changed back to its tone of wry amusement. ''Or do you think I'll kidnap you and take you to my bachelor lair, keeping you there helpless, my prisoner of love?''

That was close enough to the truth that Katie's next laugh was strained, and she felt color burning across her cheeks. ''You're teasing me,'' she said stiffly.

''Yes. I'm making light of things because the real truth of the matter is more serious. Your fear is serious. What has happened to me is serious. Katie, you may not believe it now, but the neurosurgical resident you knew in Seattle is, for all intents and purposes, quite dead.''

Katie found herself staring at Bryce and unable to look away. Her heart began thumping from all her strange, conflicting feelings. Why did he say the resident from Seattle was dead? Oh, she knew by the dramatic change in Bryce's appearance that in some way his words were true. But what had happened? There was also a sudden poignancy that squeezed at the regions of her heart. She hoped that the young doctor who had been her ardent lover in the call room in Seattle had not been totally obliterated!

''I don't understand what you mean,'' Katie whispered. ''But right now I don't understand myself very well either. I *do* believe you, Bryce.'' With her spoken words, she realized that she really did believe him. Slowly, she extended the hand she had drawn away from him. His fingers met and captured hers with a reassuring

squeeze. "Bryce, about Seattle . . ." she began painfully. "I never blamed *you* for what— Well, yes,
dammit, I have! You should have told me you were
married. Believe me, that would have stopped things in a
hurry!"

"And you should have told me you were a virgin and
not acted like an experienced woman of the world," he
retorted, but his eyes were kind. "I'd been living a
chaste and thoroughly deprived life. You looked like
manna from heaven that night!"

"Me—manna?" Katie repeated incredulously. Then
she laughed again.

"Let's quit blaming ourselves and each other. It was
all a very long time ago. Friends, Katie?" Bryce's
words held a note of eager hope.

"Friends," she agreed, her heart lightening. "And I
won't be afraid of you anymore."

Then, as the warm touch of his hand radiated up her
arm, Katie thought to herself: Now the only person I
have to be afraid of is myself, and the way he makes me
feel!

Behind them a car horn suddenly honked, loudly and
insistently. Simultaneously, Katie and Bryce burst into
laughter. Bryce still had not pulled through the raised
steel barrier of the gate, and, behind them, another
apartment resident had grown weary of waiting for them
to move.

Chapter Five

$\mathcal{K}$atie gave Bryce directions to Cee's house in the Oak Cliff section of Dallas, and, while they rode, they talked easily and companionably. Katie leaned her head back against the comfortable leather seat and watched the play of expressions on Bryce's lean face. Gradually, she relaxed, feeling a sense of welcome release as the accumulation of tension drained slowly from her.

"How in the world did you happen to become a hospital administrator, Katie?" Bryce asked.

"Oh, it just evolved," she answered quietly, studying the clean-cut line of his jaw and admiring his thick, stubby black eyelashes. "I did my undergraduate work at Ashwood College near St. Louis and went through most of the four years without the foggiest notion of what my career should be. I was too proud at first to admit that hospitals attracted me. Because of Dad, I didn't want to get mixed up with the medical profession—''

"Ouch!" Bryce said and faked a wince.

"Well, it's true! So I took a lot of business courses that I wasn't very interested in. Then I heard about the Health Administration and Planning Program at Washington University, which is also in St. Louis. I started work on my master's there. Maybe part of it was to spite Dad—I don't know. Certainly he'd been at war with administrators most of his career, and I'll admit that he howled most gratifyingly when I told him what I planned. But, to my surprise, the studies did tie together my various interests. By the time I was at my first hospital, a small one in Illinois where I did a structured internship, I realized that I really liked my career. Furthermore, I was good at it. Now what about you, Bryce?"

"One more question. What about your other career?" he inquired.

Katie looked at him blankly.

"Woman, wife, mother." He took his eyes off the road to glance at her, and she saw the enormous question in his eyes.

"Just never have met the right man," she replied lightly.

"A woman who looks like you?" Bryce appeared shocked. "Why, I'll bet you've had to beat your suitors off with a club!"

"You flatter me." Katie laughed. "Oh, I've dated, of course. Through the years there have been a few men that I knew were interested in me, but I've never needed to buy a club to hold them off. I was even engaged briefly. I returned his ring when I realized he just wasn't the right man and I couldn't settle for less.''

''Oh.'' Bryce nodded understandingly, then his face turned curiously back to her again. ''But even if you can do without a husband, haven't you missed children in your life? Haven't you wanted your own?''

Yes, so much that in eighty-seven days I'll be at a rehabilitation center that treats them, were the words that sprang immediately into Katie's mind. Not, of course, that she would utter them. Only Cee knew of her future plans, and, until Katie gave her required one-month's notice to Harwick Memorial, she wanted to keep it that way. Nothing could undermine an administrator's effectiveness more than being known as a ''short timer.'' Also, the hospital had the right to know her intentions first.

So Katie chose a careful answer to Bryce's question. ''There's been Eric, you see. I'm close to him. And I adore my niece, Jessica, even though I don't get to see her very often. It appears that the family line is continuing very well without my active participation.'' Brightly, she said, ''Now, it's your turn, Dr. Emerson. How did you wind up first at Stanford, and now here in Dallas?''

''I suspect my path has been more circuitous than yours,'' Bryce replied. ''During the difficult days of my residency, all I could think of were the usual prizes and rewards to come. I planned a lucrative private practice, with myself as a leading society doctor. I wanted a house as big as your father's, a Florida condo, European trips and a fast Jaguar.''

''But you didn't become a society doctor,'' Katie

noted. "You chose to teach medicine as well as to practice it under the difficult and trying conditions of a trauma hospital. And that, I know, is a lot more work, as well as a lot less lucrative, than a society practice. Of course, I don't suppose you've missed many meals."

"You might be surprised." A hint of a smile played around his mobile lips, and, involuntarily, Katie's eyes were drawn to the attractive hollows of his cheeks and the slight indentation at his temple. Her eyes lingered on the occasional thread of gray hairs scattered among his more abundant dark ones.

"Actually, a number of things happened to me within a relatively short period of time," Bryce related. "My divorce was one of them. You were another, Katie, and there were two or three more. Most of them painful, but they all proved great learning experiences. They set my feet on a different path."

Katie got the rather disquieting feeling that while Bryce was trying to be scrupulously honest with her he was also carefully not revealing exactly what these things and their emotional impact had been.

"It's all a long story, Katie. Maybe I'll tell you someday, if you're interested." Bryce had apparently sensed her knowledge of his reserve. "Now . . . aren't we pretty close to Cee's house?"

"It's two more exits away," Katie said automatically. She felt as great a curiosity nibbling at her as she'd earlier seen written on his face when he had questioned her. "One more question, Bryce," she said, insisting he play fair. "Why haven't you married again? What about your other career?"

"Been too busy," he said promptly, then darted her a

teasing look. "It's been an awful struggle to stay single, though. All those eager women I've had to beat off with my club!"

"Frankly, I don't doubt it," Katie retorted.

"Doubt it," he urged. "I'm too serious—perhaps even too strange, in some ways, for most women's taste. I just can't relate to a lot of their interests now, especially the purely materialistic ones. Though I would like very much to meet the right woman and have a home and family at last."

"Take the next exit," Katie instructed as another green expressway sign flashed by. Her curiosity about Bryce had only deepened with all he had carefully neglected to reveal. "What have you got against material possessions?"

"Actually, nothing," he said slowly. "I just mean I don't get very excited about acquiring and buying—or which brand names are more important than others. Naturally, I have what I really need and want. I also have a financial counselor and a sensible investment program—"

"I'm glad to hear it," Katie interjected. "From the way you were talking, I wondered if you were building a church or feeding the poor. . . ."

Bryce chuckled. "Nothing so dramatic and self-sacrificing as that! I simply took a different path; I didn't vault into sainthood."

"Turn at the next corner, then right at the first stop light," Katie directed as Bryce's car moved more slowly through a quiet, middle-class neighborhood.

"Now you see why women don't find me very fascinating," Bryce went on wryly.

I'm fascinated, Katie thought to herself. I want to know just what is going on with you, Bryce Emerson!

Aloud, she spoke kindly. "So far, at least, I haven't found you excessively serious and dull."

"Good!" Bryce flashed his earlier radiant smile at her, and once again Katie's heartbeat went into overdrive. She felt her mouth tugged gently by a slow, answering smile, and their eyes met and clung.

Then, abruptly, Bryce pulled his car over to the side of the quiet, tree-lined street.

"I want to tell you one thing now, Katie," he said rapidly, turning in his seat to face her. "At the risk of scaring you all over again, I want you to know this. Before I ever came to Dallas, I knew you were here. I knew you were one of the administrators at Harwick Memorial."

Katie felt her mouth drop open, forming an O of astonishment. "Why, Bryce!" she managed to say at last.

"It happened when Ash Blakely first visited me at Stanford to see if he could recruit me for my present position. Ash was getting nowhere fast, so he started telling me about a number of people who were now enjoying life in the Sunbelt. He dropped three or four familiar names, then he said, 'Oh, another person is Max Brentwood's daughter, Kathryn.' That was the first news I'd had of you for years."

Katie felt her astonishment deepening. "Bryce, you don't mean that just because Dr. Blakely mentioned my name—" She stopped. Of course, it wasn't the mention of her that had lured Bryce here.

"It wasn't you solely," he confirmed. "Ash made me

a good offer—a challenging offer. To rebuild a presently understaffed department and ultimately turn it into a school of neurosurgery. Still, your name was certainly a powerful lure. I'd never forgotten you, Katie.'' Bryce's eyes blazed with emotional intensity, and he stretched out his hands to enfold Katie's numb ones.

''So that's why you weren't at all surprised to see me,'' she remarked in amazement. ''That's why I didn't see any recognition of me in your eyes. I thought, at first, that you'd forgotten me completely.''

Slowly, Bryce drew her hands to his chest, pressing Katie's two small palms there. ''I wasn't likely to ever forget,'' he said softly, parroting the words she had said to him that first night in the cafeteria. ''I wanted very much to see you again,'' he continued slowly. ''To see what you'd become. You had such a wonderful, beautiful strength even as a young girl, Katie.''

His eyes were twin pools of soft gray blue, and she was drowning in their warm depths. Beneath her hands, which rested on his shirt, she could feel the warm vibrancy of his skin and the regular, steady beat of his heart. ''I never dreamed that you thought of me that way,'' Katie said faintly.

''Oh, yes,'' he returned evenly. ''Some people pass through my life and scarcely leave a trace. There have been women I knew much longer and more intimately than I ever knew you, but six months or a year later I could barely remember their names, much less their faces. Other people, and you were one, sometimes engrave themselves on my memory.'' His dark head dipped, and his lips grazed Katie's fingers ever so lightly and tenderly. "Now have I scared you to death all over again?"

Her pulses jumped, and her heart pounded but not from fear. Not now. Her veins began to send forth tiny currents of hot liquid fire. "No, you haven't," Katie breathed. Suddenly, she wanted to feel the insistent pressure of his mouth on hers, wanted to run her fingers through his hair and press her face in the inviting crook of his neck. Such a pleasant aroma exuded from Bryce: a clean, healthy male fragrance. It beckoned to her, drew her like a flame attracts a moth.

His lips touched her fingers again. Then, as though Bryce sensed the wordless invitation, he pulled Katie gently into his arms.

Her face fit perfectly into the hollow of his neck, and her fingers, now sliding upward to his hair, throbbed with the delightful sensations of touching him, of feeling again the crisp aliveness of his hair and skin.

Bryce held Katie in that gentle embrace for several long moments. He was being very careful not to alarm her, she sensed, but she knew that as soon as she raised her face he would try to capture her lips with his.

For a moment she tried to resist her own desire, burrowing her face even more deeply into his shoulder. But his hands began tracing delightful patterns on her back, and Katie knew she would, *must,* respond to his touch and the warm sweetness of his breath brushing her ear.

The silence, the stillness, built in intensity until she could fight her feelings no longer. She wanted him to kiss her. Beneath her left palm she felt the speeded-up rhythm of his heart. She knew her own was beating just as rapidly.

Slowly, she drew back and looked up. Bryce's face was so near to hers that she could count each separate hair of his thick, black eyebrows. Carefully, almost gingerly, he let his mouth drop down to hers, and Katie's lips parted in anticipation.

His lips covered hers, softly yet firmly, tenderly yet tinglingly. And she knew again the hot fire that even his lightest touch or kiss could spark within her.

Why is it like this? Katie wondered, feeling the leap of her heart, the rapid awakening of her body and her arms rising and closing instinctively around him. Why do I always melt when he touches me?

And how can I help doing anything else? she thought in one last reflection before she began to sink and drown in sheer sensation. I can't seem to help myself! I just want this moment to go on and on. . . .

Bryce's lips now claimed hers completely, pressing and exploring, his tongue darting past the barrier of her teeth and into the welcome warmth within. Katie sagged against him, helplessly and hopelessly aroused.

Bryce had called her strong, but he was the chink in her rigid armor, her constant weakness, her own particular Achille's heel, and she couldn't even despair over that fact. With his mouth so possessive and tender by turns, her body could only hum and sing, responding to old, never-forgotten depths of passion and glory.

For a few magic moments they simply gripped each other, kissing mindlessly again and again. Their mouths clung, unable to part. Then, slowly, Bryce's lips on Katie's broke the spell, first with a lighter imprint, then with a sigh that seemed to echo in the stillness of the car as his arms, clutching her to him, began to loosen.

"It takes . . . every bit of strength I have to let you go," he said breathlessly. Then she saw chagrin begin to change the rapturous expression of his face. He drew back into his own seat, his breathing still ragged.

"I don't know what happens to me when I kiss you, Katie!"

Bryce's words sounded so plaintive and their surprise so equaled her own that Katie gave a short cry.

"Oh, Bryce, I don't know what happens to me either!"

His abashed eyes met hers, their dark concern beginning to lighten with relief. Their hands linked again, naturally yet loosely, and after a moment they laughed together, no self-consciousness in the sound.

"You responded, you know," Bryce said to her in mock reprimand. "The next time I try to give you a brotherly kiss, you mustn't part your lips so invitingly or hold me so tight. . . ."

"That's right, blame the woman," she accused, but already her still-tingling body welcomed his promise of a next time.

Bryce looked down at their joined hands, her hand swallowed up in the largeness of his. "It's rather wonderful, isn't it, Katie? To find a person who makes you feel so gloriously, marvelously alive?"

"Yes," she admitted, for at that moment she could do nothing less. Then, slowly, her eyes translated the numbers on his dashboard clock. They were already late for their dinner engagement.

"Bryce, we're due at Cee's!" she cried.

He glanced at the clock and whistled. "We sure are."

They drove the rest of the way in silence, but Bryce still held Katie's hand in his free one, and she was happy, oh, much too happy, to protest.

Eric opened the door to them. With a war whoop, he hurled himself immediately into Katie's arms and began talking a mile a minute. Behind him stood Celia. "Bryce!" she exclaimed in joy and flew to embrace him.

Abruptly, Katie thunked back to earth. Automatically, she tousled her half brother's bright blond hair and tried to remember what his last question had been, but her eyes watched the other two adults who were hugging each other eagerly. Just a moment ago *she* had been in Bryce's arms; now Cee was there. The green-eyed monster that was jealousy took a small, sharp bite on her heart.

Katie's instinctive emotion appalled her. She had never been jealous of another woman before, and to experience such a primitive, barbaric feeling was unnerving. Katie felt even more ashamed when, after a moment, Cee turned to give her a hug. Sweet, dear Cee, how could she have been jealous of her? Katie felt closer to Celia than she'd been to any other woman except her own mother. Guiltily, she returned her stepmother's hug, and it was a relief when Cee directed them to follow her down the hall and into the family room.

Still, Katie found herself viewing Celia not just as her beloved friend but as a very attractive woman in competition for a handsome, desirable man. Cee was tall and slender, with strawberry blond hair and a pert, intelligent face. Although she looked her age, thirty-seven, she had such a vibrant air that one immediately forgot the tiny lines around her eyes and mouth and saw only the splendor of her twinkling green eyes and smiling countenance.

What's wrong with me? Katie thought with another pang. I can't let myself be interested in Bryce—I mustn't! My future is already planned! I'm leaving Texas soon and moving back to Washington. That's what I want—it's what I've been working toward for years. There's no place in my life for a neurosurgeon. Nor was there really any indication that Bryce even wanted such a place!

Oh, sure, he and Katie had shared several heated kisses, but people did that all the time, then left each other without a qualm. And that's what I'll do, too, Katie vowed. It was time for her to backpedal *now* and leave Cee a clear field with Bryce.

Indeed, Celia was so joyously happy to see him that as Katie got her feelings in hand, she could not avoid being pulled into that charmed circle of warmth. While she sipped the drink that Cee had poured for her and answered Eric's innumerable questions, one of her ears remained attuned to Cee's and Bryce's enthusiastic recollections.

"Goodness, I'm about ready to talk your ear off and you've scarcely had a chance to meet Eric," Cee said to Bryce. Proudly, she stretched out an arm to draw Eric into their circle. "Well, Bryce, what do you think of my son?"

As Bryce stared at the charming tableau presented by mother and son, Katie tried to see her half brother through his eyes. Eric was tall for his age and sturdy. He had Cee's grass-green eyes; she had also given him that glint of red in his blond hair. But for the rest, in features and stance, he bore a haunting resemblance to Max Brentwood.

"I think Eric's a fine-looking boy," Bryce said sincerely. "I see a bit of you, Cee, and quite a lot more of Max."

"Do you really think I look like my father?" Eric said to Bryce eagerly.

He was proud of the father he had scarcely known, for Dr. Brentwood had shown scant interest in his children while they were still young. Because a boy needed a father-figure to admire, both Cee and Katie had been careful not to reveal too much to Eric of Dr. Brentwood's unpleasant personality. At the same time they had attempted to moderate those traits in Eric. He, too, was impulsive, hot-headed and quick-spoken, with a temper that could be ferocious. Katie's brother, Wade, had once seen Eric in a raging tantrum and ever since had regarded the child with an almost hostile distaste.

Balancing those destructive traits of Eric's were others that his mother and Katie sought to nurture: his intelligence, his genuine compassion for people who were ill and suffering and his love of pets. There was also a certain native sweetness in Eric that his father had never possessed.

"I've got to check on dinner," Cee said, running a hand through her long, carelessly styled hair. "Katie, will you help me while these two men get acquainted?"

"Sure." Katie rose obediently to follow Cee, but she couldn't resist throwing a last glance over her shoulder. Although Bryce was engaged in earnest conversation with Eric, his eyes followed her. He flashed Katie a smile.

Warmed by the memory of his smile, Katie tossed salad with equal mixtures of vinegar and oil and listened to Cee talk excitedly about Bryce.

"Katie, when I heard his voice I was speechless—and you know that I am seldom rendered speechless! I recognized that it was Bryce right away and I just couldn't believe it. I used to have a crush on him years and years ago—all the neuro nurses did. 'The handsome one,' that's what they called Bryce because he seemed to have it all: good looks, money, talent. Also, a very pleasant disposition, and you know how damned temperamental surgeons can be! But Bryce was . . . well, sort of a shining light. We absolutely *fought* to work with him! Oh, I can't believe he's in Dallas now!" Cee's voice turned wistful. "I just hope we'll have the opportunity to see a lot more of him."

Katie's heart plunged downward with each one of Celia's bubbly words even as she continued to toss the salad. Oh God, this was worse than she'd thought. Already Cee was spinning fantasies of herself, Eric and Bryce.

Celia was eager to remarry, Katie knew. She needed a husband and Eric a father. She had already married one neurosurgeon, and although that marriage had not turned out well at all, Cee was still willing to gamble on another one. In that, she was unlike Katie, who had never wanted to marry a surgeon.

I certainly won't stand in her way, Katie vowed anew, giving the salad yet another grim toss. Bryce is also eager for a home and family, and he and Cee are practically the same age. They share the same interests. It all ought to work out well for them.

Katie's logic was infallible. Why did her emotions create such tumult at the thought?

"Goodness, Katie, you're going to whip that salad to pieces!" Cee exclaimed and stepped over to rescue it. She next assigned Katie the task of filling the wineglasses.

At dinner Katie was subdued, but the others were talking so much she felt sure her near silence would not be observed.

"Mom, Bryce has just rented a place on a lake 'bout forty miles from here," Eric informed Cee excitedly.

"Darling, don't talk with your mouth full," Cee reprimanded Eric, then she turned to Bryce eagerly. "You have? Which lake?"

"Lake Watachee," Bryce replied. "Before I'd been here twenty-four hours, Josh Weaver, another surgeon at Harwick Memorial, was showing me snapshots and doing a good selling job. His wife is tired of the place, and Josh is trying to unload it. I've only been there one weekend. Josh says the bass fishing is good."

"Bryce says it has three bedrooms and he says there are a lot of water-skiers on the lake. You know how I've been wanting to water-ski," Eric went on in his high, young voice. "I want to learn to bass fish, too."

"Eric, quit hinting," Cee said bluntly and looked across the table at Bryce. "Please excuse my less-than-subtle son."

"No need." Bryce gave a lazy shrug of his shoulders. "I've already offered to take Eric fishing and to teach him to water-ski as well. We've settled on this weekend. Of course, I'm counting on both of you ladies to join us."

"Oh, Bryce, we mustn't . . ." Cee stammered, but Katie, aware of every nuance, saw her stepmother's heightened color and realized that the invitation had pleased Cee greatly. "We'll impose on you!"

"It's no imposition at all," Bryce insisted. "I'd be delighted to have you there. Katie—" He turned pointedly to regard her. "You'll be able to join us, won't you?"

"I don't know if I—" She was cut short by Eric's howl of dismay. Both he and Bryce wanted Katie to come!

"We all want Katie to come," Celia said in her kind and generous way. "Don't tell me you have to work this weekend, dear?"

"Well, no, but I—"

"Good! Then it's settled," Bryce said, his voice sounding almost as young and happy as Eric's.

Oh God, what am I getting myself into now? Katie wondered, chewing distractedly on a piece of delicious barbecued beef. Then she consoled herself with a thought: I can always back out at the last minute if that seems wiser.

Wiser. Right now wisdom seemed to dictate that she keep her mouth shut and just listen quietly and observe. Through the rest of dinner Cee and Bryce talked on about old times and mutual acquaintances, pausing politely to identify the cast of characters for Katie and Eric.

Dessert was a superb flan, then Cee served coffee and brandy. She also ordered Eric to his room to do his homework.

"But, Mom—" he protested.

"No 'buts,' " Cee said firmly. "Tell Bryce and Katie good night."

Reluctantly, the child bid them farewell. Cee's eyes followed Eric fondly as the child left the room. "Don't be surprised if he's back in twenty minutes," she warned her guests. "Eric zips through homework with the speed of light."

"He's quite intelligent, isn't he?" Bryce observed.

"Almost frighteningly so." Cee sighed. "He's in a special program for intellectually gifted children. I sometimes have nightmares in which he graduates from college at fifteen." Then she turned back to Bryce. "How is your mother? I've never forgotten meeting her."

"I'll bet you haven't," Bryce said wryly, a slow smile playing around his beautifully formed lips. To Katie, he explained, "My mother, known to everyone as Mimi, is a shallow, flighty woman who is usually quite charming but can also be equally unpleasant when things don't suit her. Cee once had the unfortunate experience of meeting up with Mimi when she was in the latter state."

"I didn't blame her!" Cee shot back. "If I was ever told that my only child was dying, I'd scream the hospital down, too!"

Katie was so startled that her coffee cup clattered back into its saucer. "Your mother once thought you were dying?" she repeated to Bryce.

"We all thought he was! Why—" Cee stopped at the negligent wave of Bryce's hand.

"Clearly they were all misinformed," Bryce said lightly, even humorously, his eyes twinkling across the table at Katie. Then he looked back at Cee. "At present Mimi is doing just fine in Miami. She knows a lot of other rich widows, and they lead an exhausting life of cocktail parties, bridge games and afternoons at the race track. Mimi is always glad to inform me about the *strain* of it all. I guess squandering a fortune does take work."

"Oh, I'm sure." Cee laughed.

"I usually fly down to help her celebrate the new year and, frankly, I don't know which one of us dreads it most," Bryce went on.

"We can't choose our parents, can we?" Katie said softly. It was difficult to try and reconcile Bryce with his serious side and his commitment to excellence in medicine with a mother such as he'd described. But even more surprising was the subject of his previous critical illness that he'd obviously tried to forestall.

Katie was having none of that. Since Bryce knew all about *her*, why shouldn't she be equally well informed about him? "What's this about how you almost died?" she pressed him.

"Oh, the summer after I first met you, Katie, I flew down to South America with a friend of mine, Bud Slavens, and I think we hit every bar in northern Brazil."

"Bud was an orthopedic surgeon and a red-haired terror!" Cee filled in. "He was also not known for leaving many maidens untouched!"

"Ah, yes, there was a bit of that, too," Bryce

admitted, his eyes holding an almost wicked glint. "Boys will be boys, you know."

"Humph!" said Cee with mock indignation. "You were both supposedly grown men."

"I considered that I was celebrating my divorce, and Bud . . . well, he was just celebrating."

"As usual!" Cee interjected.

"Anyway, Katie, I remember that as Bud and I floated down the Amazon, we had quite an earnest medical conversation on how the quantity of alcohol we were consuming would doubtless kill any germs that we might acquire. As it turned out, we were wrong about that," Bryce related.

"Katie, they came back to Seattle wearing broad grins and looks of utter dissipation," Celia continued with the story.

"I know I felt rotten for about a week," Bryce went on thoughtfully. "Then I started running a fever. Lo and behold, one of those quaint South American microbes had survived the alcohol bath."

"I'll say it did." Again, Cee picked up the thread of the story. "It practically burned out your brain. Katie, Bud phoned Bryce late one night. Bryce managed to answer the phone, but he was delirious. Bud came over and broke the door down. After that, Bryce spent six weeks in isolation, and even with all the tropical medicine specialists gathered at his bedside, he almost died a half-dozen times. Meanwhile, poor Mimi had hysterics daily."

"Good heavens!" Katie said to Bryce. "Was that one of those learning experiences you mentioned?"

"Sure." He smiled, but his voice was sober. "Every

doctor should know firsthand what it's like to be help-lessly dependent and desperately ill. It gives you a whole new concept of your patients. They stop being 'the tumor in Bed 3' or 'the aneurysm' and become real, live people who are too weak to even scratch their nose when it itches, too weary to answer questions that people shout at them and too sick and scared to care whether they live or die.''

"That's a rough learning experience," Katie said, then she waxed indignant at the thought of the red-haired terror. "Whatever happened to that dreadful friend of yours who got you into such a mess?"

"You mean my very good friend who also saved my life?" Bryce corrected gently. "Well, my illness shook up his life as well as my own."

"He didn't get sick, too?" Katie questioned.

"No. You see, Bud had grown up in Brazil. He was born to missionary parents, and the theory is that he had already acquired a natural immunity to the bug that almost carried me off." Both Bryce and Cee laughed at Katie's visible start of surprise.

"They say the only people wilder than a preacher's kids are a missionary's," Bryce said, his dark eyes alight with fond memories. "Of course, another saying is that the apple never falls very far from the tree. Bud went back to Brazil. He's been at the mission hospital his father founded for almost ten years."

"But not without absconding, in typical fashion, with one of my good friends and fellow nurses, Bev Harper!" Cee lamented.

Bryce turned to Celia. "Say, did you know that Bud and Bev have four kids now?"

"Four red-haired terrors?" Cee shuddered and rolled her eyes to the ceiling.

While Cee and Bryce went on talking about Bud and Bev, Katie found her hands were clenched around the napkin in her lap. At least she knew now. She knew what had changed Bryce so dramatically. She knew why he was different, not only in his appearance but in his outlook as well. A man who had come as close to death as he had could never be quite the same as other casual, careless, take-life-for-granted human beings. In that sense, indeed, the man he'd once been was dead.

At least tonight had solved the riddle of Bryce Emerson.

Chapter Six

$\mathcal{B}$ryce drove Katie home at a leisurely pace, allowing faster cars to pass them on the busy expressway.

"Bryce, why didn't you want to tell me about your nearly fatal illness?" Katie asked tentatively.

In the light from the dashboard she could see the grimace that tightened his face. "For several reasons," he said, and his voice sounded taut, too. "First, it resulted from stupidity. With a few simple health precautions it needn't have ever happened. Thousands of people visit Brazil every year and never get sick."

Katie waited. "Second," Bryce went on after a moment's hesitation, "comes the mystical aspect. With all the attention focused in recent years on near-death experiences, people always ask if I saw lights, heard voices or experienced any of the other widely recorded phenomena."

"Well, I'm not going to let you off the hook either,"
Katie said, confessing her own curiosity. "Did you?"

She was watching Bryce closely enough that she could
see his hesitation. "Mostly, it was just a dark, empty
void. I remember the tedious time of recovery far more
clearly. But to answer your question, yes, in a way. I saw
several faces when I was very close to death. Both my
grandmother and my father seemed to appear to offer
comfort and encouragement. That's interesting, I suppose, because they had both died several years earlier.

"The last reason," he continued slowly, "is that other
people have apparently seen more of a change in me than
I have. I did decide to go into teaching, but I'm still a
neurosurgeon and still a man."

"And just what does that mean, Bryce?" Katie asked,
finding herself fascinated.

"I'm normal and human, smart and stupid, kind and
thoughtless," he said, his voice ironic.

Katie made no reply, but, silently, she thought that
Bryce *was* unusual just to admit to all of that.

During the rest of their drive, Bryce asked questions
of Katie about the other hospital administrators who he
would gradually come to know.

"It's not necessary to walk me to the door," Katie
said hastily when they were back within her apartment
compound.

"Nonsense," Bryce said briskly. "Of course, I'll
walk you to your door." He shot Katie an appealing
smile. "Some other clever character might have talked
his way inside these walls!"

"Actually, Bryce Emerson, I think you're the only

one who has gall enough to manage it," Katie fired back, and Bryce chuckled.

She had intended to insert her key in the door, then turn and offer Bryce a good-night handshake. He intercepted her motions by taking the key from her and swinging the door open wide. Katie stepped through it and realized belatedly that Bryce was right behind her.

"It's late," she said defensively. "Unless you want a cup of coffee—"

"No." Bryce closed the door and leaned back against it. "What I want is to kiss you good night, Katie," he said softly.

Her startled eyes flew to his face. Before she could begin to frame any words, he reached out and drew her to him. "I'm not going to wait for you to answer me," he whispered. "I might not like what you'd say."

His warm hands went to either side of Katie's face, framing it, while his eyes, pure blue now in the dim glow of the single lamp, magnetized her, mesmerized her. Slowly, Bryce's head came down toward hers. Katie had no time to even think of her response, much less control it, for her chin lifted spontaneously, making it easier for him.

Bryce's mouth closed over hers so purposefully and so passionately that Katie's heart gave a leap of joy. His warm lips on hers, pressing and arousing, sent flames darting wildly through her body. For a single, singing moment she yielded unconsciously, allowing him access to her mouth and tongue, letting her body be supported and cradled against the long, hard length of his.

"Bryce—" She drew back for a moment and tried to

think, although her head was swimming. "That—that was no brotherly kiss!"

His thumbs moved against either side of her cheekbones while his long fingers entangled themselves in Katie's hair. "No, thank God, it wasn't!" he agreed, then crushed her mouth beneath his once again.

He had kissed her so tenderly and beguilingly earlier that Katie was now stunned by the sudden forcefulness of his lips, of their hunger and passion, but her treacherous heart only gave another bound of delight. At the core of her being lay a strange, new, feminine desire to give and yield, to melt and succumb, to become a vessel that answered his passion and brought him to ecstasy.

This new feeling was more frightening and threatening than any Katie had known so far. Why, she was actually trembling with her eagerness to give and her fierce longing to sink with Bryce into warm, heated darkness.

His arms moved to bind her closely to him while his mouth plundered hers as though he could no longer be restrained. Even through their layers of clothes Katie could feel his aggressive need and desire for her, and her spirit soared ecstatically.

She kissed him back in a frenzy, feeling his arms around her like a haven and a heaven on earth. Unconsciously, she surrendered to the needs and desires churning through them both. Her neck arched, her body strained against him and her arms clutched him almost as tightly as his held her.

She was scarcely aware of his moving, drawing her down into the inviting depths of the sofa. Swiftly, Bryce lowered Katie there and lay beside her, his lips leaving hers to bury themselves in the softness of her neck.

"Katie . . . beautiful, beautiful Katie," he murmured.

His words transported her back across a barrier of time and space. He had said those same words to her once before, in the call room in Seattle, and suddenly it was as though Katie were back there with Bryce once again. She wanted nothing more than to feel his hands on her bare skin, so she welcomed their swift movement down her blouse to free the buttons. She wanted his lips, now moving against the soft column of her neck, to kiss each vulnerable pulse point where desire licked with fiery fingers.

She had never really forgotten him—she had never ceased to want him. Now, at last, they were together again. The past decade had passed like the flick of an eyelash for all the difference it had made to Katie's feelings for Bryce.

His weight half-covered her as his hands opened her blouse and found the front clasp of her bra. It dropped open with his touch, and when the cooler air struck her nipples, Katie felt them harden.

His hands dropped to them, stroking and kneading gently yet powerfully, his thumbs flicking the taut nipples. His mouth continued to press hot, passionate kisses along her neck and throat even as words seemed wrenched from him.

"I want you so! I've always wanted you, Katie. I couldn't forget you, though I tried. Oh, believe me, I tried! But always you stayed there in the corner of my mind—always the taste of your softness, your sweetness, your fire . . ."

"Bryce . . ." Katie's hands combed through his

hair, and it clung, crisply and electrically, to her fingers.

His mouth moved lower to kiss her shoulders, his tongue tracing their smooth contours. "Beautiful Katie!" His hands cupped her breasts lovingly yet urgently. "Everything about you is so beautiful." His body shifted, covering hers fully, and a gasp escaped Katie at this closer, fuller contact with all of him.

"Don't be afraid!" Bryce urged, his mouth swooping downward to settle over one rosy nipple while his fingers continued to excitingly rotate the nipple on her opposite breast.

"You said I . . . had nothing to fear . . . from you." The words returned to Katie from some recess of her mind where they had lodged.

"You don't, darling! I just want to love you, to hold you in my arms all night long, to watch you sleep and to make love to you when you're not asleep. . . ."

Katie wanted his lovemaking, too. With his words, her body began trembling even more powerfully and uncontrollably. An ache of longing opened up deep within her, an emptiness avid to be filled, thrilling now to each of his passionate promises.

His mouth began to suck softly on her breast, driving her half-wild with desire, and she shifted to allow Bryce's hands to move downward. They stroked her stomach and thighs, then rested at their juncture, while his mouth moved to her other nipple.

Katie felt herself going crazy with all the delirious sensations he aroused. She heard her heavy gasps and knew them to be the sound of surrender. Bryce knew that as well. He could now take her and use her as he wished, whether for love or merely for his physical pleasure and satisfaction. She was too intoxicated with desire to resist.

Groaning, Bryce feasted a moment longer at her breast, then, slowly, he raised himself up on one elbow to peer down into Katie's glazed eyes.

His own eyes glittered, and his face was flushed by emotion, but when he spoke, his voice had steadied. "Katie, I want you more than I've ever wanted any woman, but I swore I'd never hurt you again. Right now all I want to do is carry you away to your bedroom, but *you* must give me the answer to that."

Katie's body trembled again. Then, with the moment's distraction and his strangely touching words, she was able to stop and think. In the flash of a second her stepmother's vibrant face drifted across the screen of her mind. Earlier that evening she had promised herself that she wouldn't stand in Cee's way.

One of her shaking hands came up to touch Bryce's face. "Bryce, there's . . . there's Cee," she whispered.

He frowned, his breathing uneven, his body still tense from its own arousal. "Celia? What . . . ?"

"Bryce, she's—she's interested in you." Painful though the words were to say, Katie forced herself to speak them.

His hands boldly stroked her breasts again. "Oh, you're surely wrong!" Bryce's face held consternation, which changed immediately to disbelief. "Why, Cee and I love each other as friends, but there's nothing else. I've never felt like this about Cee. I never will. Oh, Katie, I want *you!*"

Still, the mention of the older woman's name and the

interruption of their lovemaking had the effect of returning Katie to earth. Although she drew a still-ragged breath, her hands fumbled for the edges of her open blouse.

The spell was broken, and Bryce didn't struggle to recapture it. Although Katie could see that a muscle leaped uncontrollably in his lean jaw, he allowed her to draw her clothes around her half-naked body. Abruptly, he swung his long legs off the sofa and sat up.

Katie sat up, too, her mind alert and functioning again while her face flushed from embarrassment. "Bryce, I—I never intended for things to go this far!" she protested, then bit her lip to stop herself from saying more.

He turned back to slant a look at her. "I know that, Katie darling," he said ruefully. "I don't know what gets into me either when I hold you in my arms. Do you think this is love?"

Emphatically, Katie shook her head, her fingers racing to refasten her blouse. "No. We don't know each other well enough," she said primly.

"Perhaps not yet." He reached out a hand and playfully, ruefully tumbled her hair. A hand that was not quite steady.

"Bryce, are you all right?" Katie said with some concern, for a wry, regretful expression played over his mouth.

"No. I'm very frustrated and aching from discomfort, if you want to know the truth," he said to her candidly. "I'd like to kick myself for opening my big mouth at the wrong moment and yet . . . yet I really don't want to take advantage of you or rush you into a relationship before you feel ready. I find I feel very protective of you, Katie. That's what makes me distinctly suspicious that I really am falling in love with you.''

"Oh, Bryce!" Katie scoffed, trying not to let his words affect her. "We feel an attraction for one another, but—"

"I think it's always been more than that," he contradicted gently. "At least it has been for me." He sighed, the sound seeming to come from the depths of his being. "Do you know that when I was hallucinating, one of those faces I saw was yours?"

"Oh, Bryce!" Katie's voice was suspended between a cry and a jeer.

"It's true," he said with such intensity that she could no longer doubt him. "It almost drove me mad while I was recovering. Since the other faces were of people who had died, I was filled with this morbid fear that you were dead, too. As soon as I was strong enough to dial a phone I called your house and asked for you. Your maid said you were away at college. That still didn't satisfy me, so I made discreet inquiries among the nurses. One of them thought you were at Ashwood College, but she wasn't sure."

"Why, Bryce!" Katie felt her eyes widening in amazement.

"As soon as I could walk, I dragged myself down the hall and confronted your father, who hadn't been to visit me. I asked him about you and how you were doing."

"What did Dad say?" Katie asked, her heart thumping again against the wall of her chest.

"He gave me a distinctly fishy look and said you were fine. End of conversation." Another sigh escaped

Bryce. "So I dragged myself back to my room and phoned the college."

"You did?" Katie felt her heart give an even harder knock at this story of his persistence. "I never knew that!"

"I know." Bryce nodded. "That college battle-ax I talked to the first time would neither confirm nor deny that you were there."

"You mean you called more than once?" Katie said, incredulous.

"I called a couple of times more. I had to know you were all right! Finally I reached a human being, a student who worked in the office, I believe. She whispered that you were indeed enrolled there and quite well. She said you were playing in a tennis match that afternoon."

"When did you finally come to your senses?"

"I wonder if I ever have," Bryce said reflectively. "Oh, after all that, I thought it was better that I stay out of your young life and get on with mine. Before the year was out, I had moved to Stanford. I thought of you much less often with the years, of course. Still, occasionally, all through those years, something would happen to remind me of you. Maybe I'd see a woman with dark brown hair like yours or the same curve to her face, and I'd find myself thinking, 'Why, she looks like Katie!' Tell me, did anything of that sort happen to you, too?"

"No," Katie said firmly. It was true. She had worked very, very hard to forget Bryce completely. And she'd succeeded.

Then, belatedly, she remembered the splash of rain against a windowpane and the memories that always came back, unbidden.

"When Ash Blakely mentioned your name, Katie, after so many years, it was like something clicked into place inside of me," Bryce recalled. "Usually, I'm a practical guy. I'm not given to psychic experiences or mystic revelations, but I can't tell you how strongly I felt that you and I were *meant* to meet each other again."

Katie was a practical sort, too, and now her head whirled from all the things that had happened tonight and all she had learned. "I must say, Bryce, that this has been a very eventful evening," she hedged.

His eyes searched her face. "You don't believe me, do you?"

"I—I don't know," Katie said with painful honesty. She had always preferred to think she controlled her own fate. Discussions of destiny and fated happenings made her feel uncomfortable.

He leaned over and dropped a kiss on her forehead. "I understand. It's too much to take in all at once, so I'll go now. I have to be at the medical school quite early in the morning." Bryce stood up and extended a hand to help Katie up off the sofa. As soon as she was on her feet, she dropped his hand reluctantly.

"Remember this weekend," Bryce said when he had reached her door. "I expect you, Cee and Eric at my lakeside place."

This was as good a time as any to take a stand and draw away from a relationship that disturbed her as much as it attracted her. "Bryce, I don't think—" Katie started gamely.

He stopped her words by dropping his fingers across her lips. "Don't say it, Katie! Please! We need to see each other until what is still alive between us has been worked out. We need to know, one way or the other."

Mutely, she gave her head a shake, unable to deny the truth of Bryce's words but unable to entirely agree with his suggestion either.

His hand dropped from her lips, then he reached to open the door. "And don't be sorry about tonight either!" he ordered and left her with that instruction.

Eighty-six days . . .

Sorry? Katie wasn't merely sorry. She felt wretched and thoroughly miserable. All morning she had castigated herself repeatedly and remorselessly.

How could I? she thought, feeling angry and embarrassed by her behavior the night before. All Bryce Emerson has to do is kiss me a couple of times, breathe a few sweet nothings, and I tumble into his hand like a ripe plum!

Katie had spent another restless night, finding it difficult to sleep, and even when she had dropped off into an uneasy slumber her dreams were a confused jumble of past and present. They had been filled with Bryce and more of Bryce. She had awakened determined to forget the man and never to see him again outside of professional encounters, and discovered instead that there were reminders of him everywhere.

Her traitorous body, in particular, failed to cooperate. Katie had only to remember Bryce's hands and lips on hers, and the familiar excitement set her senses churning all over again. Her breasts tingled, and their sensitive nipples tightened just from the memory.

She had discovered this morning that her breasts were

reddened from his loving assault and slightly abraded by his beard. The sight had made her flush from shame as well as anger. How could she? Oh, how *could* she have let him go so far?

Then her reaction infuriated her further. She was like some mid-Victorian maiden, making a big deal out of a little bit of heavy petting. Half the teenagers in Dallas would go further than she had on their Saturday-night dates! At least nothing more serious than petting had happened. Why wasn't she grateful for that?

Deep in her heart Katie knew it was because Bryce, not she, had been the one who stopped and spoke, giving her a chance to reconsider and to come to her senses. Next time, if there was a next time, she might not be so lucky.

At least she was resolved not to go to the lake this weekend and it didn't matter that Eric would be disappointed. It didn't matter that she was disappointed in a way, too, because she always enjoyed weekends out of the busy, bustling city, especially if she could sit beside a tranquil lake. None of that mattered—she wasn't going!

It didn't even matter that she wanted to be with Bryce. No matter how she tried to color it and serve it up to herself, Katie always came back to that blunt truth. A part of her soul yearned for the man, but . . .

I can't fall in love with him again! she thought in near despair. I'm leaving, and he's staying. Certainly, Katie did not want to begin her desirable new life in a new setting carrying the leftover baggage of a broken heart. Yet every time she allowed herself to see Bryce Emerson she was increasing the risk, the danger.

When the telephone rang, Katie welcomed it. Some instinct told her that Bryce was busy at the medical school and in any event would not phone her this early.

She answered and then heard the voice of the secretary to the executive hospital director. The woman informed Katie briskly that there would be a special operations meeting that afternoon. Could she come in at three?

"I'll be there," Katie assured the secretary. She replaced the receiver, thinking that some problem had obviously come up. Usually problems were the last thing hospital administrators wanted, but today—today she was ready to welcome them.

The executive director was a relatively young man to have achieved his present eminence. At thirty-five, Robert deSilva ran a tight ship with a deceptively casual and breezy manner. He insisted on informality among his staff, and while the other administrators accorded him the deference due his high position, they also obligingly called him Bob.

The meeting was in the conference room and they all took their usual seats. Katie sat between Steve Wills, who had also arrived to attend this special session, and Darrell Harvey, another junior administrator.

"OK, folks, I've called you here because we have entirely too many empty beds in this hospital," Bob announced. "Since we're starting a new building program before the end of this fiscal year, we need to keep the patient census high. Now let's review the census by departments . . ."

For the next three-quarters of an hour, the administrators discussed the various hospital areas as well as

economic policies that could be implemented. Throughout the lengthy discussion Katie had trouble concentrat-
ing. Her mind managed to leap off on tangents of its
own. In one moment she was locked in Bryce Emerson's
embrace, surrendering to his overpowering masculinity.
In another she was standing tall and proud as she bid him
farewell and left for her new position in the Pacific
Northwest. *I've seen too many grade-B movies!* Katie
thought in disgust when she forced her mind back to the
conference room after yet another flight of fancy.

Still, her thoughts simply wouldn't focus on business,
and she found herself thinking of the children instead.
Those beautiful, wonderful little kids who could be
salvaged and rehabilitated.

Crippled, twisted limbs could often be slowly and
tediously taught to refunction. Plastic surgery could do
wonders with birth defects and burns. Katie remembered
a determined, little blond girl she had met during one of
her tours of children's hospitals. Originally, it had been
thought that the child would never walk again, but hours
of muscle stimulation by physical therapists and hours of
boring, tedious exercises practiced by the child had put
her on her feet at last and paved the way for her first,
unsteady steps. . . .

"OK, folks, let's watch the expenditures and supplies." Bob deSilva was winding up his meeting as Katie
jerked back to reality. "And remember, keep those
helicopters flying! They bring us patients." Virtuously,
he added, "And we save their lives."

Katie walked out of the meeting and clipped on her
beeper, which soon came chattering to life. "Ms.
Brentwood, call Dr. Gloria Ashton—"

Katie went right back to "troubleshooting and stomping out fires," as she had often described her duties. She met with an unhappy patient who claimed he was being overcharged. She talked with a disgruntled employee who thought he was being overworked. She answered a page from Security about a small amount of barbituates missing from the Pharmacy. Returning from her last summons, Katie rounded a corner and collided with Stella Hopkins, a tiny woman who was reputed to be the toughest flight nurse at the hospital.

"You'd better cool off your heels, Katie," Stella advised as she brushed her green jumpsuit and retrieved the scissors that had toppled out of her shoulder pocket.

"Busy night," Katie said apologetically and sped on her way.

At least there was no evidence that Bryce was at the hospital tonight, Katie reflected, half gratefully and half wistfully, too. Of course, there was also no evidence that he wasn't here.

At 8:40 she received a STAT page. A Dallas police officer had been shot in the line of duty. Critically injured with a bullet near his spine, he was being transported to the hospital by helicopter.

That meant that the news media would soon converge on the hospital. Katie hurried away to Flight Operations and then to the Shocktrauma Unit's waiting room to check on the policeman's condition. Thirty minutes later she faced a live TV camera and reported tersely that while the officer's vital signs had been stabilized, he remained critical and was presently undergoing surgery for the removal of the bullet.

It was 10:15 before Katie finally reached the hospital

cafeteria for another delayed dinner break. She ate slowly, resisting the impulse to bolt her meal, and was not particularly surprised when a breezy voice greeted her.

"Hi, lady administrator. You sure looked cute on TV!"

Katie looked up to see Doug Sears and discovered that she was actually glad to see him. Her eyes crinkled, and her mouth tugged upward into a smile. "Hi, flyboy," she said. "Grab a chair."

Doug was already doing that without waiting for her invitation. In his dark blue uniform he was a dashing figure. His hair, which always managed to look wind-whipped, fell raffishly over his forehead.

"I told you I'd see you around, Katie," he said, treating her to a flash of white, even teeth.

"So you did. Are you on call tonight, too?" she asked.

"Not for another hour. Actually, I came in early just hoping to see you." He grinned.

"I'm touched," Katie said, forking through her salad.

"Not too deeply, I'm sure."

"Why, you misjudge me, Doug. I'm really rather fond of you," she protested.

His mouth turned down. "The last time a woman said that to me she was my third-grade teacher. She decided to forgive me for the frog I'd left in her desk drawer."

"I'll bet you have a surprise up your sleeve for me, too!"

For several minutes they bantered back and forth, then Doug veered off to the topic of his split from Sheila Rigley. "Look, I really *like* that woman, Katie. I'm not going to say I don't. But Sheila's reached the all-or-nothin' stage. Like wedding bells and lifetime commitments. I told her I'd tried it once and it didn't take.''

"Oh, I didn't realize you'd been divorced," Katie said, thinking that there was quite a lot about Doug that she'd never known.

"No divorce. An annulment. It was a high school thing, but I did learn one thing about myself," he proclaimed.

"Let me guess. You're fickle," Katie said, only half teasing.

"That's partially true," Doug said. "Or was. But, most of all, I learned that I have to be up and away, doing something that's exciting. It was motorcycles in high school and hot rods in college. Now it's choppers. Most women can't take the suspense of wondering whether a guy is coming home that night or whether she should crawl into her basic black and start making funeral arrangements. Like that policeman's wife right now must be wondering.''

"Sheila wanted you to give up flying?" Katie guessed.

"You've got it. Feet on solid ground and home every night by six. Katie, I'd go nuts!"

"Yes, you would," she agreed slowly, looking into his reckless blue eyes that were bracketed by a few attractive squint lines. A pilot has to fly. . . . A neurosurgeon has to operate. And God help the woman who loves either one of them! she thought to herself.

"See? I knew you'd understand," Doug said triumphantly. "That's why I wanted to see you again, Katie.

Because you're that one woman in a million who knows what people are really like and is strong enough to stand 'em that way.'' Casually, Doug reached out and took her hand.

''Gee, thanks,'' she said ironically, wondering why people kept commending her for her strength. Bryce Emerson had only to touch her and that steel in her soul dissolved to mush.

Doug went on talking for several minutes, then Katie saw him glance briefly over her shoulder, then glance once again. He turned back to her, and his voice lowered. ''Say, there's a tall character over there in greens who is boring a hole through you, Katie.''

Her heart speeded up in an almost frightening way. ''Oh?'' she said and managed to keep herself from turning.

''Neurosurgeon, from the looks of him,'' Doug went on. ''He's got his little reflex hammer poking out of his lab coat.''

Slowly, Katie turned, and her eyes met those of Bryce, who was seated alone across the room. So he was here tonight!

Bryce's face was carefully noncommittal. Courteously, he gave her a nod.

''That's Dr. Emerson,'' Katie said to Doug and wondered at her suddenly breathless tone. Briskly, she pushed away her plate and stood up. ''Come on, I'll introduce you.''

After all, it's only the polite thing to do, she thought, as she wove her way through the tables to where Bryce sat by the wall. He rose at their approach.

Why was her heart racing so? Katie wondered as she drew nearer. Now that she was closer to Bryce she could see the flicker of something in the depths of his gray blue eyes. Was it disapproval? Anger? No! Her heart contracting even more, Katie recognized the expression and identified it. *Pain*. Bryce must have seen Doug reach for her hand, and he'd misconstrued the gesture.

Well, dammit, what did the man expect? That she'd spend the last ten years of her life just waiting for him to reappear?

By the time Katie introduced the men that expression in Bryce's eyes had been carefully masked. "You're one of the pilots?" he said to Doug as they exchanged a quick handshake.

"Yeah, I fly 'em in so you fellows can patch 'em up," Doug said in his lighthearted way.

"You do a good job," Bryce commended, then his eyes returned to Katie. "You also do a good job, Ms. Brentwood. That statement on TV was great. By the way, I think our policeman will make it with no paralysis, but that's not for publication just yet."

A few more pleasantries were exchanged, then Katie and Doug walked out of the cafeteria, and Bryce sank back down at his table to finish his cup of coffee.

"Let me take you to dinner Saturday night, Katie," Doug offered, smiling down at her as they walked back toward Administration.

Had the invitation come just a few minutes earlier, Katie knew she would have accepted. With Doug things would be fun without being complicated by a lot of threatening feelings and unseemly emotions.

But that look of pain in Bryce's eyes, however brief,

had been so sharp that Katie couldn't disregard, or forget, it.

Still, she was absolutely astonished when she heard herself telling Doug in a perfectly calm and natural voice that she had already agreed to spend the weekend out of town.

Chapter Seven

Eighty-four days . . .

Bryce was the image of a happy man as he turned his car off the main highway and onto the side road that led down to his lake house. Eagerly, he pointed out landmarks to Katie—a convenient grocery store that provided supplies, a marina a few miles farther and various houses set back beneath huge spreading trees.

Katie leaned her head against the leather seat, enjoying the sight of Bryce's pleasure. In fact, she couldn't seem to tear her eyes away from him. In faded jean cut-offs and a tan polo shirt made limp from frequent washings, he seemed entirely different from either his hospital image or his dressed-for-dinner appearance. He wore positively disreputable-looking sneakers, and Katie couldn't resist a smile over his youthful, near-boyish

128

enthusiasm. Bryce actually looked younger, too, here in the bright daylight with the sunshine and fresh air.

He turned his head and intercepted her smile. "If you keep looking at me like that, I'm going to have to pull off this road and kiss you!" he threatened softly.

Her pulses leaped. "Oh, no, you don't! We need to reach your place before that great block of ice in your trunk melts away," Katie teased.

"That's not the only thing that's melting," Bryce muttered. Then, his voice growing excited again, he said, "Look, Katie! There, through the trees, you can see the lake."

She looked obediently and saw serene, blue waters encircled by willow trees, elephant ears and tall grass. "How beautiful," she murmured.

"It sure is," Bryce echoed, but glancing back at him, Katie saw that he was watching her rather than the lake.

A rush of delight swept over her. She knew she looked nice today in crisp white shorts that belted over a red-and-white sleeveless shirt. Her own white sneakers were new, bought just for this occasion.

Despite Katie's resolve that this weekend was to be nothing very special or unusual, she had anticipated it with unaccustomed zest. Indeed, as she worked the rest of Thursday night and Friday, she'd been able to think of little else. It's just that I need a respite from the hospital, a couple of quiet days to rest and unwind, she told herself, but her whirlwind shopping expedition bore little resemblance to her logical thinking. Packed in her overnight case were a new swimsuit and another shorts set just as attractive as the one she presently wore. In the large picnic hamper she'd brought lay a cake she had baked herself, a large salad of marinated tomatoes and cucumbers and a dish of baked beans that would taste better when they were reheated.

Bryce had been delighted with the hamper and had poked around in it, sniffing appreciatively at the combination of aromas. "How very thoughtful of you, Katie!" he'd exclaimed.

"It's nothing much," she had said depreciatingly. "It ought to go with the sandwich stuff and chips you're bringing. Cee has some edible surprises as well."

"We'll have a real feast!" Bryce had said delightedly.

Now, glancing down at his lean, tanned legs, lightly covered with dark masculine hair, Katie thought that Bryce could certainly use some good meals. I'd like to see a few more pounds on him, she thought with a sudden rush of tenderness. See those hollows in his face filled out just a bit.

What a wifelike thought! That it had crept through her mind astounded Katie, and even more disconcerting was the effect his scantily clad body had on her. She could almost feel the power and warmth radiating from that strongly muscled body, and the delightful scent of him—soap and clean clothes and a dash of aftershave— wafted toward her in appealing waves. For a moment she yielded to the sensations, wishing she could feel his lips on hers, could lie across his lap and run her fingers through his crisp dark hair and explore the doubtlessly tantalizing feeling of his bare legs against hers.

Oh God, what was she thinking? Fiercely, Katie wrenched her mind back to her surroundings. She looked again at the lake and exclaimed over a graceful waterskiier who had appeared from around a bend. Aloud, she said, "I wonder when Cee and Eric will get here."

"Oh, I think they're probably a couple of hours behind us," Bryce replied.

That was the only hitch that had arisen this weekend, for the original plan had called for all of them to drive down together. And a lot *safer* that would have been for me, too, Katie thought privately. With a chatterbox like Eric in the car, she knew she would have had little opportunity to dwell on Bryce's physical attributes.

But Eric had wanted to bring along his bicycle since he rarely had a chance to ride it in the midst of a bustling city. Then he had discovered that the front tire was punctured. Cee had called Katie at the last minute to explain that she'd have to buy Eric a new tire and that she'd phoned and gotten directions from Bryce, so she and Eric would arrive a bit later.

Now, Bryce turned off the winding lake road and pulled into a gravel drive. "Here we are," he announced to Katie, then added with a trace of anxiety, "I hope you're not too disappointed."

Katie saw a rather weathered house in need of paint, but there was a long, screened porch in front and, from the peek she saw of the back, an outside deck and a pier that led down over the water.

"I'm not disappointed at all," she said warmly to Bryce. "I think it looks charming."

Inside, the furnishings were casual yet pleasant. A large main room served as both the living and dining area while a small kitchen was tucked into an alcove. Bright blue and white drapes accentuated the blue sofa and chairs; rag rugs dotted the hardwood floor.

The rooms were filled with an almost eerie golden light, which crept in from around the drawn drapes, and there was a faint smell of dampness that Bryce set about immediately to rectify by pushing the curtains back and flinging the windows open. Katie unpacked her picnic hamper and refrigerated the perishable items, while Bryce finished preparing the house for his guests.

After the ice and food had been stored away, Bryce extended a hand to Katie. "Now let me show you around."

She took his hand without conscious thought, and only when his fingers curled warmly and strongly around hers did Katie question the wisdom of allowing Bryce to touch her. But clearly he was intent only on showing her the place.

He threw open a door and she saw a bedroom with four bunk beds. A room for children, her mind registered. "I thought Eric and I would stay in here," Bryce said. "There's a small bathroom just beyond with a shower stall. You ladies can have the larger, more luxurious bath."

"How gallant of you," Katie said lightly.

"Your room is across the hall." Bryce led her over there and flicked on a light switch. Twin beds of simple, early American style were covered with soft white spreads while more rag rugs lay on the gleaming floor. "Why, Bryce, this is charming!" Katie exclaimed.

"Your bath is here." He turned on another light switch and she saw a modern bathroom decorated in soft mint green.

"Good heavens, there are even makeup lights!" Katie

exclaimed as another switch illuminated the vanity area. "What a great big tub!"

"Yes, I soaked in it last weekend after a hard day of fishing," Bryce commented. "The room where I slept is just beyond."

He opened a connecting door and Katie's breath caught in her throat. She saw a large, masculine-looking bedroom dominated by a huge king-sized bed. Like the rest of the house, the room wasn't furnished extravagantly, but its colors of rust and tan, accentuated in the geometric-patterned bedspread, were quite attractive.

"Oh, Bryce, you shouldn't give up your bedroom and bath," Katie protested. "Cee and I can take the bunk room and Eric could—"

"I want you to be comfortable," Bryce insisted. "Also, Eric might awaken in the night, and children are often confused by strange surroundings." His hands rose slowly to cup Katie's face. "Anyway, I'm afraid I might have lurid thoughts, not to mention lurid dreams, if I'm all alone in this big bed . . . without you."

"Bryce—" Katie could feel the pounding of her heart. Why did it insist on going mad every time he said a personal or suggestive word?

"I want you, Katie," he said huskily. "I want you so very, very much. I never knew the need for one woman could be so overpowering!"

She stood still, unable to move or speak, but she began to tremble when Bryce's mouth dropped down to cover hers. At the firm touch of his lips, her whole being came alive in a swift rush of soaring joy. Katie arched into his arms, suddenly aching with the need to be close to him, and she heard Bryce gasp at her instinctive and uninhibited response.

He swept her up against him. As their bodies ground together and their lips fused even more deeply, he moaned softly. I'm going to lose control again, Katie thought, but the thought held no significance for her at all. When his tongue plunged into her mouth, she wanted nothing more than to sink down and drown in all these wonderful, rapturous feelings.

Did Bryce move first or did she? Katie wasn't sure, but she felt the edge of the mattress of the king-sized bed against the backs of her knees, then she was falling with Bryce across the mattress, straining toward him, gripping him to her as though she would never let him go.

"Oh, Bryce!" she murmured when his mouth moved enough to allow her to speak.

"Just let me hold you, Katie!" he said, his voice and hands feverish. He clutched her even closer, as though fearing she might escape him, while his lips rained hot, moist kisses down her face and neck.

Escaping from him was the last thing Katie wanted to do at that moment. She moaned with delight as she felt his hair-roughened legs on hers, felt the shelter of his arms holding her to him and the passionate delight of his kisses.

Against the firm yet yielding mattress, they rolled even more closely into each other's arms so that Katie seemed to feel Bryce against her everywhere. His skin, now damp with desire, met hers in a hundred separate places. Wrists, ankles, throats—all rubbed insinuatingly against each other until the force of Bryce's ardent desire grew unmistakably evident.

"Can you feel what you do to me, Katie?" he said in a choked voice.

"Yes!" she answered, and then their lips clung again in a violent, almost heated response to each other. I want him—oh, how I want him! Katie found herself thinking and heard little cries of delight building in her throat as Bryce's hands moved rapidly over her. He kneaded her breasts through the bright shirt, his aroused breath burning her skin.

Her breasts ached and throbbed, needing his closer and more intimate caresses. Without being aware of what she was doing, Katie thrust her shirt upward and almost frantically guided his warm, exploring hands to the softness of her bare skin.

Bryce gave a wordless exclamation of delight at her eagerness, and his hands encircled her rib cage. Then, with tantalizing, almost agonizing slowness, they rose upward, each finger in gentle motion. He caressed her until Katie felt faint with desire.

When Bryce reached to draw the shirt over her head, she helped him with impatient hands, and, a moment later, her bra was snatched away. "You, too, Bryce," she urged, her mouth finding a small dimple of skin just inches from his lips.

His tan polo shirt followed her blouse to the floor, then he caught Katie against his bare chest. Oh, how gorgeous he was! The thick, silken mat of chest hair tickled and teased her nipples, and she cried out from the utter, sheer pleasure. Slowly, she guided his head down to her upthrust breasts. Under the ministrations of his lips and tongue and fingers, they swelled and tautened.

His mouth fastened on one pink crest, and he tugged

there gently, sweetly, while new cries of delight escaped from Katie. She felt her legs moving and parting beneath his, and, a moment later, Bryce's hands were fumbling at the waistband of her shorts.

He wrenched his head from her breasts to give a short, shaky laugh. "I'm trembling so, I can't get these things undone!"

She felt the tremors rippling through his strong frame and his sudden awkwardness was touching. "Here, darling," Katie whispered and reached down to help him.

"Please say that again!" Bryce pleaded.

"Darling . . . my darling Bryce!" Katie's smaller fingers made fast work of undoing the elusive buttons, and then she felt his hands on her smooth belly. They dipped below the waistband of her panties, encircling her navel.

"You're like satin everywhere!" he marveled. "I want to touch you everywhere, Katie. Kiss you—"

"Yes, please!"

For a few seconds of breathless, heart-stopping desire he explored her, his trembling fingers edging ever closer to the very center of her being. Katie gasped and clung to him, and soon his lips crushed hers once again.

"I love you, Katie! I love you, love you—"

Bryce's words were almost anguished in their urgency. They fired the fever already stirring Katie's blood and sent forth that hot, languid gush of pleasure that threatened to dissolve her bones.

In her state of mindless, heedless rapture, while they moved ever closer to the awesome moment of becoming one, Katie might have thought herself blind and deaf to everything but overpowering desire. But, apparently, her subconscious mind had remained attuned to a predictable sound that arrived suddenly with a jarring, nerve-rending impact. The sharp squeal of brakes and the sound of a car pulling into the driveway froze her.

Cee and Eric! Katie went rigid, then she tore her lips from Bryce's and pushed at his powerful shoulders. "Bryce, stop! They're here!"

He gazed down at her uncomprehendingly, his eyes smoky and desire-glazed. Katie gave another frantic shove at his rocklike shoulders. "It's Cee and Eric!"

"Oh, God!" Comprehension flared in his eyes. Slowly, Bryce lifted himself from Katie and turned to lie, gasping, beside her.

"Bryce, hurry. Get up!" Already, Katie had bounded off the bed and began, with frantic fingers, to pull on her clothes. Outside she could hear Eric's bright, piping voice.

"Katie! Katie, where are you? Bryce?"

"God!" Bryce swung his long legs to the side of the bed and stood up, his mouth quirked. "It's enough to give a man cardiac arrest!"

"Bryce, hurry!" Katie begged.

"OK, sweetheart." In a flash, he swept up his tan shirt and put it back on, then smoothed down his hair. Katie gave a desperate tug to right the tumbled bedspread.

A moment later Bryce plunged into the bathroom where he splashed his face with water. Then as Katie pattered in behind him, feeling disheveled, frustrated and out of breath, Bryce handed her a cold, wet washcloth.

"Thanks," she said briefly, patting it over her flushed face and throat, then handing it back.

Bryce dropped the cloth over a towel rack, then turned to frame Katie's face in his hands. His voice still shaken and awed, he said softly, "I love you. Never forget it!"

With his words, every trace of apprehension and shame dropped away from Katie. She felt only a glorious, glad spreading of warmth inside her that was every bit as powerful as their passion had been. Why, he really means it: He loves me!

Then Bryce turned and went striding through the door to greet his guests.

Eighty-three days . . .

Katie lay on her stomach in the sun, her mind full of thoughts and her heart alive with feelings. It was impossible for any woman to remain unaffected by those three magic words, "I love you," she reflected. Yet everything had happened so fast that she was suspended somewhere between disbelief and complete confusion. Did *she* love Bryce? He stirred her powerfully, as no other man ever had, but it was still too soon for her to know. Only a few short days ago she had said "hello" to him. Matters had escalated so rapidly that she was still waiting for her head to catch up with her feelings. And, of course, always lingering in the back of her mind like a cautious reminder was the fact that she would soon be leaving Bryce.

To distract herself from the thoughts that kept churning around like squirrels in a cage, Katie cracked an eye open and gazed out at the peaceful blue lake. Bryce and Eric were out there fishing, their boat a small dot on the horizon. They'd left hours ago, and if today was like yesterday, they'd come back smelling of sweat and sun, proudly bearing a long string of smelly fish.

Yesterday, Katie and Cee had cooked their catch, and the fish had tasted delicious when coated in a cornmeal batter and fried golden-brown. Everything, in fact, tasted delicious here by the lake. The sandwiches at lunch yesterday, the fish dinner last night and Cee's homemade sweet rolls and fresh fruit that they'd had for breakfast.

Exercise, sun and food had left the adults lazy and lethargic, but Eric still had enough energy left to ride his bicycle around the lake after dinner.

Now Cee, who was sprawled on a beach towel beside Katie, sat up, grumbling. "It's time to smear on more sunscreen, or I'll go home looking like a broiled lobster. Katie, do you mind?"

Obligingly, Katie rolled over on an elbow and began massaging the lotion into her stepmother's splotched shoulders. Cee's fair, thin skin burned easily, and the sun had brought out quite a number of freckles.

"You're getting a gorgeous tan, Katie," Cee complimented enviously. "All nice and toasty brown. And you look fantastic in that swimsuit! Bryce hasn't been able to tear his eyes off you."

Katie felt herself flushing. How much did Cee know? How much had she guessed? Had she deduced that her arrival yesterday had interrupted a pretty hot and heavy love scene? Or did she merely think the two flushed, breathless people who greeted her and Eric had been out jogging around the lake or something?

"You look nice yourself," Katie said generously, for

it was true. Celia's figure was still slender and firm, high-breasted and long-legged. With her bright hair and bubbly personality, Cee was so attractive that Katie wondered if Bryce were really indifferent to the older woman's physical charms. Probably not. But she certainly wasn't going to allow herself to start feeling jealous all over again.

"I wish we didn't have to leave so soon," Cee said with a little sigh. "What time do you think it is, Katie? Two o'clock? Three?"

"About three," Katie murmured and rolled over onto her back.

"The men will be coming in soon. My, hasn't Eric had a fine time!"

"Yes," Katie agreed with a grin. Her young half brother had managed to get up on water skiis the second time he tried. He had baited a hook correctly on the very first try, having watched Bryce intently. The child was a remarkably quick learner, and Bryce had appeared to enjoy Eric's company even, Katie wondered, if he wasn't also growing exhausted by it. Eric's unlimited energy could wear one down in a hurry.

"Eric needs to spend more time with a grown man," Cee went on, her voice turning wistful once again. "Oh, Katie, I do hope I'll marry again. I'd even like to have another child or two—but it will certainly have to be soon! That old biological clock is ticking away. When you get to be thirty, you'll know what I mean."

"Um-hum," Katie said noncommittally.

"I hope Bryce decides to buy this place," Cee continued. "Wouldn't that be nice?"

Katie gave another murmured assent, and Cee fell

silent. A minute or more might have passed, then she spoke again, hesitantly. "Katie, have you told Bryce yet that you're moving back to Washington?"

"Why, no," Katie said in surprise. "I haven't told a living soul but you, Cee. I don't want word leaking out before I give formal notice."

"I really think you ought to tell Bryce now," Cee persisted.

"Why?" said Katie bluntly.

"Because . . . well, he can certainly keep a secret! And . . . er . . . he might be getting the wrong idea about . . . well, various things."

So that was it! Katie was not the only woman present to have felt the bite of jealousy. With the dreary realization, her spirits nose-dived.

"Of course, it's your business," Cee went on hastily.

"Yes, it is," Katie agreed, "and right now, Cee, I don't want to tell Bryce. Not that I think for a moment he would blab, but sometimes secrets just slip out."

No, I can't tell him yet, Katie thought decisively. Not when I still have to work with the man for almost three months. If, God forbid, Bryce and I find ourselves arguing over something at work, like the helicopter flights, I don't want him looking at me and thinking "short-timer," or possibly holding that fact over my head.

"It's too soon," Katie told her stepmother emphatically.

"All right, dear." Cee shrugged her shoulders.

Silence stretched taut between them. How transparent Cee was! Katie thought, shielding her eyes from the sun with her forearm. She could practically hear every whirl and click of her stepmother's brain. Cee longed to remarry, to give her child a father and to have other children to fill those bunk beds here at the lake house. She and Bryce really would be an ideal couple.

But it was to her—Katie—that Bryce had said those extravagant words yesterday: "I want you the way I've never wanted another woman!" Oh, sure, he had a friendly, affectionate feeling for Cee, but even Katie could not read more into Bryce's attitude than that.

Still, Cee was also right in a way, because Katie knew she had to do *something*. Was it fair to let Bryce continue having "ideas"? Fair to keep seeing him and letting him kiss her? That was leading the man on unfairly, and Katie always tried to be fair.

Yes, she had to do something. Soon. Right away. Even today.

"Look, Katie, here comes the bass boat." Cee stood up and began to wave as the dot that was the boat moved slowly toward them. "Eric's sitting in front. Oh God, it looks like they've caught another mess of those damned fish! Well, I'd better go inside and get our stuff together."

"I'd better, too." Reluctantly, Katie pulled herself erect and began to fold up her beach towel. The men had returned, the afternoon was waning and the weekend was coming to an end.

Bryce was the laggard who delayed their departure. Of course, in fairness to him, he was also the one who had the most to do, Katie thought. He and Eric cleaned their fish and stowed them away between layers of ice. Then Bryce presented Cee with the styrofoam cooler.

"Thanks just loads!" she cracked.

"Mom, we can cook 'em on our barbecue grill," Eric said excitedly.

"I'm thrilled." Cee ran a hand through Eric's tousled hair. "Now go shower, fisherman. I want to get home before dark."

Meanwhile, Bryce was busy securing the bass boat, hauling in lawn chairs and recliners and locking various doors and windows. He threw an apologetic look at Katie, already waiting in a chair by the door with her overnight bag and picnic hamper. "Just let me grab a shower, too. I know I'm reeking from bait and fish."

Katie hadn't noticed that he reeked at all. Rather, Bryce's faint aroma of sun, warm water and perspiration was a natural, healthy one. "What can I do to help?" she offered.

"See if there are any perishables left in the refrigerator," he instructed. "Carry out the garbage, too, if you don't mind."

Katie didn't mind, but when she returned from garbage duty she found that Cee and Eric were getting into their car. Indeed, Eric was shouting, "Mom, c'mon!"

"Just try and stall an impatient kid," Cee said wryly. "He wants to watch a rerun of 'Star Trek' on TV. Well, I guess Bryce knows we've had a dandy time. Eric's told him often enough!"

"Oh." Katie's throat tightened with apprehension. So she was to be left here alone again with Bryce.

For a moment she shamelessly debated whether to ask Cee to take her with them. She could call to Bryce that she really needed to get back. Resignedly, Katie knew she couldn't do that. Bryce had gone to a great deal of trouble to make the weekend an enjoyable one and he would be hurt if she ran out on him. Also, it would take Cee out of her way and might make Eric late for his precious program.

But Katie was already dreading the necessary scene to come while she hugged her stepmother and Eric, then waved them away. She walked slowly back inside the lake house to wait for Bryce.

When he emerged, crisply clean and smelling of soap and aftershave, Katie informed him that the others had already left. "I know. I heard them drive off." Bryce's mouth quirked in a smile. "Eric told me the complete plot of two 'Star Trek' episodes while we were fishing today. I had a feeling he wasn't going to miss another installment."

"Thanks for being so nice to him," Katie said sincerely.

She wished Bryce didn't look so appealing. In clean jeans and a striped knit shirt, he made the breath catch in her throat. She wished she wasn't so dangerously aware of their being here alone. "Ready to go?" she asked nervously.

He came nearer, and Katie saw the purposeful look in his eyes. "Oh, no . . . no, Bryce," she stammered and moved swiftly to put a chair between them.

"Don't run away from me," he said softly, starting to circle in on her. "Come here, Katie . . . darling."

"No!" she said fiercely, biting her lip in agitation.

"Why?" Bryce said, his eyes clouding with bewilderment. "I've had a hard time thinking of anything this weekend but the way you felt in my arms. Don't tell me you haven't thought about it, too!"

"We need to get back," Katie protested.

He stopped inches away and sent her a slow, steady smile. "Why? What does it matter if we get back late tonight—or even tomorrow morning?"

"Bryce, I'm not available for an affair!" The words blurted out far more sharply than Katie had intended. Then she drew an unsteady breath. At least she had stated her position.

Bryce's handsome, tanned face tightened with consternation. "An affair!" he repeated. "Katie, is that what you think I have in mind?"

For a long, stark moment they stared at each other, then Bryce gave a short laugh. "Maybe you thought when I said I loved you it was just the thrill of the moment. That's not true!" One of his strong, large hands shot out and imprisoned hers, and even that brief contact of their flesh set Katie's senses ablaze.

"Katie, I love you," Bryce said earnestly.

"You don't—you can't! You really don't even know me," she half wailed, struggling to free her hand from his.

His hand tightened, refusing to release her. "I know all I need to know about you. And I don't view making love with you as an affair or a fling or anything else. I see it as a very serious commitment."

"I'm not ready for such a commitment," Katie protested.

"Why not?" Bryce's face grew strained. In his gray eyes she again saw that look of pain. "Don't you want to get married? Have a family of your own one day? Maybe even a smart little boy like Eric or a pretty little girl?"

"No, I'm not at all sure I do," Katie flashed back,

although her heart hammered relentlessly both from anxiety and despair. *Why did I have to meet him now . . . at this particular point in my life? A few years ago I would have loved hearing every word he's said!* Aloud, she replied carefully, "Bryce, I've worked hard to get where I am. It hasn't been easy. I don't want to do anything that will jeopardize my career."

Abruptly, he released her hand as though his own had suddenly gone nerveless. "Is that what you think would happen?" he inquired evenly, yet the distress in his eyes and face was unmistakable. "Would it make any difference if I said I was proud of you and all you've accomplished? I wouldn't try to turn you into a hausfrau, Katie!"

"Maybe you wouldn't intend it, Bryce, but I have the distinct suspicion that's exactly what would happen," Katie rushed on. "Doctors have such demands made on them with their own careers that it would be exceedingly hard for you to be supportive of mine."

He didn't reply, only stared at her steadily with that deepening pain in his eyes. Oh God, why should it hurt her so much to think she'd hurt him?

"So that's it," Bryce muttered. "It's because I'm a doctor."

Avidly, Katie seized at the excuse he offered. What did it matter that this wasn't the real reason; it served as a handy and convenient one. "I always swore I'd never marry a doctor, Bryce. I've gone to considerable lengths never to get mixed up with one! Not only do our careers often put us at swords' points, but doctors are slaves to their phones and beepers. Their family always comes a poor second. It's true—you know it's true! Look how many nights you're at the hospital now."

"I've been learning the setup. Every hospital is different from every other one. But my methods are very different from Ash Blakely's, and things will change when I'm the chairman of the department, Katie. Also, as long as I've waited for a wife and family, they will never come a poor second! I'd be very, very involved every step of the way."

"You say that now," Katie whispered, "but what happens when there's an emergency?"

"You're saying you don't trust me to work things out." Bryce's voice went flat and the lingering hope drained from his eyes.

For a moment, wavering and torn, Katie simply looked at him. A part of her wanted to reach up and stroke his tense cheek and take away that look by pressing her lips to his. But how fair would that be? She had known all along that she couldn't get involved with Bryce and now was the time to make her stand. If she didn't cut things off decisively right now, she might not be able to later.

So she made herself turn away from her inner longings and head toward the door. "I'm sorry, Bryce," she said over her shoulder, quietly, inadequately.

"You'll never know how sorry I am, Katie!" he cried.

"Are you coming?" she asked tersely.

"Oh, yes. I brought you here and I'll deliver you safely home." Then his voice tightened, growing hard and inflexible. "But I'm not giving up, Katie. I want you—I need you! You were born to lie in a man's arms—my arms! Maybe I've rushed you. If that's the case, I'll back off and give you time to think. But I know what I want and I won't give you up!''

Again she felt a terrible conflict of emotions. A part of Katie thrilled to the determined passion in Bryce's voice while the other part recognized and identified that tone of voice. She had heard that rigid, inflexible note before in other doctors' voices, in her father's voice.

By the time they were halfway to Dallas, Bryce began talking to her again about very mundane affairs. Was she a football fan? No. That was too bad. He looked forward to seeing the Dallas Cowboys in action.

Katie was not deceived by his idle chatter. Bryce had made up his mind, and once a surgeon did that, his opinion was set in concrete. He might be smilingly determined to get his own way, even sweetly determined, or, as in the case of Max Brentwood, roaringly and ragingly. But, in his own way, Bryce was just as determined as her father had ever been.

"You don't need to walk me to my door," Katie said stiffly when they'd reached her apartment.

"Don't be ridiculous!" Bryce said, his voice suddenly snappish.

At Katie's doorway, he seized her, imprisoning her within the hard circle of his arms. "Bryce, please don't!" she said, anguished.

Ignoring her protests, he forced her head back against his arms and caught her mouth with his. For a long, almost endless moment he kissed her deeply and searchingly. Katie stood stiffly, willing herself not to respond while she tried to retain the memory of his voice gone so curt.

Bryce's tongue plunged into her mouth, as though hungry to snatch one last taste of sweetness. And despite all of her unhappiness and mute resolve, Katie felt her carefully constructed defenses against him beginning to crumble. She wanted to wrap her arms around him and urge him, with her own lips and tongue, to be gentler and more loving . . . the way he had been before with her.

Instead she pushed futilely at his strong shoulders until he was done with the almost punishing kiss. Slowly, his dark head lifted and she caught one last glimpse of the pain he was now trying to hide.

"I won't give up, Katie," he said again, then reached for her hamper and overnight case and set them inside her door.

But, of course, she had never doubted that for a moment.

Chapter Eight

Seventy-eight days . . .

The sullen, ominous rumble of thunder was loud enough to penetrate the thick hospital walls. "Ms. Brentwood, call Flight Operations STAT," Katie's beeper chattered.

What now? Katie thought as she dashed out from a waiting-room lobby on the fourth floor in search of a phone. The nearest one, at the nurses' station, was presently being used by a white-clad nurse. "STAT," Katie mouthed at the nurse, who hastily began winding up her conversation.

What a week! Each night had presented special problems for her. On Monday there had been a VIP admission to arrange. Elise Engel, star of TV and films who had been in Dallas on a movie location, was hospitalized with a stomach virus. Katie had arranged

Ms. Engel's admission under an alias, not that anyone would have recognized her anyway. After several hours of throwing up, the young actress had looked pale, wan and certainly less than beautiful.

On Tuesday night a technician sent to run an electro-cardiogram balked when he found his patient confined to the isolation wing with suspected hepatitis. "I've got a pregnant wife at home and I'm not taking any chances!" he told Katie flatly.

Although Katie sympathized with the young man's fear, it was still his job to go where he was sent. She put the employee on report and located another braver tech to run the necessary EKG.

Wednesday was one of those unpredictable nights when, for no discernible reason, the kooks and crazies came out of the wall. The helicopters took off and landed repeatedly, bringing in a stream of patients who had been shot, stabbed or beaten. Even ordinary law-abiding citizens were exceptionally careless. Figures on automobile accidents and home injuries took a sharp turn upward. The Emergency Center was packed, and the Shocktrauma Unit was busy all night.

"At least this improves the hospital census," Doug had said cynically, and Katie, who felt infinitely weary, shot him a dirty look. No, she definitely did not enjoy being troubleshooter at a trauma hospital. Thank goodness this would all end for her soon! How much better she would feel when she was administrator of a children's rehab center, watching the luckier ones put braces and wheelchairs aside and helping the less fortunate to adjust to their disabilities with grace and courage. What better thing could she do with her life?

She and Doug had snatched a quick bite together in the cafeteria that night and then he'd escorted her out to her car. There Doug took advantage of the dimly lit, deserted area on level Five to steal a couple of kisses. Katie had tried to respond to those kisses, for they weren't unpleasant. Doug was an experienced enough lover to know how to kiss, so it wasn't his fault that he couldn't flood Katie's heart with warmth or accelerate its beat appreciably.

What had happened on Thursday? Oh, yes. That night Katie had to arrange for a patient under police guard to be transferred to the nearest prison hospital. The patient did not relish the transfer and had spewed out a number of very ugly words to his doctor, Katie and the armed policeman who accompanied him.

Now it was Friday, dark and stormy with rain, and Katie had just been paged by Flight Operations.

While she waited impatiently for the phone to free up, Katie knew in her heart that Bryce Emerson was the real reason this week had proved to be so awful. How could she forget the man when he was always here, there, everywhere until there appeared no escape from him?

On Monday night she had seen him in the hall, striding along purposefully. Bryce sent her a polite nod and a quiet smile, but just the sight of him made Katie feel weak.

He had also been present on Wednesday night when Dr. Ash Blakely summoned Katie to meet him outside of Shocktrauma and, once again, made his familiar pitch to either shut down the helicopters or divert neurosurgical patients elsewhere.

"I'm sorry, Dr. Blakely, but this very matter was discussed just last week in Operations." Firmly, Katie kept her eyes on the short man and tried not to stare at Bryce, a long, lean figure in green scrubs, with paper booties over his shoes and a surgeon's cap on his head. Still, she had been aware of a subtle emanation that seemed to flow forth from him. The strange inner warmth almost reached out and touched her. Katie tingled all over even as she repeated her position to Dr. Blakely. "Administrators have been instructed to keep the helicopters flying. Period."

As usual Dr. Blakely could see only his limited point of view, and Katie had left him fuming. *Neurosurgeons!* she thought in exasperation, but her heart ached when she thought of how tired Bryce had looked. He was spending long days at the medical school teaching and long nights in surgery. Katie knew the decision she had made would do nothing to ease his heavy load, but she could do nothing else.

Bryce was at the hospital again tonight, Katie suspected, even though she hadn't actually seen him. His very aura was here. Katie could sense the invisible connection as though a silver cord tugged and pulled her toward him. She could brand the notion ridiculous and herself as fanciful, but she *knew* he was here.

"All right, doctor," said the nurse on the telephone. She broke the connection and handed the warm receiver to Katie.

Quickly, Katie dialed Flight Operations and reached Terry Kendall, the dispatcher. "We've just had a report from the weather bureau, Katie," he informed her. "A cold front has met a mass of warm gulf air and tornadolike conditions are developing. We're going to have to shut down for the night."

"Terry, you can't do this to me!" Katie wailed.

"Can't do anything else, Katie. We're starting to tie down the choppers right now so that they won't blow off the pad."

So much for keeping the helicopters flying! Katie could scarcely argue with a weather bureau bulletin. Oh, why did weather predictions have to be so inexact and uncertain? Although rain had been forecast for the area tonight, there had not been any previous mention of a possible tornado.

She sighed, then became aware that Terry was still on the line. "What's the problem?" she asked, for she had lost track of helicopters taking off and landing. "Is anyone still out?"

"Doug is," the dispatcher said quietly. "He went over to Arlington with Stella Hopkins to pick up a neonate."

Silently, Katie digested that fact. A neonate was an infant whose age ranged from birth to six weeks, and the very fact of its being flown here indicated that it had probably been born prematurely and was critically ill. Such babies were frequently transferred to Harwick Memorial where expert facilities for pediatric critical care existed.

Stella . . . Katie's mind conjured up the fierce, little flight nurse she had collided with a few days ago. One of the many hospital stories about Stella related how a man injured in a car wreck momentarily regained consciousness to find her crouched over him. "I knew I was close to death," the patient had said. "I wouldn't have been surprised to see an angel bending over me—or a devil either! But I couldn't figure out why this little green elf was there cutting off all my clothes!"

Katie was glad that the cool-headed Stella was flying with Doug tonight. "Terry, is he going to set down the chopper?" she said anxiously to the dispatcher.

"You know Doug. He's coming on in."

"I'll be right there," Katie said. She dropped the phone onto its hook and sprinted for the elevator, her palms already clammy with perspiration.

Of course, this was Doug's shot to call, not hers. The pilot always made decisions such as this. Still, Doug was reckless. Maybe she could persuade him to set the helicopter down in a cleared area. He, Stella and the baby could be brought here by ambulance. Yes, maybe she could convince him to do that. . . . Yet even as Katie flew down the hall toward Flight Operations, she doubted it.

She found the dispatcher already engaged in a static-filled conversation with Doug. The small room was filled with other concerned pilots and flight nurses.

Terry glanced up and shook his head at Katie. So Doug was proving adamant. "Let me talk to him," she urged.

"Doug, here's Katie Brentwood," Terry announced and thrust the mike into her hands.

"Set down, Doug!" she begged. "We can send an ambulance to pick you up."

"No good, sweetheart. We've got a sick little tot

here, and Stella says she'll never make a long ground trip." Doug's familiar voice crackled from excitement as well as with static.

"Oh, Doug—"

"Katie, it's a helluva mess up here. If I've got to set down anywhere I'd rather risk the helistop. At least it's all lit up and there aren't any high wires around."

Silently, Katie digested those logical facts. "How's Stella?" she asked.

"Green as her jumpsuit. But just before she buried her head in a barf bag, she told me to go for it!"

Oh, *damn!* "Doug, please be careful," Katie pleaded and was distressed to hear her voice quiver. Grimly, she got a grip on herself. "If you crash our million-dollar helicopter, I'll deduct every cent I can from your death benefits!"

"You sweet thing, I always knew you cared!"

Then there was only the crackle of static and the anxious circle of faces. Katie handed the mike back to the dispatcher and reached up to wipe away a trickle of perspiration that had seeped down her temple. "I'll be back," she said to Terry and went immediately across the hall to Administration. This was something "just-call-me-Bob" had to know about.

She reached the executive director at home, informed him of the situation and promised to keep him advised. Then she walked back outside into the corridor and sagged against the wall beside Flight Operations. For the moment she could not bring herself to go back inside.

"What is it, Katie?"

She looked up, amazed, to see that Bryce stood before

her. She'd been so distracted by her thoughts and fears that she hadn't even seen his approach.

"It's Doug," she said through tight, stiff lips. "He's caught in the middle of the storm, trying to fly in a neonate."

"Doug?" Bryce said blankly, then she saw recognition tense his strong, too-thin face. "Oh, the helicopter pilot who's your friend?"

Katie gave a mute nod, and Bryce's face suddenly tightened. "So *that's* it," he said, almost as if speaking to himself. "He's more than your friend, isn't he, Katie?"

Her taut nerves snapped. "Oh God, Bryce, what if he is?" she cried distractedly.

Bryce's face whitened and looked almost gaunt. When she saw him go so pale and still, Katie could have bitten off her tongue.

Good grief, he thought she was romantically involved with Doug and that wasn't the truth at all! She would be just as worried and frightened if it were any other Life Copter pilot in this jam, flying with any other nurse and infant.

"Bryce, you've misconstrued—" she began hastily.

"It's all right, Katie." Stiffly, his mouth framed the words. He even managed a small, strained smile. "You should have told me before. Now that I know, I'll keep my distance."

"If you'd let me explain—" she blurted.

He interrupted her again. "There's no need. I certainly hope Doug makes it back safely. He should. He's sure got a lot to come back to!"

Then Bryce strode away, leaving Katie leaning against the wall and feeling even more stricken than before.

Why didn't he listen to me? she wondered almost despairingly, for she knew that her involvement with Bryce Emerson had now been quite effectively ended. But, of course, she wasn't running after him, insisting he listen to her explanations either. It's better this way, Katie thought numbly. But why does it hurt me so badly whenever I hurt him?

She didn't know, and no answers floated up from her mind to help her. There was only pain, knotted like a cold, aching ball in the pit of her stomach, pain over Bryce and pain over Doug.

At least she need have no more fear of Bryce's determined, relentless pursuit of her. Why wasn't she relieved? Why did she ache with misery instead?

She forced herself to go back inside Flight Operations and found that another person had joined the tense, waiting group gathered there. Katie's stricken eyes met the equally distraught ones of Head Nurse Sheila Rigley.

"How did you know about Doug?" Katie asked awkwardly.

"I just felt it." Sheila's mouth twisted crookedly. "Isn't that the darndest thing, Katie? That I can feel it whenever he's in trouble."

That invisible cord, Katie thought, and patted Sheila's arm automatically. Together they stood watching through the dispatcher's window as dark rain beat down on the brightly lit helistop.

Seven long, long minutes later the hum of an incoming helicopter rose above the sounds of the storm. The hum advanced rapidly to a clatter. Then they could see the green and silver helicopter nearing the pad. It slowed, hovered momentarily, and then Doug set it down with such perfect precision that Katie could almost forget how badly buffeted by strong winds the small aircraft was. More long, long moments passed as the rotors slowed and stopped. Finally, the door to the helicopter popped open and Doug leaped out. He was soaked immediately by rain as he leaned back in to assist Sheila. Several flight attendants in yellow rain slickers rushed out to help. The little green elf's face was contorted, and Katie could guess that Stella was blistering the air with her curses, but she and Doug had a firm clutch on the portable isolette, and a tiny baby, born too soon, would now have an excellent chance for life.

A hesitant hand touched Katie's arm. She turned to see Sheila Rigley sagging with relief. "Don't tell Doug I was here," she whispered, then turned and left.

Katie stared after the slender, white-clad figure, and for the first time in the last tense quarter of an hour, she smiled. She fully intended to tell Doug that Sheila had been here. He deserved to know. After that . . . well, it would all be up to him.

Seventy-one days . . .

A week of stormy weather followed. The hospital quieted as human beings were forced to stay inside and they wreaked less mayhem upon each other. The rain only permitted the helicopters to fly sporadically. Still, hospital security and administrators like Katie had to stay vigilant against the denizens of the nearby park as they crept in seeking shelter. Their plight and their wasted lives depressed Katie.

Other things depressed her, too. The near-constant rain. Her own lonely, empty hours. She had even lost, temporarily she was sure, her zest for the new and exciting life that awaited her back in Washington. What's wrong with me? Katie wondered, amazed by her brooding.

She knew the answer to that lay with the lean, green-clad figure who still haunted the halls and cafeteria and haunted too many of her thoughts as well. Bryce was always perfectly polite when their paths crossed, but his gray blue eyes had not lost their look of pain. Katie wished that Bryce were a better actor. Or was he acting with this pretense of pain? She wished she knew.

Other things tugged strangely at her heart. Katie found herself keenly aware of pregnant women. Many were patients, women of all ages and races, walking proudly down the halls, their loose dresses billowing out over their distended stomachs. Others worked at the hospital as nurses, secretaries and doctors. Katie had never particularly noticed expectant mothers before, but now she caught herself frequently watching other women's waistlines.

She was also made aware of which people wore wedding rings and which ones did not. There were so many different rings! Gold and platinum rings, wide and narrow ones, diamonds or nuggets, they all seemed to proclaim: "I belong with someone."

Since the flow of Katie's thoughts ran from puzzling to painful, she welcomed every bit of hospital business, whether it was ejecting Bessie, who had been caught showering in the nurses' dressing room, or soothing unhappy patients who disliked their doctors, nurses, hospital food or all three.

On Friday the weather cleared and the pace of city life grew surly once more. The helicopters flew, the Emergency Center filled with patients and, predictably, the available neurosurgeons found themselves stretched thin. At 10:00 that night Katie was summoned to meet with Dr. Emerson outside of Shocktrauma.

Bryce was alone, and that look of pain about his eyes and mouth had vanished utterly. His face could have been carved from stone and his eyes were hard as marbles as he confronted Katie.

She felt very nervous under his harsh gaze. She found herself swallowing and clutching her clipboard as though it were a shield. "Ah . . . where's Dr. Blakely?" she began.

"Away," Bryce replied tersely. Then, as though he could gauge Katie's discomfort and her flicker of disapproval that Dr. Blakely was unavailable, Bryce added a postscript: "His mother is quite ill."

"I see," Katie murmured. It was impossible for her to even imagine Dr. Blakely having a mother. She gripped her clipboard until its edges cut into her fingers. "What's the situation?"

With an economy of words Bryce described the patients who had arrived and their various injuries. "Ms. Brentwood, I'll have a better arrangement worked out in a couple of weeks—a month at most," Bryce said formally. "But tonight any further candidates for neurosurgery should be diverted to a Fort Worth hospital."

Katie drew a breath through lungs that ached. Bryce's

coldness was harder to take than either his persistent pursuit or his revelation of pain. "I can't do that, Bryce," she whispered and felt further unnerved to hear herself use his first name.

He stared at her with an expression so censorious that Katie quailed. Like a parrot, she repeated the hospital's stance. "It is neither our policy nor our philosophy to turn away emergency patients. Many of them might not survive a longer flight to Fort Worth since a trauma victim—"

"I am well aware of how long it takes a trauma victim to expire," Bryce stated ironically. "Indeed, I am probably far more cognizant of the time limit than you, Ms. Brentwood!"

Katie felt her face flush. *That* was certainly putting her in her place! The omniscient doctor had now spoken derisively to the hospital's hireling. So much for Bryce's respect for her and her career!

"I will not, under any circumstances, order flights diverted to Fort Worth!" Katie flared.

Bryce stared at her incredulously. "You mean that's your final word on the subject?"

"You bet it is, Dr. Emerson!" Katie snapped and heard an unpleasant edge to her voice.

"You are being completely irrational and unreasonable!" Bryce's voice grew as sharply unpleasant as Katie's, and she could feel his own suppressed fury. "Furthermore, that is an entirely *immature* decision considering that the situation here could easily worsen."

Katie knew she should not have said "under any circumstances." A smart administrator would have left herself an escape hatch. But those damning words—

irrational, unreasonable, immature—put the seal on her stubbornness.

"I'm prepared to take the responsibility, Dr. Emerson," she replied stonily.

"You will also take the official reprimand," Bryce shot back. "I can promise you, Ms. Brentwood, that the first task I'll undertake in my office Monday morning is a letter to the executive director of this hospital reporting your hostile and uncooperative attitude!"

Oh God! Although Katie's body still felt encased in ice, her heart began to sink. Such a letter from Bryce could provoke a full-scale investigation into Katie's actions tonight, and, in her heart, she suspected that she might not come off looking very good. Of course "just-call-me-Bob" had directed his administrators to keep the helicopters flying, but still the administrator on call was supposed to use common sense. Patient welfare was always the first consideration.

Katie knew she should shamelessly retract her statement to Bryce. She should ask him to notify her if the situation changed for the worse. In fact, she might be cutting her own throat by not doing this. But staring into the hard face of the tall man in greens, Katie simply could not utter another word. She turned instead and marched away.

When Steve Wills arrived to relieve Katie two hours later, he found her hunched tensely over the telephone. "What's going on?" he said curiously, and Katie raised her strained face to him. She knew she must look as awful as she felt.

"I've screwed up, Steve," she admitted and thought how easy it was to confess her misdeed to this man who was her friend. Why couldn't she confess it as easily to Bryce?

"*You?* Why, I don't believe it, Katie," Steve said in mild protest while he drew up a chair. "Tell me."

Katie did, relating the incident as honestly as she could. When Steve's face colored with annoyance she realized that his irritation was directed at Bryce, not her.

"Neurosurgeons!" Steve said, almost explosively. "I thought Emerson was going to prove a different sort. Well, it just goes to show—"

"Steve, I was *wrong*," Katie said painfully.

He peered at her troubled face. "I don't think so," he said staunchly. "Even if you were . . . Hell, you're only human and you've got your own orders to follow. I'm glad you told the smug sucker off!"

Katie gestured toward the telephone. "I've already called the Shocktrauma Unit twice to keep tabs on what's happening. I can't keep pestering them, but—"

Steve caught her meaning immediately. Since Katie had taken such an adamant position, she was trying to stay posted on the neurosurgical situation so that she could, if necessary, reverse her decision.

"Let me scout around," Steve said conspiratorily. "I've got a few odd friends in strange places."

"Thanks," Katie breathed and bent her head down into her hands.

Steve was back in ten minutes. "It's A-OK so far," he said to Katie cheerfully. "The only new admission is a kid who can wait until tomorrow. Now go home and get some sleep, Katie."

She shook her head. "I can't, Steve. Not yet. Not

until I absolutely know there aren't going to be others . . ." Her voice trailed off.

Through the next couple of hours while Steve continued his surveillance, he phoned his reports to Katie and they grew steadily more encouraging. "Hey, it's past two, and all our birds are sitting quiet on the pad. Not a rotor whirring! Dr. Almighty Emerson has finished his case and he and the neurosurgery resident are twiddling their thumbs. You *did* make the right decision! So go home, gal."

"All right," Katie said wearily. "Thanks." She hung up the phone, stood up and swung her purse over her shoulder. What a night!

Her heels tapped echoingly as she walked down the corridor that led out to the parking garage. Involuntarily, she shivered. After midnight the hospital corridors always seemed so spooky. There was something ominous about the dimmed lights and the absence of traffic.

Katie had stepped outside into the humid spring night before she realized that she had no security escort. She could have phoned for Elliot Wainwright if she'd remembered in time, but she felt too tired to retrace her steps.

Unconsciously, she walked faster. How eerie and deserted were the hospital grounds!

The concrete parking garage stood silent and clammy cool, but an elevator was waiting. Katie stepped inside and pressed the button for the fifth level. Silently, the elevator whisked her up.

Was Bryce preparing to leave soon, too? Katie's mind flew to him again and she shivered once more, remembering his granitelike face, his cold eyes and his anger. Would he carry through on his threat to report her to the executive director? Katie rather doubted it now, for the night's events had proven that, by sheer luck, her decision had not been unwise. But how about her attitude?

The elevator eased to a stop on Five, and Katie stepped out automatically, her thoughts still on Bryce. Tonight they'd certainly seen the worst in each other for something more than professional concern had egged him on. Had his hurt and disappointment over *her* been transmuted into anger? Would he become her outspoken enemy? Katie drew another painful breath. To think of herself and Bryce remaining at odds with each other throughout the next seventy days was another source of pain.

She heard the echo of her footsteps in the dungeonlike silence of the garage and suddenly Katie was seized by uneasiness. How late it was and how dark way up here! The shadowy illumination concealed as much as it revealed. Oh, why had she parked so far from the elevator?

Abruptly, the hairs on the back of her neck stood up and she could feel them rising on her arms as well. Was that a *moving* shadow, flitting noiselessly from behind the parked cars? No, it was only her imagination. She was still nervous and overwrought from the night's events. How she wished her heels didn't make so much noise! She also wished she could walk faster, but her straight, professional skirt restricted her steps.

What was that noise? Had there definitely been one? A

noise louder than the soft click of her purse when she opened it to draw out her car keys? Katie's heart pounded ominously in her ears as she reached the side of her parked car.

Her hand searched the depths of her small purse. She faced the locked door of her car, but she couldn't find her car keys! Where were they? Oh God, why hadn't she had her keys in her hand when she stepped off the elevator?

Katie's apprehension increased as the key ring continued to elude her. She had no recourse but to stand, alone and exposed, while she frantically burrowed about in her purse.

The keys simply weren't there! Oh, dear God, what now? Katie thought desperately. Then she remembered the deep pockets of her blazer. She often dropped her keys there. Her free hand went scurrying into the blazer's right pocket. *Nothing.* Wildly, she shifted her purse, her breath shallow and rapid with fear, but the left pocket of her jacket did yield the elusive keys.

Before she had time to savor the small victory, she felt herself seized from behind, a wiry, strong arm going tightly about her throat. Katie's instinctive cry was muffled as that arm constricted her windpipe. A sour, hot breath blew in her ears, the excited breath of an animal aroused by the scent of blood—or lust.

As Katie felt herself gripped about the waist by a second, equally strong arm, her whole being exploded with panic. Tentacles of horror drove deep and embedded in her brain as she confronted every woman's deepest terror and flailed out against it. She struggled with a strength she had not known she possessed, but all she got for her efforts was the mocking sound of her car keys as they dropped from her hand and struck the cold concrete floor.

She was going to be raped! Another strangling cry of terror rose from deep within her but was cut short by the relentless arm at her throat. In Katie's frantic mind the events translated into one word: rape. Even as the terrifying realization slammed into her, she felt the hand at her waist rise roughly to her breasts. They shrank beneath the harsh touch. Then she heard a ripping sound as her blouse was rent and buttons popped loose to dance and bounce on the garage floor.

Desperately, Katie tried to kick out at her assailant, but he evaded her sharp pumps with a growling sound deep in his throat. She could feel his damp hand groping inside her blouse and could smell the scent of excitement and rancid sweat on him. Nausea rose churning to her throat, the bile of fear and near-disbelief choking her almost as much as the man's fierce arm was. A wave of dizziness followed. She couldn't breathe—his arm was suffocating her! She was going to be raped, here in this deserted garage, by one of the nocturnal beings who had drifted over from the park, and all Katie could hope for at this point was that she wouldn't be murdered as well.

Of course, dead women could not identify their assailants. A silent body allowed a rapist to go free.

At the thought of her life ending here, in a parking garage at two o'clock in the morning, Katie struggled with renewed vigor against the fierce clutch. Oh, what a waste! she thought despairingly, and on the heels of that thought came another: I've scarcely *lived!* I haven't accomplished what I wanted to do as an administrator!

I've never been a wife and a mother! Blindly, she flailed in the harsh grasp, trying to bite, scratch, scream—anything!

A sharp blow to Katie's head left her reeling. Stars exploded behind her eyelids and the blackness of oblivion threatened. The arm at her throat had tightened remorselessly until she could no longer breathe at all. Katie felt herself sagging, her knees buckling, and heard a triumphant grunt of pleasure.

Her assailant lowered her to the hard concrete floor. Katie was still conscious enough to feel its uneven ridges scratching her legs and snagging her stockings. She blinked against the threatening blackness and saw the male figure crouching over her. Her throat, released at last from his pressure, yielded up a thin, little scream.

The man looming over her cursed savagely and gripped her throat between maddened fingers. This was it, Katie thought despairingly. Lights out. Curtains. End of scene—end of life.

Then, incredibly, she heard the sound of her own name. "Katie? Are you here, Katie?"

It was Bryce! At the sound of his familiar voice, Katie summoned a last ferocious burst of energy. Strength poured into her, propelling her limp hands upward, her thumbs driving hard toward the rapist's eyes. She made contact with one eye and heard the man squeal in pain. His hands jerked away from her throat, and, with a great gasp of air, Katie managed a final weak scream.

But those sounds were loud enough to send footsteps pounding toward her. "I'm coming, Katie! Hang on!" Bryce cried.

She blinked and her vision cleared just enough to see

the rapist leaping back from her. In a flash Katie saw his pallid face, streaked with sweat and grime, and his eyes, now glittering with fear. Then he sprinted away on sneakered feet that made only a soft, slithering sound on the cement floor.

Bryce's heavier footsteps pounded closer, then stopped. "Katie! Oh, my dearest Katie!" he cried.

His voice sounded muffled to her, but that was because of the ringing in her ears and the wave of fresh dizziness that was sheer relief sweeping over her. For a moment Katie blacked out completely. Then, with a gigantic effort, she swam back to consciousness to see Bryce kneeling before her. In the dimness of the garage his face was a ghastly, ghostly white while his hands moved rapidly over her body. Despite the fear that still gripped her, Katie did not resist Bryce's touch; she recognized that those warm, steady hands were making a swift, professional inventory. He was checking her for obvious injuries and broken bones.

"Katie, are you all right?" Bryce said urgently, his voice hoarse with fear.

She managed to nod, then winced at the pain the gesture caused her. At once Bryce's warm hands began to explore the tenderness of her neck and head. "That man—" Katie said fearfully and heard her normal voice reduced to a frog's croak.

"He's gone, the slimy scum!" Bryce said grimly. He stared at Katie, his eyes enormous with their concern. "Was I . . . in time?"

"Yes," she croaked and grew aware of her sprawled position. Her skirt was twisted beneath her and hiked immodestly high on her thighs. With a groan, she attempted to sit up and right her clothing, and Bryce aided her deftly.

He rocked back on his heels as, with shaking hands, Katie buttoned her blazer over her nearly bare breasts and fumbled with her skirt. Her throat ached miserably, and her head throbbed. The adrenaline released throughout her body by fear made her feel nauseous. Still, she had to have one answer to a very important question. "How did you know?" she asked Bryce, her voice still almost comically deep.

Bryce's hands were no longer exploring the back of her neck, but he massaged the tense muscles there. "I left the hospital just in time to see you enter the garage," he answered unsteadily. "It was so late . . . so dark. I waited to watch you drive out." A small, shaky sound escaped him. "Maybe I sensed trouble, who knows? When you didn't come back out, I went looking for you. I stopped on every floor, calling your name. . . . Oh, Katie!" All at once Bryce's professional aplomb deserted him. For just a moment he clutched Katie close to his heart. She could hear its rapid beating, then he rose slowly, lifting her up with him.

When she attempted to stand, Katie discovered that her legs were as weak as water and trembled uncontrollably. She had to lean heavily against Bryce for support.

"Let's go back to the hospital," he urged. "We'll get you checked over in Emergency—"

"No, please!" Katie begged. Her voice was almost back to normal. "Bryce, I'm all right now and—I just want to go home!"

She saw uncertainty wavering on his face. "Please!" she urged.

"All right," he said with a reluctant sigh. "I'll drive you. You're certainly in no shape to drive yourself."

To that very obvious fact, Katie had no argument. "I dropped my car keys down here somewhere. . . ."

"I see them. Here—lean against the car door." A moment later Bryce opened the door and helped Katie inside. Since she was on the driver's side, she edged over on the seat to make room for him. Then she dropped her head back against the seat. Almost impersonally she observed the tremors running through her body, causing her legs and arms, knees and fingers to jerk and tremble. It was delayed reaction to fear and stress.

Bryce pushed the car seat back to accommodate his longer legs, then drove out of the garage slowly, exiting by the brightly lighted Emergency entrance. He braked for a moment. "Katie, are you sure . . . ?" he began.

"Bryce, I just want to go *home!*" she insisted.

Slowly, Bryce nodded, accepting her decision, and the car shot forward into the night.

Chapter Nine

$\mathcal{T}$en minutes later when the car stopped, Katie opened heavy eyelids and peered around in bewilderment. "This isn't where I live," she said, staring at the unfamiliar apartment complex.

"No, it's my place." Bryce threw her a brief, encouraging smile. "I can't let you stay by yourself tonight, Katie, and it's much too late to call Celia to come stay with you. I know your neck is wrenched, and it's even possible you have a concussion. You might also go into shock."

Since Katie was still trembling all over, she made no objections. She realized that she didn't want to be alone—that, indeed, she wanted to be with only one person in the whole world and that was the anxious man seated beside her.

"I'm sorry to be so much trouble, Bryce," she said softly.

"Trouble!" he exclaimed. "My God, Katie, I *always* want to be with you when there's trouble."

Bryce's heartfelt words sent a welcome rush of warmth and strength through her. When he helped her out of the car, Katie was able to walk almost normally.

His apartment was only a few steps away, and Bryce switched on the lights as he walked through the living room. Katie was still too shaken to take much note of her surroundings. She saw modern furniture, a few paintings and wall hangings, and a number of small sculptures of modern art.

Bryce apologized for the magazines and medical journals stacked on tables and lying all about. "My long-suffering maid is forbidden to toss them out," he said, half-jokingly, to Katie.

"Everything looks fine," she said and glanced around for a telephone. She found one on an end table and phoned hospital security, giving them a terse report. When she hung up, Katie's skin was crawling again with the realization of how that—that *creature* in the garage had touched and mauled her. The need to bathe, to scrub her body completely clean of his contaminated touch, was overpowering.

"Can I fix you a . . . No!" Bryce stopped himself abruptly. "No drinks except water and no drugs stronger than aspirin until I know for sure that you're all right."

"I just want to take a bath," Katie said faintly.

"Sure." He nodded understandingly and led her back

to a bathroom that was pristine clean and sweet smelling. Swiftly, Bryce started water running in the tub, then found towels and soap for Katie. He even provided her with one of his bathrobes.

"Call if you need help," Bryce said kindly. He left, closing the door behind him.

A minute or two later, Katie realized belatedly that she did actually need help to bathe. For the first time in her adult life, she was unable to remove her clothes. The mechanisms of buttons, zippers and hooks baffled her, for her hands were trembling again and so weak they refused to obey her commands. Yet she wanted a bath so desperately! She needed to feel clean again! At the dilemma this posed, she began to cry hopelessly, huge tears rolling down her face until the sound of her choked sobs finally escaped.

"Katie, what is it?"

Bryce's voice came from just beyond the door. Katie realized that he had been standing there, waiting to hear the sounds of her splashing and had heard her tears instead. "I—I can't!" she wailed and sobbed aloud.

"May I come in?" he called.

"Yes," she said helplessly, and when he stood over her, anxiety written on every line and plane of his strong-featured face, Katie dissolved completely.

"My hands . . ." she sobbed, showing Bryce their tremors. "I can't even get my clothes off."

Bryce's face cleared with relief. "Let me help you, Katie," he said gently. "I once spent a summer working in a nursing home. I've bathed many, many people. You can trust me."

"I do trust you," she said, mopping at her streaming eyes and realizing the strange, wonderful truth of her words. Yes, she trusted Bryce completely. The realization came as a welcome surprise.

Bryce began carefully, making no sudden moves to alarm her. With his eyes holding her own, Bryce removed Katie's garments by touch. When he slid the jacket off her limp arms and then raised the skirt over her head, his touch was as delicate as any loving mother's. Katie's slip followed her skirt, and she felt a sudden flush go over her when she realized that she stood in only her shredded panty hose and dainty, revealing bra. But Bryce seemed to take no notice. He turned away to adjust the water filling the tub before turning back to hand Katie a thick towel, which she held like a curtain before her. Matter-of-factly, Bryce reached around the curtain to unfasten the bra and slide her panty hose down over her rounded, still quaking hips. Then, allowing Katie the modesty of shielding herself with the towel, he led her to the edge of the tub. Only when she slid down into the protective froth of soap bubbles did Bryce slip the towel from her hand.

The warm water lapped over her comfortingly, easing the tenseness of her muscles and taking the soreness from her scraped legs. Deftly, Bryce wielded a washcloth. "Let me wash your face now," he said calmly, his eyes still meeting and holding Katie's. "Good! Now, bend forward, knees to your chest, and I'll soap your shoulders and back."

She was infinitely grateful for his calm, measured voice, his innate decency and delicacy. Bryce even made a game of it as one would in bathing a little child. "Want me to shampoo your hair?"

"Yes, please," Katie answered.

"Close your eyes and here we go! Golden drops of lather that moisturize, add body and reduce the static of flyaway locks. That's all right here in this one dandy bottle!"

Incredibly, Katie heard herself giggling at Bryce's nonsense. He soaped her hair twice and rinsed it, his fingers gently massaging her scalp and neck. "Umm, you're better than any hairdresser," Katie said, relaxing under the brisk, nonthreatening touch.

"You think so? Maybe I'll give up medicine and become a hairstylist. I expect the pay is about the same, if you're good at your job, and I can't think of anything nicer than being surrounded by beautiful women all day!" he joked back.

"Women aren't beautiful in shapeless smocks with their hair in rollers," Katie retorted.

"*You* would be!" Bryce shot back. Then before Katie could react to that, he rose and headed toward the door. "Soak for a bit but no sinking beneath the bubbles," he warned. "I'll be back in a few minutes."

"Ummm . . ." Katie said again, letting herself enjoy the sensation of the warm, bubbly water lapping over her. She leaned her head on the edge of the tub, closed her eyes and had almost fallen asleep when Bryce returned.

He carried a cup of steaming herbal tea and two small white tablets that he told Katie to swallow. "You know the routine, take two aspirins and call me in the morning," Bryce joked.

Obediently, Katie swallowed the pills and washed them down with tea. Then she let Bryce help her up and swaddle her in the depths of a huge, thick towel.

While Katie sat in a vanity chair, the towel clutched about her, Bryce blew her hair dry. He glanced away carefully as he replaced her towel with his robe. "Sorry I don't have any pajamas your size, but mine would swallow you," he remarked.

"What? You mean there aren't any nightgowns in this bachelor's pad?" Katie said with a feeble attempt at humor.

"Nary a one," Bryce replied, his voice so rueful that Katie knew he spoke the truth. For some reason she felt absurdly glad, although she was certainly woman enough to know that a man of Bryce's attractiveness and obvious virility could have had any number of women.

His arm about her shoulder, Bryce led Katie back into his bedroom and turned down the sheets of the bed. She slipped gratefully between the cool, crisp sheets. Then a thought struck her.

"Bryce, you're always giving up your bed for me," Katie said sleepily. "Where will you sleep?"

"On the sofa. It's quite comfortable. I know—I've fallen asleep there plenty of times."

"But—" Katie started to protest.

He held a finger to his lips to silence her. "It also makes out into a bed. Call me if you need anything."

"Bryce . . ." Katie stopped, torn by the absurd, strange need that gripped her.

"What, Katie?" he asked quietly.

"Oh, nothing," she muttered, turning away from his

penetrating look. He had done so much for her already, how could she ask for more?

He sat down on the edge of the bed and turned her face with gentle fingers that were nevertheless insistent. "What?" he repeated softly.

"Would you give me a . . . a good-night hug?" The strange pleading in her voice was that of a child, not of a competent hospital administrator. "It would feel so good after . . ."

He understood immediately that she needed, from him, the reassurance that most men were decent, caring individuals. That she needed a gentle touch to blot out the memory of the harsh one. Katie watched the comprehension in Bryce's eyes as he reached out and swept her to him.

He held her, hugging and stroking her as if she were a small, petted child. There was no demand in his touch, no clutch in his hold on her. His marvelous hands stroked her hair, her cheek, her shoulders while he cradled and cuddled her. But there was still something undone and some very important words unsaid. Held in the protective circle of Bryce's arms it was easy for Katie to say these words that had earlier stuck in her throat. "Bryce, about tonight . . . when we argued, I was unreasonable. I was wrong! I'm so sorry!"

"Shh," he soothed her. "I was just as unreasonable and just as wrong. I've been uptight over— Well, it doesn't matter now."

Katie relaxed, sighing with contentment. She had apologized and so had Bryce. They were friends once again. Dimly, she felt his lips brush her forehead and nestle in her hair. Slowly, his lips dropped lower to press small, loving kisses across her neck.

Suddenly, the easy warmth Katie had been feeling caught fire. Small flames, triggered by his gentle, passionless kisses, burst within her like miniature explosions. She turned her face just as Bryce lifted his head and abruptly their lips met.

It was like a collision of comets. Fierce and fiery their mouths crushed together. For one breathtaking second, Katie thought, Oh, no! I didn't intend *this!* Then her brain blanked out, overcome by the sheer delicious sensations he evoked within her.

Bryce's lips, pressing on hers, sent rapturous feelings soaring through her. His lips were so tender yet so wonderfully desirous, and the clean, sweet taste and smell of him flooded her senses. In a sudden need for surrender, Katie felt herself sinking, melting. She caught him closer, gripping his broad shoulders with small, urgent hands, letting her mouth soften and part invitingly beneath his.

Bryce gave a muffled groan and caught her even closer, his tongue plunging in her mouth to outline longingly each curve and contour. His hands moving against her body were no longer those of a fond uncle or doting father but a lover's hands that sought out her softness, her willingness, her yielding.

I can't fight this anymore, Katie thought with relief. I can't fight my desire for him, my overpowering need just for him!

Abruptly and unexpectedly, Bryce thrust himself away from Katie. A small cry of loss escaped her.

"Not tonight!" Bryce said, his voice sounding as if he

were strangling. "I *won't* have it on my conscience that I've taken advantage of you a second time, Katie!"

Then before she could react with embarrassment or chagrin, Bryce's less than steady hands pressed her down into the softness of the bed. He dropped a kiss on her forehead and closed Katie's eyes with kisses on both eyelids.

"I'll be in the living room," he said, his voice still uneven. "Shall I leave the lamp on by your bed?"

"Yes, please," Katie whispered, not wanting to be plunged into pitch darkness.

I was ready to make love with him, she thought as she heard Bryce leave the room. She didn't know whether she was glad or sorry that he had stopped them. Then, as exhaustion began to slip over her, she realized that the bad memories of tonight had faded far away, leaving only a faint nightmarish residue. Thanks to Bryce, they had been overpowered by the much more important memories of kindness, tenderness and the healthy, physical needs of a man and a woman.

Katie slept about two hours and awoke, tingling all over. The taste of Bryce still lingered on her lips, and her body throbbed with remembrance. A wave of longing swept through her, a longing as intense as any she'd ever experienced.

Katie sat up, aware of her muscles' fatigue, but the utter exhaustion that had gripped her earlier was gone. She slipped out of bed, stretched to test her body and discovered that, while her throat still felt sore, her head no longer ached.

Silently, on bare feet, she padded to the living room,

hoping to catch a glimpse of Bryce. What did he look like when he was asleep? She didn't know, for she had never seen him sleeping.

To her surprise he was awake, sitting up and reading. He had shed his shoes, and his stockinged feet were propped up on the coffee table. He had loosened his shirt by undoing its first several buttons. Golden lamplight burnished his hair, making the silver threads in it gleam. His face looked tired, almost worn. But what surprised Katie most of all were the glasses that had slid down the bridge of his nose.

"Bryce, I didn't know you wore glasses!" Katie blurted.

He glanced up at her with a smile; then removed the glasses and set down the medical journal he held. "I only use them for reading and operating," he explained and patted the sofa cushion beside him. "Come over here. Did you have a bad dream?"

"No," Katie said. She moved toward him slowly yet steadily, as though she were being irresistibly drawn forward. At closer range Bryce's thick hair looked rumpled and she saw the weary lines etched in his face. "Why didn't you go to sleep?" Katie asked in concern as she dropped down beside him on the sofa.

Bryce made a small deprecating motion of his hand. "I wanted to stay alert in case you needed me."

With his quiet words, Katie was deeply touched. A lump rose in her throat, and the intense longing she felt for him deepened until it was practically intolerable. "I feel fine now," she said, her voice hushed. Then her hand moved of its own volition, reaching out to stroke

Bryce's cheek gently. It felt a little scratchy from his new growth of beard.

He turned his head to press a kiss against her hand, and Katie's heart lurched and felt wrenched by his tender, loverlike touch. Incredibly, she heard herself saying words she had never planned to say: "Bryce, I need you now."

There! She had said it and she wasn't sorry. Maybe she would be sorry later. Maybe, with the dawn of a new day, she would be filled with the bitterest of regrets. But right here, at this moment, it seemed natural and right.

She felt Bryce's start of surprise. Felt him look at her so searchingly that Katie turned, burying her face into the warm crook formed by his neck and shoulder. Oh, how good it felt just to yield, to allow her emotions to have the upper hand. How good *he* felt!

"I need you, too, Katie." Bryce's voice was roughened by emotion. "Do you have any idea how much I need and want you?"

Her heart pounding, Katie drew back to look at him. The earnestness and intensity in his gray blue eyes literally took her breath away. Her throat was too tight to allow her to speak, and her arms ached from the need to hold him and then rose to link fiercely about his neck. "Last chance, lady," Bryce said softly, and she felt his arms sliding around her. Their lips met with the same fiery, stunning sweetness as before.

He kissed her for a long, breathless time until Katie felt as though she were liquid, running and melting against him. He pulled her across his lap to let their bodies touch more closely, and the contact with his warm strength was poignant. Bryce touched her heart as no other man ever had and Katie welcomed his kisses, his touch, his obvious need of her.

She felt his hands untie the sash to the oversized bathrobe, then she shivered with delight as they slid over the smoothness of her skin. "You're so soft!" he marveled.

She felt him parting the top of the bathrobe to gaze at the same body that, earlier that night, he'd been so careful to shield. "God, Katie, how gorgeous you are!"

She closed her eyes against the blazing light of his, as though she peered into a sun too bright to endure, but as Bryce began drawing the robe off her shoulders, Katie felt modesty reawakening in her.

"The light," she said faintly and reached out her hand to switch it off.

Bryce caught her hand. "No!" he said fiercely. "Let me look at you! Don't you know what the sight of you does to me?"

Katie could feel just exactly what it did to him, and the knowledge of Bryce's arousal quickened her own. She sank back into the circle of his arms and let his hands play across her skin in dancing, delightful motions.

When Bryce parted the bathrobe fully, Katie heard his indrawn breath as the last of her secrets were unveiled for him. Then she was sliding down into the soft, welcoming depths of the sofa while he bent over her.

His mouth caressed her throat even while his hands gentled and steadied her body. Katie felt her own hands sliding up his strong back to feel the corded, knotted muscles beneath his shirt. She pressed feverish kisses against his jaw and finding the delightfully sensitive spot beneath his ear, she heard the tempo of his breathing accelerate.

Bryce caught a rosy nipple with his lips, pressing a kiss on its vulnerable softness, then his lips encompassed it wholly. Katie gave a sigh of delight and felt, at the center of her being, a rush of desire so intense that she began to tremble.

Bryce repeated the exciting caress on her other breast, then his dark head oscillated between them, arousing and delighting, evoking primitive sensations in Katie. Her sighs of delight became gasps when his hands glided down over her stomach and thighs, awakening her to all they had once shared long before.

Katie flung her head back in abandon, her mind enveloped by needs so intense they overrode all rational thought. I want him, I want all of him! she thought hungrily.

"Your clothes . . ." she managed to whisper.

He gave a pleased, shaky laugh. "Don't move!" he ordered, his face alight. Swiftly, Bryce stood up and stripped off his clothes, draping his shirt, slacks and briefs across the seat of a nearby chair.

Katie watched the emergence of his tanned, naked body through half-open eyes, heavy-lidded with desire. What a completely beautiful man he was! she thought, watching the rippling muscles that were toned to supple strength.

She welcomed his return with open arms, but he drew her up to him. "The bedroom," he said, through desperate kisses. "More comfortable . . ."

A minute later she was back again in his extra-long

bed while his hands played a rousing symphony across her body. She arched and stirred beneath his touch, wondering at the miracle that told Bryce just where to stroke and how to press so delicately.

His loving assault moved lower, circling to the very center of her, celebrating her femininity, and Katie caressed him boldly in return. His hard muscles and obvious virility were her body's perfect complement and together they moved toward final culmination in what appeared a perfectly orchestrated dance. At last his eager hands parted her thighs, and Katie welcomed the almost rhapsodic thrust even as it sent a little cry from her lips.

She felt Bryce stop for an instant, staring down at her in the dim glow of the bedside lamp. "You lovely liar!" he reproved gently. "I thought you and Doug— But you haven't been with a man in years, have you? Not since Seattle . . ."

"You can tell that?" Katie whispered, amazed.

"I can feel it." The happiness on his face almost blinded her.

A similar happiness swept Katie, too. She was glad Bryce knew the truth and she clutched eagerly at his shoulders.

His breath stormy, Bryce imprisoned her completely, binding her to him, claiming her in a burst of glory.

"Katie, Katie . . . my beautiful Katie!" He made her name a chant as he rocked her with him, the deep, pumping motions carrying her away, far away, where there was only splendor in the final, total union with him. Somewhere, deep in her mind, Katie remembered the splatter of rain against a windowpane. As the pleasure rushed over her, she felt as if she were where she belonged at last. No longer able to hold off the explosion of all her muscles, inner and outer, she cried out again, her hands urgent on Bryce's sweat-streaked back. Then she felt his own explosion of release, and they lay still and sated, warm and together. Their legs remained entwined while their arms continued the close embrace. Gradually, their gasps for breath slowed and sleepy contentment followed.

"I'm glad," Bryce said softly. "I love you, Katie!"

"I love you, Bryce!"

No longer were the epic words hard for Katie to acknowledge, either to herself or to Bryce. Yes, she loved him—and what a relief it was simply to stop fighting her feelings and allow that love to flow into every nook and cranny of her being. What a relief to stop running from Bryce and from herself as well. She had loved him yesterday, through all those distant yesterdays, she loved him today and she would love him tomorrow.

"It's going to be all right now," Bryce said with quiet assurance, cradling Katie's head on his shoulder, and she nodded in contentment as they drifted to sleep. She could not think of problems, troubles and difficulties now, after a passage as intense as the one they had shared. Right now she could only be happy.

Katie slept for several hours held tight in Bryce's embrace. Then she dreamed of passionate kisses, sensual and arousing caresses, and came awake slowly to a room lighted at the edge of the windows by a new dawn.

Bryce's warm body covered every inch of hers, and

rustling movements beneath the sheet indicated other delightful things as well. "What are you doing?" Katie whispered, aware of deep, stroking motions that inflamed her once again.

"Me?" Bryce whispered back in feigned astonishment. "I was sound asleep when I felt myself being seduced!"

"I did no such thing!" Katie protested in mock indignation, but her body shifted to allow him greater access to hers.

"Want to stop?" Bryce teased.

"No!" she gasped, stirred once again to quickening excitement, and his low laugh held a note of triumph. This time their lovemaking was slower, gentler and more tender, powered by love and less by driving need. Finished, they toppled headlong into sleep.

When Katie awoke again, Bryce was gone, but the room was bright with sunshine, and the appetizing smell of frying bacon made her crinkle her nose appreciatively. She stretched languorously, more aware of her body than she had been for years, glorying in its contentment. Then she glanced at the clock. It was past eleven! Hastily, she scrambled out of bed and dashed away to take a quick shower.

Even her face looked different today. Its glowing peach-colored softness and radiance revealed a blissfully happy woman. Katie emerged from the shower wearing a towel and found the discarded bathrobe lying across the sofa in the living room. She smiled as she picked it up and belted it around her.

"Good morning!" In the kitchen Bryce greeted her with a sunny smile. "How do you like your eggs?"

"Just a lot of them." Katie smiled back as renewed awareness of each other flashed between them. "I'm ravenous!"

"Good. The biscuits will be done in a few minutes." He walked over and dropped a lingering kiss on her lips. "You look cute."

"So do you," she said approvingly. Bryce wore tan shorts with a tank top and looked more like an athlete than a neurosurgeon. "Nice legs, too!" She let her fingers run up and down one long, hair-roughened leg.

"You'd better not say that to the rest of the guys," Bryce threatened and kissed her again. Then he smiled with a boyish eagerness. "Can you spend the weekend with me? I'm off duty and we could go to the lake."

"That sounds wonderful," Katie agreed, releasing him so that he could rescue the bacon. Then a practical thought occurred to her. "Bryce, what in the world am I going to wear?"

"Nothing, I hope!" His smile became a leer.

Katie felt her cheeks turning pink. "Be serious!" she implored. "How am I going to get out of this apartment and over to my own to pick up a few things?" She couldn't bear to think of putting on the torn, dirty clothes she'd worn last night.

"Relax," Bryce assured her. "I've already given the matter some thought. One of the scrub suits returned to me recently by the hospital's laundry happens to be a petite. I discovered it when I pulled on the pants and they stopped at midcalf."

Katie laughed at the picture he painted and eagerly accepted the cup of steaming, aromatic coffee he handed her.

An hour later, Katie wore the small green scrub suit back to her apartment. She felt ridiculous, especially since she'd had no choice of footwear except her dress pumps. But at least she was decently clad as she made her way up the outside stairs. To deepen her chagrin, she and Bryce met one of the apartment's security guards, a tall black man in a gray uniform. "Hi, doc," he greeted Bryce.

"Hello, George Parker," Bryce said in recognition. The guard tipped his cap to Katie as she tripped past him on the stairs.

"Was that the guard who let you in without a card?" she hissed to Bryce after Mr. Parker was out of earshot.

"Yes. I hope you didn't report him as you threatened to. As you can see, George and I are on practically a first-name basis."

"No, I didn't report him," Katie admitted.

Her telephone was screaming as they walked inside Katie's apartment. For a moment she debated answering it, then reluctantly scooped up the receiver. "Hello?"

"My goodness, Katie, where have you been?" Celia's voice said in exasperation. "I've been trying to reach you all morning!"

"Is something wrong, Cee?" Katie replied.

"Oh, no. We had a letter from Wade yesterday that I wanted to share with you. He and his family are fine."

"May I call you back tomorrow night?" Katie asked, thinking that a fond stepmother who kept tabs on her was almost as bad as having a jealous lover.

"Oh, sure." Then curiosity got the better of Cee. "Are you going somewhere or something?"

"Bryce is here. We're about to leave for his lake

house," Katie said evenly. She hoped this knowledge wouldn't devastate Celia. On the other hand, her stepmother would have to know sometime.

"Oh!" said Cee. Dashed hopes and disappointment were contained in the single word. Then she rallied quickly. "Well, have a good time, you two. Phone me when you get back, Katie."

"I will," she promised and promptly thrust Cee out of her mind as she hurried around gathering up a few things to take to the lake.

Chapter Ten

$\mathcal{K}$atie had ceased to count the days until she would leave for Washington although she wasn't as yet even conscious of it. For one golden, enchanted weekend her consciousness was centered completely on the handsome, dark-haired man who was always beside her.

She and Bryce sunned by the lake and swam. They slept locked together in the large bed of the lake house and awoke to make ardent love. Bryce even took her fishing with him the next morning and baited her hook with plump, pink worms, but they set their captive fish free and watched them flash back into the silvery water. It was a time without time, the minutes flowing effortlessly into hours, and the hours sealed by love.

Soon, too soon, it was time for them to return to the city. They peeled off their swimsuits and took a last shower together. Then they dressed, closed up the house and started the drive back.

In Dallas they stopped for dinner at a steakhouse where they weren't out of place in their casual weekend clothes. Their steaks, grilled over mesquite wood and served medium rare, were delicious, their taste enhanced by the bottle of red wine that Katie and Bryce shared. Katie felt pleasantly full and a little light-headed by the time she and Bryce returned to her apartment.

Encroaching nightfall had cast shadows in Katie's pleasant living room, and while she walked around, switching on lights, she could feel Bryce watching her. "When do you go to work tomorrow? Four?" he asked.

"That's right." Katie nodded, already suspecting the reason for his question. "You?"

He made a grimace. "By six tomorrow morning, I've got to be at the med school, ready to take students on rounds. So I ought to go." But their eyes caught and held, and Katie read the reawakened desire in Bryce's. His eyes glowed down on her and the desire in their depths made her legs feel weak. I want him again! she thought, marveling at the upsurge of passion that swept over her body like a warm wave.

"If you'd like to stay here tonight, I can set an alarm," Katie offered. She had never felt more aware of the tug on that invisible cord that seemed to draw them closer together.

"I'll run down and get my bag." Bryce smiled.

He had never seen her bedroom before. It was a feminine room with a bright, coral-colored spread on the bed and vases of silk flowers, which picked up the same hue and mingled it with soft yellow and blue. Much of the furniture—a carved chest of drawers, a comfortable ottoman and a mirrored vanity—had once belonged to Katie's mother.

Bryce seemed fascinated by the room. He strolled around inspecting the paintings of peaceful forests and gardens and even investigated Katie's bottles of perfume set atop the bureau. "Nice," he said, breathing the fragrance exuded when he removed a cap.

"Just girl things," Katie said, enjoying his curiosity.

"You're such a beautiful girl. No—you're a beautiful *woman*," he corrected. Slowly, he walked to Katie, and when his head bent down, his lips poised over hers, Katie's arms went up instinctively to encircle his neck.

They made gentle love, then fell asleep in each other's arms. Shortly after four the following morning, Katie awoke to find that they were welded in a far more urgent embrace. Already her breath came in deep, passionate gasps.

"Bryce!" she whispered, aware of his warm weight covering her.

"You woke me up, you insatiable woman," he whispered sleepily while his deep, powerful motions brought Katie to full wakefulness.

"I did not!" she protested even as she clutched his broad back avidly. "But don't—don't stop!"

The encounter was startling in its intensity and the passion that swelled recklessly and relentlessly between them. Their lovemaking grew wild, primitive and barbaric, until they were crying out ecstatically beneath a tangle of sheets. Afterward, the bed looked as though an explosion had struck it: pillows tossed on the floor, a light blanket twisted awry, the damp sheets falling off the mattress.

When their gasps for breath had slowed, Bryce smoothed back Katie's wildly tumbled hair with his hands and pressed a slow, almost reverent kiss on her lips. "I never knew *anything* could be like that," he breathed, his voice awed.

Katie smiled up at him tremulously while tears pricked her eyes. She had never known that lovemaking could be quite like that either. Such enormous, overpowering rapture made her want to cling to him forever and yet she would be leaving him soon . . . so soon! As reality began to intrude on her timeless enchantment, Katie began to tremble inside until her stomach seemed to quake. How could she bear to leave Bryce now? Yet how could she bear to turn her back on a dream come true for her career? What she'd worked so long to achieve lay within her grasp at last.

"I'll make coffee," she murmured since it was time for Bryce to get up. She eased out of his embrace, found her robe and drew it about her as she went into the kitchen. The apartment was small enough that while the coffee dripped through its filter she could hear the drum of water that indicated Bryce was showering.

He came in fully dressed and shaven, his hair neatly combed, and looked his immaculate self once again. Gratefully, he took the steaming cup of coffee that Katie handed him.

"Shall I cook bacon and eggs?" she asked.

Bryce shook his head emphatically. "Not at this ungodly hour! Just coffee now. I'll eat later."

"All right." Katie walked over and took a chair at the

breakfast table. She sipped at her own coffee and tried to conceal her inner turmoil.

Bryce joined her at the table, taking the chair opposite her. "Katie, we have to talk," he began, his voice urgent.

"About what?" she said warily.

"You and me. Us. Our future. That subject on which you were very lukewarm once before," he warned her.

Katie felt that shaking, sickening sensation return to the pit of her stomach. She almost knew what was coming.

Bryce leaned over and covered her hand with his. "Katie, I want to marry you," he said earnestly.

She looked into his eager, hopeful face and her heart took another downward plunge. I'm going to have to tell him now, she thought.

"Katie, listen to me," Bryce went on, speaking more urgently than before. "We were meant to be together. Why, we want each other so much we wake ourselves up making love! When two people share an experience as special and wonderful as that, it certainly means marriage to me. Please don't say no!"

"Bryce, I have to," Katie said, but her voice wasn't steady and she felt her lips tremble. "There's something I haven't told you—something you need to know."

He went very still, as though frozen in place, but his hand slipped away from hers. "What?" he said, his lips scarcely moving.

She could not bear the sudden devastation in his eyes. "Don't look like that!" Katie blurted. "It's nothing terrible or sinister! It . . . it started on that weekend when I was to meet you in Victoria. I sat on a cold bench in Butchart Gardens and vowed that I was going to find something special—something of my very own. That's what my career has been to me, something special that's my own, and I've worked so hard—''

"I told you I would never expect you to give it up," Bryce interrupted impatiently.

"Will you listen to me?" Katie flared, her own nerves frayed.

He sank back into his chair, his face growing cooler and more aloof. When she saw that expression, Katie began talking desperately. She told Bryce just how it had been for a young, single woman breaking into a field that was predominantly male. The weekend and night duty that had played havoc with her social life. The dirty, old charity hospital where she'd worked first that was encrusted by years of grime and despair. The male director at her second hospital who thought making passes at her was just part of the duties she'd agreed to assume. An agonizing three months of unemployment that had followed after she had abruptly quit that job. Then the two long years at Harwick Memorial where she'd faced most nights with dread.

"OK, so you've had it rough," Bryce said, his voice not entirely unsympathetic. "My career—medical school, interning and residency—wasn't exactly a lark for me either. It cost me my marriage. What—''

"Bryce, before we ever met again I'd already accepted a job offer that's exactly what I want—what I've always wanted," Katie rushed on.

Then she told him of the Port Angeles Children's

Rehabilitation Center. Of the cool, green, mountainous country where forests loomed high above the sea. Katie talked of the modern new facility being built there and of the children it would house. Those frightened little children in wheelchairs and face masks . . . the ones whose small bodies had been seared by radiation treatments . . . those whose limbs had been amputated or had cancerous eyes removed. Because of the fervor that filled her voice, Katie saw new comprehension flash on Bryce's face.

"Yes, I can see why you'd want to go there," he said heavily when Katie fell silent at last. "It's a gorgeous part of the world, and career-wise, you'd feel needed and fulfilled. But, Katie, that's not the only such job in existence! We could find you another one that you'd like just as much right here in Texas. Why, just the other day I heard about a proposed new rehab center for brain-damaged patients and those with spinal injuries. Such patients are usually teenagers—"

"Bryce, I am going to Port Angeles!" Katie said emphatically.

For a moment he stared at her, as though by sheer dint of willpower and eye contact he could force her to see things his way. "Oh, damn." He sighed, breaking the contact at last. He rose to stand by his chair, and now Katie saw anger tightening his mobile lips. "Doesn't it mean anything to you that I love you with all my heart?"

"You'll never know how much it means," Katie said, and her voice held a tremor. "I love you, too, Bryce."

"I'm beginning to doubt that!" he snapped.

Katie felt her taut nerves stretched to the utmost. "Oh

boy, here we go,'' she muttered. ''Just because I'm a woman I'm supposed to forget my own 'secondary' aspirations and plans and should stay here to accommodate *your* career!''

''I can scarcely accommodate yours,'' Bryce flashed back. ''What would a neurosurgeon find to do in that part of Washington? Fish for a living? Fell trees? God, Katie, the only reason I ask you to stay here, with me, is because there's nothing for me there! It has nothing to do with the importance of your career versus my career!''

Now Katie was the silent one. What else could she say?

''So this is where we tear it all up?'' Bryce said bitterly.

''Why?'' she cried out wildly, unshed tears beginning to burn her eyes. ''We still have two months—''

''I don't like having a death sentence hanging over my head, Katie,'' Bryce shot back.

''Why do you call it that?'' Katie cried. ''Even after I go back to Washington we could still see each other occasionally. Vacations and holidays—''

''Have you looked at a map recently?'' Bryce said sardonically, his eyes steel-gray and blazing from anger. ''I'll be close to Mexico and you'll be practically in Canada! I don't want a continent between me and the woman I love!''

As Katie watched Bryce demolish her frantic schemes to keep them together, her own temper ignited. ''You 'don't want'—you 'don't like.' Has anyone ever told you, Bryce Emerson, that not everything is going to go *your* way?''

"This will," he said evenly, "or I'll have no part of it."

Katie felt her breast heave with the effort to stay calm. She bit her lip to forestall more angry words and blinked her eyes rapidly to hold back the threatening tears. She was losing him . . . losing Bryce! The dismal feeling around her heart had nothing to do with the cool logic of her brain which reminded her that she'd known all along that there could really be nothing between the two of them.

"I think you'd better go now, Bryce," Katie whispered.

"All right. But just as a matter of curiosity, Katie, why didn't you tell me about all this before?" His voice was ironic, and only the pallor of his face revealed that he was feeling any emotion at all. "When you lay in my arms making love with me, didn't it occur to you that your big news just might be pertinent to our situation?"

"I'd been trying to keep it a secret," Katie said painfully, her hands twisting in her lap.

"You didn't trust me to keep your precious secret?" he demanded.

"No. I mean yes! I trust you." She swallowed hard. "Oh, Bryce, I didn't know we were going to get involved so fast or I would have told you much earlier."

"I see." His voice was heavy with sarcasm and his mouth twisted unpleasantly. "Yes, I think I'm beginning to get the picture now. Except for that unfortunate incident in the garage you would have kept me at arms' length. Tell me something, Katie. Would you have let anyone who rescued you make love to you?"

Her head jerked up. Stunned with disbelief, she could only look at him in horror. Bryce's voice was clipped, and he stared condemningly at her out of eyes that were hard and hostile. At that moment Bryce looked exactly like Max Brentwood when matters had not suited him.

At the thought, anger flooded Katie, tightening her lips and stiffening her spine. She was not going to be bullied, insulted and overpowered—no, not even by the man she loved. Especially not by him! "How dare you?" she gasped.

For a long, long moment Bryce stared at her out of chill gray eyes. Then he turned and walked out of the kitchen.

Katie leaped up. Was this it? Would he give her up so easily?

Bryce's decisive slam of her front door as he left was his own quite eloquent statement.

They had parted once before and each had survived. They would survive again, Katie reminded herself. It was just getting through the miserable time in between that seemed so impossibly difficult.

Two weeks had passed. For Katie they were weeks of sleepless nights, tasteless food and tears that came unexpectedly in floods. Why had she so rapidly reacquired a taste for one man's kisses and the texture of his skin against hers?

From four until midnight Katie dealt with hospital problems although even they seemed drabber and far worse than usual. Sewage backed up. A respiratory therapist was found sleeping on duty. A physician's locker was ransacked. As the petty problems mounted, Katie felt as if she were being overwhelmed on several occasions. Often, things seemed almost too much for her to cope with and that was a feeling that the efficient and indomitable Ms. Brentwood was not used to encountering.

The worst incident happened in the cafeteria when Katie carried her dinner tray toward her accustomed place. Suddenly, she saw Bryce seated at one of the small tables set against the wall.

It was her first glimpse of him in almost two weeks, and her eyes ranged over him briefly yet hungrily. Katie saw his crisp hair, his ruggedly handsome features and his long legs wound back about the legs of the chair. Her heart contracted painfully when she recognized the woman seated across from Bryce.

She was Dr. Gloria Ashton, a pediatrician. Dr. Ashton was about thirty, divorced and attractive enough not to bother with her hair or makeup. Her flawless skin glowed with health, and her long, ash blond hair was fastened with a large, decorative clip at the base of her willowy neck. Although she had an excellent reputation as a doctor, Gloria Ashton didn't let her profession prevent her from wearing quite feminine attire. Tonight she had shed her white coat, revealing a bold red, sleeveless dress with which she wore high frivolous red sandals. To Katie, feeling the crunch of jealousy as well as the pain of loss, Dr. Ashton appeared a very formidable rival indeed.

Her appetite disappeared in a flash. Automatically, Katie set her tray down and cast another furtive glance at the twosome by the wall. They were laughing together at some private joke and she didn't think they had seen her. Katie turned toward the nearest exit, abandoning her dinner. Once she was safely back in a tiled hall corridor, she discovered that she was perilously close to tears.

This won't do at all, she told herself firmly as she blinked the tears away. When she reached her office she immediately phoned Cee and Eric, inviting them to lunch the following day, which happened to be Saturday. Then Katie drew a deep breath and phoned Flight Operations. She left word for Doug Sears to call her.

She hadn't seen Doug lately, but if he and Sheila were still on the outs . . . Katie let her thought trail off unfinished. She really didn't care about seeing Doug. Still, she had to do *something* to pull her life back together! She was beginning to sink into a depression.

Doug didn't phone her back, but, at midnight, as Katie prepared to leave, she glanced up and saw him standing at the door. Doug was his usual dashing self in his flight uniform and suave grin.

"Like a walk to the garage, lady?" he offered, and when Katie accepted Doug took her hand quite nonchalantly in his. They strolled out together.

It was just plain bad luck or bad timing that the only person they saw as they walked down the quiet corridor was Bryce. Hastily, Katie dropped Doug's hand, but she was afraid she hadn't been quick enough. Bryce was alone now and he threw them a curt nod. Katie thought she saw his jaw tighten with anger or disapproval, but the movement disappeared so quickly that she wondered if she had imagined it.

After Bryce had walked on, Katie's rocketing emotions gradually steadied. Wearily, she forced her mind to focus on Doug's breezy words.

". . . know I've been out of touch lately, but a lot's been going on."

"What?" Katie asked without feeling any real curiosity.

Doug stopped and shot her his raffish grin. "Look, at the risk of breaking your heart, I'd better tell you that Sheila and I have gotten it on again. This time we're going for broke."

"You're going to get married?" she said, surprised.

"Yeah. I'm afraid it will definitely have a dampening effect on my social life, but the gal begged me and I do hate to see a grown woman cry!"

"Doug, be serious!" Katie said. "You two are really getting married?"

"Next Friday in the hospital's chapel," he said promptly. "Sheila thinks it's romantic to be wed in the place where we met."

"You met in the chapel?" Katie teased.

"Oh, hell, you know what I mean." He grinned. "You're invited, by the way. Sheila's own suggestion since jealous she isn't. A little scaredy-cat she may be, but she's decided she can live with the idea that I might topple into a treetop one day."

Katie felt an unexpected warmth go through her. "Oh, Doug, I'm glad," she said sincerely. "I think you two belong together."

"Funny, so do I," he agreed.

Impulsively, Katie reached up and kissed Doug's hard

cheek, and he gave her an affectionate pat on the behind. "Doug!" she cried reprovingly.

They entered the parking garage and went up to the fifth level in silence. Involuntarily, Katie shivered. Just being here in this dark, deserted garage gave her the willies, and she knew she would never again dare to enter it alone. She was more vulnerable than a man simply because she had been born a woman. No longer did she mind that thought, for she had learned just how glorious it could be, that business of being a woman. At least, she thought miserably, Bryce has given me that much.

She drove home slowly along the accustomed streets, wishing for all she didn't have, wishing for just exactly what Doug and Sheila had found together. Why did you have to run Bryce off, Katie Brentwood? she reproached herself. He was right, you know, there *are* other jobs in this area that would suit you almost as well. But, surely, it wasn't all her fault! Wasn't Bryce to blame, too? He had expected her to drop all her long-range plans and dreams after less than a month's reacquaintance with him. He'd turned hard, inflexible and adamant, refusing to negotiate with her at all.

If I'd spent just a little more time with him, I could never have left him, Katie realized, dashing fresh tears from her eyes. If I love him this much after just one passion-filled weekend, how much more I would have loved him after a few more weeks! The realization had come to her too late.

But what kind of husband would he have been, a man who couldn't compromise? A man who always had to believe he was right? Katie shuddered. She knew just exactly the kind of husband and father such a self-righteous man became.

The thought brought her no comfort, and by the time she was safely locked in her apartment, Katie's depression had only deepened. She missed Bryce so badly that she felt lonely and lost. He had appeared again in her nice, settled life, had turned it upside down and wrung it inside out. Memories of the two of them together when he had held her, kissed her, claimed her as his own were burned in her brain. He's left memories I'm never going to be able to erase, Katie thought dismally. Tears pricked again behind her eyelids as she slid between the smooth sheets, and she sensed that sleep would be elusive for her again tonight.

Just as she reached out a hand to her bedside lamp there came an abrupt, loud knock on her door.

Katie gave a startled jump and the motion carried her halfway out of bed. Her heart pounding, she seized her robe and dashed to the door where another knock had already resounded.

Who on earth could it be at this hour of the night? A neighbor in trouble? A visitor who couldn't get his car started? A crazed sex maniac?

In her heart, Katie knew that it could only be one person. "Who is it?" she called out through the door and heard the tremulous sound of her voice.

"Bryce. Let me in, Katie."

She hesitated, torn by indecision. She wanted to see him—oh, how much she wanted to see him! And yet . . .

"Katie, if you don't open this door I'll make such a

racket your neighbors will all come out!'' Bryce threatened.

Defiantly, she threw the door open and looked up into his taut face with its ominous, glittering eyes. Good God, was he drunk? Angry? Completely, certifiably insane?

They spoke simultaneously. "Are you alone?'' he demanded, his hands balled into fists.

"How did you get into this complex?'' Katie cried over hard, hammering heartbeats that shook her chest wall.

Bryce strode inside; and they answered each other simultaneously. "George let me in,'' he said.

"Of course I'm alone!'' Katie flared indignantly; then they simply stared at each other.

"I really am going to have that man fired!'' Katie gasped, and her overwrought nerves snapped like a twig. She began to cry, and when the hot tears spilled down her cheeks, she dropped her face into her hands.

"Katie, oh, Katie—'' Fiercely, Bryce's arms clamped around her and Katie couldn't help herself. She yielded to that welcome, familiar touch even as more tears continued to fall.

"I didn't mean to make you cry,'' Bryce said desperately, his lips against her ear. "I think I'm going nuts! Oh, Katie, just let me hold you for a moment. I've missed you so much! I—'' His voice wasn't quite steady and words failed him then. He crushed Katie against the long, hard length of his body, and she seized him with shaking arms, famished and ravenous for his touch. She felt his lips tasting her tears, drinking them from her cheeks.

"I've missed you!" Katie sobbed. "Oh, Bryce, why are you so inflexible? So—so—"

"I don't know! I'm like another, different person with you!" She felt tremors shaking the strong body she clung to and despite her own anguish, mixed now with relief, Katie was astonished by the effect she had on him.

She looked up at Bryce out of wet eyes and saw what she hadn't seen on his face earlier. He was tired. Exhausted. Strain had deepened the shadows under his eyes and etched harsh lines on his face. Womanlike, she sought to ease his own anguish. "Bryce . . ."

His lips stopped her before she could say more, those same warm lips she'd hungered and thirsted for. Katie felt her mouth part beneath his and knew she was inviting and enticing him, but she seemed unable to stop herself.

Bryce whispered an endearment and swept her up into his arms, his lips reclaiming hers. He carried her into the bedroom where they sprawled across Katie's bed, locked in each other's tight embrace.

"Katie, I don't understand what's happening to me," Bryce said bewilderedly, each painful word wrenched from him. "The last thing on earth I ever wanted to do was hurt you!"

"Just hold me," Katie whispered, straining even closer into his arms. Her bathrobe, belted hastily and carelessly, opened.

"I need you so much!" Bryce's firm hands sought and found the softness of her breast, and, a moment later, she felt his warm breath as he pressed his lips over the thin fabric of her nightgown. The nipples of her breasts tightened, tingling with excitement.

Slowly, Bryce's hands and lips celebrated her in a glorious rediscovery that left Katie gasping. She felt Bryce slide the robe off her shoulders, then he lifted the hem of her nightgown. She raised her arms to aid him in removing it, then sank back again into the rapturous, sensual sensations he evoked.

His fingertips moved gently, tenderly to trace the lines and curves of her body, then slipped beneath her hips to cradle and knead their rounded softness. His mouth moved in rhythm with his hands, sucking and tugging on her nipples, then dipping down to trail hot kisses across her stomach. She felt his warm tongue explore the small indentation of her navel, and then his breath burned lower while his hands cupped her buttocks.

"Bryce, no!" Katie murmured, alarm darting through the excitement she felt.

"Shh," he soothed, and his mouth resumed its daring downward trek.

She felt her knees quivering under his warming, awakening assault. He rolled his face against her soft skin, arousing and demanding. His fiery fingers plunged further, deeper, until flames licked through her body with savage sweetness, until Katie felt herself quivering and heard the cry of wonder that broke from her. There was no way to defend herself against so powerful a caress, and she felt no desire to resist it. She writhed, craving the shattering pleasure of release as Bryce carried the caress even further. This tender aggression, which went on and on, was more powerfully exciting than anything Katie had ever dreamed of. Rapturously, she flew off the edge of the known world and soared high above the familiar and charted peaks of passion into a whole new dimension. While gusts of pleasure lifted her, she sailed above a new earth and across a new sky until her whole self leaped and shuddered and glory burst through her. Moaning, Katie thrashed in Bryce's hold until yet another shattering cry tore from her lips. Then she sagged against him, filled with a lazy lassitude and an incredible, swelling tenderness and love for him.

Bryce drew away to strip his own clothes off rapidly, and Katie watched him through what seemed to be a veil of that otherworldly mist. She heard the heaviness of his breathing as he turned back to her, and her shaky legs entwined about him, her hands stroking the muscles of his hard, broad back, finding and tracing each perfect rib. They moved together, deep in the final closeness, her breasts flattened against his chest and his large, agile surgeon's hands gripping her delicately. He led and guided her in the instinctive and erotic motions that have forever bound man to woman. For days she had ached so emptily for him, and he filled her, bringing her to yet another world of ecstasy, even greater and more shattering than the one before.

Bryce cried out at the instant of his own release, and Katie's every cell vibrated to his primitive sound. His body shook so convulsively that she held him, speaking soft love words against his lips, trailing her hands gently, gratefully, over his damp, exhausted face.

Gradually, the clutch of his arms loosened and he turned to lie beside her. "Oh, Bryce," Katie breathed, cuddling against him.

He turned her head with fingers that still trembled, searching her face for the meaning behind her words. She drowned in the depths of his eyes. They were very blue at this moment, and his mouth trembled slightly. Then as a great sigh escaped him, Katie pressed kisses across his cheeks, his throat, his shoulders, aware again of the depths of his exhaustion. "Sleep now. Sleep," she whispered, almost hypnotically. Obediently, his eyes closed, concealed by their thick, dark lashes, and soon his breathing grew regular and deep, although his arms continued to encircle her.

For long, long moments Katie studied him, marveling at the way the lines of tension and strain began to fade from his face. She saw it soften with sleep, his lips parting slightly. With his dark brown hair tumbling down across his forehead, she could see the small boy he had been long ago. Waves of tenderness, as powerful in their own way as passion, gripped and stirred her very soul. Fiercely, she longed to keep him safe and happy, well fed and well loved. She yearned to be the woman who answered his needs, filled his bed and bore him the children he desired. The magnitude of their encounter tonight had forever sealed her future to him and with him. She could never leave him now, for to do so would cut out her heart.

Gradually, she grew aware of her own deep exhaustion and stretched out a hand to the bedside light. When the room plunged into darkness, Katie lowered her head back to the hard pillow formed by Bryce's shoulder. No downy, feather-filled pillow had ever felt so good! Her weary eyes closed, and, sated, she slept beside him, knowing that in some mysterious way their very body rhythms had synchronized.

Katie never stirred until nearly dawn when she grew aware of a soft murmur of words. Bryce was talking to someone on the telephone. "Continue the medication," she heard him say. "I'll be there as soon as I can."

She struggled to awaken fully, but her eyelids felt too heavy to lift. She was dimly aware of Bryce moving about the room, then she heard the quiet opening and closing of her front door and knew he had gone. He was off to the hospital, she surmised from the snatch of conversation she'd overheard. Katie wished Bryce had kissed her good-bye, but undoubtedly he hadn't wanted to disturb her sleep. Perhaps he'd left her a note. If not, he would surely call her later in the day. They needed to talk about so many, many things!

But Bryce had left no note nor did he call.

Chapter Eleven

At first Katie was not overly concerned by Bryce's silence. She had things of her own to do today. First on her agenda was a phone call to the chairman of the rehab center's trustees in faraway Port Angeles, Washington. The man was obviously disappointed by Katie's decision and, for a moment, regret brushed her as well. Someone else would oversee the maimed and crippled little children. Someone else would walk through the rain forest and sit on ash-colored sand by the sea.

The moment of regret passed as quickly as it had come. She had only to remember the searching expression in Bryce's eyes and the vulnerable way he had looked as he slept to know that this man she loved did need her. I never could resist him, she mused with a smile.

Katie thought about Bryce while she busied herself

making preparations for Cee and Eric's visit. A lunch of hamburgers, Eric's favorite food, with a huge salad for herself and Celia. There was also ice cream in the freezer.

They arrived at noon, Eric with a whoop and bound. He gave Katie a swift kiss and dashed out to the balcony to check out the state of the swimming pool. "Mom said I could bring my suit," he said and slammed into Katie's bathroom to change.

"There's no lifeguard out there," Katie warned Cee.

"Let's sit on the balcony and watch him," her stepmother suggested. "I've got to let Eric burn off some energy or he'll drive me crazy with his constant questions."

"I believe you," Katie said dryly.

"Bryce was a help. He took us to dinner Tuesday night and then to a miniature golf course where he ran Eric's little tail off!"

"*You've* been seeing Bryce?" Katie said, her voice aghast.

Her changed tone did not escape Celia. Katie saw her stepmother's eyebrows rise. "No, we haven't seen Bryce except that one time. He only called us because he was feeling very lonely. And while we're on the subject, Katie, let's clear up another point," Cee went on. "Yes, I was interested in Bryce—at first. I've been lonely, too, so I guess I started spinning a few idle daydreams about him. But it was all fantasy. Katie, the man loves you! The question is: What are you going to do about it?"

Eric, bolting out of the bathroom in his swim trunks, spared Katie having to make a reply. She certainly didn't want to reveal her intentions to Cee before she'd had a chance to tell Bryce.

She and Celia took chairs out onto the balcony where they could watch Eric swimming below. The pool lay blue and serene until Eric hit it, and a pleasant breeze stirred the warm air.

The energetic child splashed vigorously across the pool, and Katie's eyes followed his bright head. "He's so much like Dad," she mused.

"Yes, he is," Cee agreed, "and I'm not really sorry about that. With all his faults, your father also had his good points. I often missed Max after I left him."

Katie turned to look at Cee incredulously, and the older woman gave a short laugh. "Well, I did! I missed having him to talk to because we once enjoyed each other's conversation. I even missed our blazing arguments because I could be just as stubborn as he was. Most of all, I missed him in bed. He was really a very good lover."

Katie shook her head, amazed. "Surely you're kidding!"

"Why?" Celia said in surprise. "Lots of doctors are great lovers. Why, the nurses in Seattle used to have a running joke about that. They wondered whether doctors were good lovers because of their knowledge of anatomy —or whether it was just their bedside manners!" Celia's eyes were shrewd as she smiled at Katie. "Whatever, I'll bet Bryce Emerson is one of the best!"

"I don't intend to discuss that," Katie said abruptly and rose from her chair. She knew her face was probably flaming.

"Katie, I didn't come over here to offend you," Cee said swiftly. "I just want to remind you that a single life is never entirely complete. I know because I found myself missing a man I didn't even admire or love. But enough of that. I need a favor. Would you loan me your jade green blouse? I have a special date tonight and would like to wear it."

Cee's sudden switch in conversation to such an inconsequential matter caught Katie by surprise. "Of course," she said automatically. "It will look great with your eyes."

"I know," Celia admitted.

"Who's your date?" Katie asked curiously.

He was an attorney named Louis Halley, Cee related. She'd met him several weeks ago when she was doing special duty at Presbyterian Hospital with his diabetic mother. At the time, Celia had never dreamed that Louis had noticed her as anything but a nurse. She had never dreamed that he was a childless widower. Furthermore, they'd already had two delightful dates, but Cee had never *dreamed* that Louis would be so anxious for more.

The conversation was ended by Eric, who pulled himself out of the pool. Dripping, his hands on his hips, he yelled up at the two women on the balcony. "Hey, I'm starving! When do we eat?"

"Thanks a bunch, Katie!" Darrell Harvey said fervently. The young weekend administrator wore a harried look. "I can't believe you'd give up your Saturday night just to help me out."

"Give me the beeper and run along," Katie replied lightly. Why shouldn't she help Darrell out? She'd had no plans for the evening while he had both a sick wife and baby at home. She had actually welcomed Darrell's SOS since she still hadn't heard from Bryce. Why hadn't he called? It had been marvelous to be in his arms again last night, but now they needed to sit down quietly and talk.

Perhaps he was at the hospital, too, and she would see him later. Didn't he still love her, want her as his wife? Katie couldn't bear to think otherwise.

"I'll be back early tomorrow morning," Darrell promised as he handed Katie his beeper.

As soon as Darrell had left, Katie sat down at the desk and began reviewing his Weekend Report. Another busy Saturday night appeared to be shaping up, and rain peppering down had turned roads and highways slick. A helicopter flew in, the clatter of its rotors penetrating the thick walls. Idly, Katie glanced over various papers and memos on Darrell's desk until one name riveted her. She found herself staring down at a letter written by Dr. James Bryce Emerson.

Just seeing Bryce's typed name and boldly scrawled signature gave Katie a jolt. Apparently, Dr. Blakely's family problems had prevented his return and now Bryce had taken over in the senior physician's capacity.

Fascinated, Katie skimmed the body of the letter. Since it was dated yesterday—Friday—she would normally not have seen it until Monday. In official-letter language it notified the hospital's administrators that three neurosurgeons in private practice, who already had privileges at Harwick Memorial, had agreed to provide emergency backup coverage.

Pride surged through Katie as she reread the memo.

Oh, what a good doctor Bryce is! she thought admiringly. He had certainly lost no time in trying to rectify the situation he'd inherited. Now that he'd recruited three additional specialists to help cover Neurosurgery, the long-standing hassle over grounding the helicopters would be at an end. About time, too! Katie thought fervently.

Abruptly, her beeper squawked. She dropped the letter, listened, then grabbed her clipboard. Soon she was searching for a cactus plant that had disappeared from a patient's room and, after that, ordering the immediate medical care of a visitor who had slipped and fallen on a newly mopped floor. Overhead, another helicopter began to warm up. "This is Life Copter," Katie's beeper chattered. "We are leaving for an accident scene to pick up a Jane Doe with a skull injury."

Jane Doe. John or Jane Doe were the hospital labels slapped on patients whose real names were not yet known. Sometimes it took a couple of hours for the identity of a trauma patient to catch up with him or her.

She had just returned to her office when her telephone rang. "This is Operating Room 7," a woman's voice announced. "Please hold for the doctor."

Uh-oh! Katie thought, wondering what had gone wrong in the OR.

"Dr. Emerson here," Bryce said a moment later.

The sound of his voice brought Katie up sharply. So he was here! And undoubtedly busy. That was probably why she hadn't heard from Bryce earlier in the day. "This is Katie Brentwood," she said formally over her heart's happy, excited racing.

There was a pause at the other end. When Bryce spoke

again, his voice seemed to have softened perceptibly—or was she just imagining it? "What in the world are you doing here on a Saturday?" he asked.

"Covering for Darrell Harvey," Katie said breathlessly.

"Ms. Brentwood, the laser in OR 7 is not functioning properly." Bryce's voice became purely professional. "Can anything be done about it tonight?"

"I'll notify the engineer on call," Katie said in immediate response. "Is it essential for your operation, Dr. Emerson?"

"No," Bryce admitted a trifle reluctantly. "But I'd rather have it, if I can."

"I'll see what I can do," Katie promised.

"Thank you. I hope you have a quiet evening," Bryce replied courteously, then the line went dead.

I hope you have a quiet evening, too, Dr. Emerson, Katie thought with love. Swiftly, she phoned Engineering and reported the problem.

Merciful quiet descended after that. It was as though Bryce's wish for her were coming true. After a while Katie walked to the window and looked outside. The peppering rain had increased to a solid sheet. Lightning flashed, illuminating the hospital's grounds. Another spring storm.

At least her own inner storm was over, ended effectively by the man in OR 7. Katie turned back to her desk and rolled a sheet of paper into the typewriter. Quickly, she composed a brief letter, confirming her phone call of that morning to the chairman in Port Angeles.

Katie signed her letter, typed an envelope and then went to the photocopier. On impulse she ran two copies.

One was for her own files; the other she sealed in an envelope on which she wrote Bryce's name. She set both envelopes out to be picked up by the mail room on Monday, and by then, her telephone was ringing again.

It took Katie a moment to realize that the child's voice on the other end was Eric's, he was talking so fast. "She said she'd be right back, that she wanted to get some crushed ice for a drink to serve Mr. Halley. But she hasn't come back and now *he's* here—"

"Whoa!" Katie said, cutting through Eric's excited flow of words. "Slow down, honey. Start over."

Swiftly, she pieced his story together. Cee had dashed out to drive to the nearest convenience store for ice. That had been forty-five minutes ago and she still hadn't returned. Meanwhile, Louis Halley, Cee's date, and the babysitter had both arrived.

"Eric, I'm sure your mother is fine," Katie said reassuringly. "Maybe she decided to buy a few more things. Or she might have stopped for gas—"

Her beeper shrilled at her. "Eric, I'll call you back in ten minutes," Katie concluded.

She dropped the phone, pressed the button on her beeper, and a moment later dashed out to rescue a lab tech who was trapped in a stalled elevator.

Fifteen minutes had elapsed before Katie could return Eric's call. Then the phone at the Oak Cliff house was answered by a mature man's grave voice. He identified himself as Louis Halley and informed Katie that Cee had still not returned. "I called the police a few minutes ago," he said in response to Katie's worried questions. "This isn't like Celia at all!"

"No, it isn't," Katie admitted, her own concern deepening. Where in the world was Cee? She heard the clatter of an incoming helicopter, and at the back of her mind, an unpleasant thought nudged.

Louis Halley promised to stay in touch and Katie hung up, her brow furrowed. That thought in the back of her mind just wouldn't go away no matter how she tried to scoff at it. She sat staring at the large clock on the wall, watching as its second hand made one entire revolution.

This is ridiculous! Katie argued with herself. Cee is a careful, responsible driver.

But Cee was also a woman falling eagerly in love with the attorney. What had Eric said? That Cee had grabbed her keys and dashed out for crushed ice—

The clock's second hand made another revolution and then another before Katie reached for her telephone. Quickly, she dialed the Shocktrauma Unit.

"This is Katie Brentwood," she said to the nurse who answered on the second ring. "Has that Doe arrived yet?"

"She came in just a minute ago, Ms. Brentwood. They're working on her now."

"Has there been an identification on her yet?" Katie asked anxiously.

"Not yet," the nurse replied.

"What was the Doe wearing?" Katie asked next. She sensed the nurse's impatience and added, "It's important!"

"We've cut her clothes off, of course. I'll have to check and see."

Several long minutes passed before the woman came

back on the line. "Black slacks, black sandals," she rattled off. "Green silk shirt—"

Cee!

Katie would never remember clearly the next several hours or their exact sequence of events. Her first frantic phone call had been to Bryce in Operating Room 7. She had to wait until he could break his concentration enough to talk on the speaker phone, and while she waited, Katie's terror mounted with every second.

Finally, Bryce said brusquely, "What is it?"

"Bryce, Cee has just been admitted here as a trauma patient. She crashed her car! They know she has a serious skull injury!"

"Oh, my God!" Bryce said sickly. Then Katie heard him mutter to someone, undoubtedly his resident, to "take over."

"Bryce, please do something!" Katie cried when his attention was focused back on her again.

"Get a grip on yourself, Katie!" Bryce ordered, his voice roughly tender. "Cee's in the best possible hands right now. She's at a class-one shocktrauma unit, so *you* just back off and let the system function as it's designed to do."

Her brain could not even register his words. "It's Cee!" Katie wailed, beginning to sob. "Oh, Bryce— she's critical!"

"Of course she's critical!" Bryce fairly yelped. "She wouldn't be here if she weren't!"

Another gulping sob was Katie's reply.

"And stop that crying this minute, Katie! You can't afford to go to pieces now."

Katie's tears stopped, more from the harshness of Bryce's voice than from the impact of his words. Still, desperation egged her on. "Bryce, I don't want any neurosurgeon touching her except you and—and I'm going to tell them that!"

"Katie, are you out of your mind? I wouldn't touch Cee with a ten-foot pole! I'm too close, too involved. It would be like treating kin. Now you listen to me, lady administrator. You stay the hell out of this! It's a medical matter, not an administrative one. Just . . . go sit down and let me finish up here. I'll be with you as soon as I can."

Bryce's tough attitude shocked Katie back into reality. Not that she really thought she'd go to pieces; she wasn't a hysterical sort of woman. She forced herself to sit down, as he'd said. Then, as she began to think logically once more, she felt resentment mounting toward Bryce. She'd been scared out of her wits and he . . . Well, he could have been kinder. The way he'd yelled at her held a haunting familiarity.

Grimly, Katie squared her shoulders and dried her eyes. She got up and began pacing the small, private waiting room outside the Shocktrauma Unit. When she felt that her voice had finally steadied, she phoned Louis Halley and told him what had happened to Cee. He already knew. He'd just talked with the policeman who had found Cee's small car lying upside down in a ditch and then radioed for Life Copter. Louis promised to join Katie at the hospital as soon as he could get there.

Then there was nothing for Katie to do but sit and wait. Or pace and wait. Worry and wait. Only when her beeper shrilled and jabbered once more did Katie realize that she was still officially on duty. In the wake of her personal emergency, she had forgotten to call in another administrator to relieve her.

Katie answered the page to find that a burglar alarm had gone off in the Pharmacy. She left Security to deal with the problem and returned to the waiting room. She must find another administrator, even if she had to call Darrell back. Fortunately, she reached Steve Wills at home and he promised to be there in an hour.

Katie had just returned to her seat when the red double doors, which bristled with warnings forbidding anyone not authorized to enter the Shocktrauma Unit, hissed open. Dr. Jeff Ferguson, a young trauma team surgeon, stepped through, motioning to her. His face looked so expressionless! Oh God, was Cee dead?

Katie walked on shaking legs to stop at the bold red line painted on the floor, which dared her to come any farther. "We've been lucky so far, Katie," Dr. Ferguson said as he began to strip off bloodied gloves. "The policeman who found your stepmother knew just what to do. He called for paramedics, and while the helicopter was still flying out, the paramedics stabilized her. She was already intubated, an IV line started, and she was on a cardiac monitor before the chopper got there. While the helicopter team loaded her up, they got a report from the paramedics."

Katie jerked her chin in assent, but she was still too worried to be particularly grateful for the breaks Cee had supposedly gotten. "Her injuries . . . ?" Katie began fearfully.

"Looks like it's just her head. That's the main thing,

and I won't pretend it's not serious. Mrs. Brentwood is on her way to X-ray to be CAT-scanned right now, and, of course, we've called for a neurosurgeon."

CAT-scan. Katie knew about such scanners. Although Computerized Axial Tomography, called CAT for short, was a highly sophisticated, expensive diagnostic tool, many of the machines were also temperamental and went down frequently.

"Both scanners are up," Dr. Ferguson said as though he could read Katie's mind. "We'll have a more definite diagnosis for you soon, Katie."

"Thank you," she said then paused, struck by another thought. "Should I notify Celia's parents? They live in Beaumont and are elderly people. Or my brother Wade? He's in Seattle."

Dr. Ferguson hesitated for a moment. "Yes, I think you should call them," he said quietly.

The gravity of Cee's condition struck Katie anew, and as the young trauma surgeon left, she began to tremble.

Numbly, Katie sat with her arm around Eric while Louis Halley busied himself feeding quarters into the pay phone and placing calls. He had already phoned Cee's parents and Wade. Clearly, Louis was a man of action, which was just the kind Katie needed at the moment. She felt almost frozen into immobility.

Eric really shouldn't have been here, of course. Children his age were supposed to remain in the hospital lobby, but Eric wasn't quite like other children. He had demanded to come to the hospital with Louis, and Katie knew he would never remain quietly in the lobby.

Wade's wife, Janet, had phoned back to say they were flying in with Jessica, their three-year-old daughter. Louis was now making arrangements for their plane to be met.

"Katie?"

She turned to see Eric peering up at her out of red-rimmed eyes.

"What, honey?" she whispered, stroking his bright hair.

"You suppose they'll put the Brentwood shunt in Mom?"

"Eric, I don't—" Fiercely, Katie clamped down on the rest of her words. Eric's emotions had run the gamut from disbelief and terror to tears. Now the child's natural optimism was reasserting itself.

"Maybe they will," Katie agreed faintly and then looked around impatiently. It seemed like hours since Cee had been taken off to be CAT-scanned. What was happening? And where was Bryce? He still hadn't joined them.

The red doors hissed open again. "Ms. Brentwood!" called a familiar, commanding voice.

Katie looked up, then rushed to the red line and gazed across its boundary at the neurosurgeon standing there. Despite the mask and gown he wore, Katie recognized him instantly. It was her old nemesis and she reeled with shock. "Good thing I came back to town tonight," Dr. Ash Blakely remarked. "We'll take your stepmother to surgery now."

Louis and Eric rushed up to stand on either side of Katie. "You're the neurosurgeon?" Louis said eagerly since Katie, at that moment, was incapable of speech.

Dr. Blakely was pleased to introduce himself as such. "What's wrong with my mom?" said Eric tremulously.

"She has an epidural hematoma," Dr. Blakely pronounced. "That's a blood clot in layman's language."

"Is it really bad?" Eric asked, wide-eyed.

"Well, son, a subdural hematoma would be less serious. But don't you worry. I'll evacuate that blood clot, and in a few days she should be good as new. Lord, boy, but you look like your father! I knew Max mighty well."

Eric stared at Dr. Blakely, his eyes shiny with hero worship. Louis chimed in, thanking the neurosurgeon, and after basking for a moment in the glow, Dr. Blakely fairly strutted back inside the double doors.

Or so it seemed to Katie, still stunned with disbelief but growing angrier by the moment. Ash Blakely, of all the surgeons in the world, was to operate on Cee, precious Cee! That ancient strutting peacock was going to open up Cee's head!

Hot words started to Katie's lips, then died there. She could not object because to do so would alarm both Eric and Louis. Further, she could not object because she was a part of this system, too, a system in which Cee was now engulfed. The system that Bryce—*Bryce*—had told her to trust in.

Devastated by a feeling of utter betrayal, Katie groped her way back to her seat.

Steve Wills arrived a short time later. Automatically, Katie briefed him on the night's events, handed over her beeper and felt his supportive clap on her shoulder.

"Has there been any more news of Mrs. Brentwood?" he asked.

Katie shook her head. Cee was still in surgery and might be for hours yet.

After Steve had gone, Katie rubbed her eyes wearily and looked at the other two occupants of the waiting room. Eric had dropped off into an uneasy sleep. Louis Halley was feeding yet another quarter into the telephone. After a few minutes, he came over to join her.

While the next several hours crept slowly by, Katie learned quite a lot about Louis as they talked to keep their minds off what was happening at that moment in an operating room. Louis wasn't a handsome man, but his iron-gray hair and rugged features gave the impression of strength. So did his tall, stocky body. "Celia and I haven't known each other very long," he confided to Katie, "but she's someone very special to me. She has been from the moment I first saw her! Of course, I don't know how she feels about me, but I'm sure going to stay right here until she can tell me."

"Louis, she thinks you're someone very special, too," Katie told him sincerely.

He beamed, and Katie looked down at her hands, knotted loosely in her lap. How she prayed that Cee really would recover and confirm those words to Louis! Love was such an important and special thing. Then, her thoughts turning grim again, Katie thought of Bryce with renewed resentment. She could forgive his having yelled at her, but if anything went wrong and Cee died, Katie was quite sure she would never forgive Bryce for letting her stepmother fall into Dr. Blakely's hands.

There had been at least three other neurosurgeons that Bryce could have insisted upon, yet he hadn't. He'd allowed Ash Blakely to be called instead. Was he playing a cynical game of hospital politics, staying on the good side of the chief of Neurosurgery—at Cee's expense? It was a hateful, ugly thought, but, at the moment, Katie did not feel especially charitable.

Hours seemed to have passed before Dr. Blakely reappeared, crossing the red line and ripping the mask from his mouth to talk with them. Bryce was right behind him, still dressed in greens. His face was impassive, Katie noticed, but he looked very tired.

"Mrs. Brentwood is doing well!" Dr. Blakely boomed and the sound of his voice awoke Eric. The child sat up sleepily.

"What—" Katie and Louis began in unison.

"I evacuated the blood clot. She's now in Recovery. She'll be unconscious for about seventy-two hours, then she ought to wake up and be ready for some company."

"Doctor, you really think . . ." Louis's voice trailed off hopefully.

"It couldn't have gone better!"

Dr. Blakely's eyes and his voice were a marvel of self-congratulation, Katie thought suspiciously.

"Thank you," she muttered. She supposed the man really had done his best. As Dr. Blakely walked away, Eric turned swiftly to Bryce with a flood of questions. Bryce replied patiently, but Katie could feel his glance on her own bent head.

As soon as Eric paused for breath, Louis stood up decisively. "You know what we're going to do now?"

he announced. "We're all going to the cafeteria and have something to eat. Come along, Eric. You'll feel even better after you've had a hamburger and some french fries."

Katie accompanied them dutifully, although she didn't think she could possibly eat, and she was surprised when Bryce tagged along with them. "How is Cee . . . really?" Katie hissed softly since Bryce was sure to know.

He shot her a look of surprise. "Why, she's just as Ash said." Katie felt Bryce's glance sharpening on her, observing her hostile eyes and set lips. "What's wrong, Katie? Are you mad because I shouted at you? If so, I apologize. I only yell when I'm scared and your news about Cee pretty well floored me when I was already at a bad point in a sticky operation."

"No, I'm not mad about that," Katie said, sotto voce.

"Then what? I know I said I'd join you as soon as I could, but my own surgery lasted longer than I thought—"

"No, it's not that either!" Katie snapped fiercely.

"Then what?" Bryce asked, sounding surprised and perplexed.

"I'll tell you what, Dr. Emerson! I was ready to demand a really good neurosurgeon—if not you, then someone equally adept—when you shouted me down. *You* let Cee be turned over to that pompous old fossil, Ash Blakely—"

"Wait just a minute!" Bryce caught Katie's arm in so tight a grip that she winced, and while his voice was still low it was also completely furious. "I allowed Ash to be called in because he's the best damned neurosurgeon I know! Why do you think he got to be chairman of the department? He may be getting on in years and maybe he's not a born organizer, but, lady, when it comes to cracking skulls Ash Blakely has no peers! He's a master of the old school, just as your dad was—"

"If you think I consider that any sort of recommendation—" Katie interrupted hotly, but Bryce didn't allow her to finish her sentence either.

"It's a recommendation, you can bet your fancy little panties on that! Max Brentwood and Ash Blakely and a half-dozen others like them began practicing when a referral to a neurosurgeon was like a patient receiving a death sentence. Max and Ash learned by watching their patients croak, and the rest of us have built on their hard-won knowledge and the desperate techniques they devised and their inventions like the Brentwood shunt. So you're damned right it's a recommendation. Max might have been a lousy husband and a rotten father, but he was one hell of a neurosurgeon!"

Bryce's attack left Katie seething and perfectly willing to fire another volley of her own until she saw Eric looking back anxiously at them. So she lifted her head in feigned indifference and walked on to join the others. Bryce fell into step beside her, his jaw set and his eyes still full of fire.

They were all seated over hamburgers when a shadow fell over the table and Katie glanced up to see Doug Sears. Bryce was scarcely polite, just grumping by way of greeting, while Katie introduced Eric and Louis.

Soberly, Doug expressed his concern over Cee, and as

he pulled up a fifth chair at the table, Katie could see
Eric's eyes studying him eagerly. "Are you the pilot
who flew in my mom?" he asked Doug.

"No, fella, that was another guy," Doug said a little
regretfully. "I've just come on duty." He turned to
Katie and opened his hand to show her a small velvet
box. "Take a look and see if you think my favorite nurse
will be pleased."

Katie unsnapped the box and stared down at a winking
solitaire diamond. "Oh, yes, Doug. She'll love it,"
Katie said almost wistfully.

Doug looked critically at the ring. "You don't think
the stone's too small?"

"No, it's in perfect taste." Katie didn't dare look up
at Bryce, but she could tell by his utter stillness that he
was attentive to every word.

"You're getting *married*, Sears?" he said abruptly.

"Yeah. Friday. Since Katie played cupid for us, I
wanted her to be sure and see this."

"Why, that's great news!" Bryce's voice took on a
new friendliness.

"What did Katie do?" Eric asked with his usual
curiosity.

"Why, she whispered a little word in my ear that my
gal was positively pining away without me!"

"Oh, Doug," Katie protested with a sigh, but the
pilot proceeded to tell the story with a little prompting
from the others.

At least Doug's presence had lightened the atmos-
phere, and when Katie, Louis and Eric returned to the
waiting room they were all better fortified by food and
friendship.

"I'll look in on my patient and Cee," Bryce announced. Pointedly, he turned to Katie. "I'll be here all night. Call me if you need anything."

"I need *you,* Bryce!" Katie wanted to cry, but she thought of Cee, whose fate was still so uncertain, and found that she couldn't say a word to Bryce in reply.

Chapter Twelve

At six the next morning, Katie roused herself from a half-sleep and went into the nearest ladies' room where she splashed cold water on her tired face and twisted her hair up into its familiar knot. She was only gone five minutes, but when she returned she saw that Bryce, clad in fresh greens, had joined Eric and Louis on the waiting room sofa.

Bryce started to stand up, but Katie stopped him with a gesture. He looked almost as tired as she did. Had his night been sleepless, too? His eyes meeting Katie's were expressionless, but at least they looked more blue than gray. She accepted that as a good sign.

"How's Cee?" she asked Bryce.

He hesitated, just long enough for Katie's spirits to plummet. "There's been no change, but, of course, we didn't expect one yet. She's unconscious, but stable."

Katie's eyes bored into him, demanded that he tell her the truth, but Bryce only spread his hands in a gesture more eloquent than words.

"The first several hours after surgery are always critical," he added. "She's receiving the best of care."

Before Katie could ask anything more, noise erupted in the hall. There were brisk footsteps, a tired child's fretful voice, and then Janet, Wade and small Jessica burst into the now-crowded waiting room.

Hugs. Tears. Handshakes and introductions. Briefly, Katie felt her niece thrust into her arms. "Hello, honey," she said, kissing the dark-haired Jessica's soft cheek, and that extracted a halfhearted smile from the grumpy little girl.

"My goodness, who's this pretty person who looks just like Aunt Katie?" Bryce's voice was whimsical as he bent over Katie and her niece.

Jessica glared up into the face of the strange man and let out a piercing shriek.

"Reminds me a bit of Aunt Katie, too," Bryce said, almost to himself. Shaking his head, he started tiredly down the hall. Katie longed to run after him, to ask more questions about Cee and, yes, to drop her head on his shoulder and tell him that she still loved him and always would, whatever . . . whatever. But Jessica wailed anew and clutched Katie's neck in a death grip.

Janet, efficient and competent as always, caught them in hand. "We'll go to Cee's house for breakfast. The children shouldn't be here, and we all need to rest. Katie, you look positively drained! Wade darling, bring our bags."

Wade looked well and fit, and his eyes followed his

wife adoringly. In Janet he had found a benign, loving dictator to smooth his path.

After everyone had rested and eaten, Janet organized them into relays. There was no need for all of them to be at the hospital at once, she argued logically. Cee's parents, who had now arrived, could take the morning shift. Janet and Wade would stay through the afternoon and early evening. Katie and Louis could keep the night vigil.

Katie agreed gratefully with her sister-in-law's logic. She did not want to be in charge, having to think and question and weigh decisions. Katie had had quite enough of decisions for the time being! But on one very important matter she was soon forced to take a stand.

"Wade and I want to talk to you, Katie," Janet announced that night as Katie was preparing to leave for the hospital. "Of course, we're so thankful that Celia is holding her own. But if—God forbid— she *doesn't* make it, we want you to know that we'll take in Eric. Why, we'd raise him right along with Jessica. Isn't that right, Wade?"

"Of course, Janet," Wade replied obediently, but Katie saw the involuntary tightening of her brother's face and knew that Wade would never be truly comfortable with a child who was so like Max Brentwood.

Eric's future happiness was too important to let Janet settle presumptuously. "That's wonderful of you to offer, Janet, but I think Eric would want to stay with me," Katie said firmly. "He knows me better and with all the shocks the poor kid has had, he doesn't need to be uprooted again."

"Katie, we'll decide about Eric later, if we have to," Janet said, flashing a sweet smile.

"No!" Katie insisted. "I want it established here and now that *I* assume responsibility for Eric."

"Janet, I think Sis is right," Wade contributed.

Janet looked from one to the other of them in surprise, finding herself outnumbered. Then she shrugged her shoulders. "Well, it won't be necessary, anyway. Celia's tough. She's going to make it!"

But was she? Katie wondered after the second disquieting day had slipped into the third. Of course, the seventy-two hours Dr. Blakely had predicted were not quite up, but Celia still lay unconscious and unresponsive. Cee's parents looked drawn and older by at least ten years while Eric had been crying again, silently and secretly, only his swollen eyes attesting to his private grief.

Poor little Eric! Katie's heart ached for the unhappy child. Eric's plight was a reminder to her that one could never entirely plan the future. Always there existed the possibility that a sudden change of events would occur, taking no notice of one's plans and dreams.

Even if I hadn't already decided not to go to Port Angeles, Cee's accident would have changed my plans, Katie thought. Tiredly, she leaned her head back against her waiting-room chair on this, the fourth night of her vigil. It promised to be another very long night, and Katie wished desperately that Bryce was here so that she could talk to him.

He had been carefully and studiously avoiding her, Katie knew. Oh, it wasn't blatantly obvious as Bryce stopped at least once daily to give Katie and Louis an encouraging word. He was courteous and pleasant, but his eyes remained gray and distant. They tended not to look directly at her, she had observed. To Katie, even her fights with Bryce had been preferable to this.

Earlier today she had shamelessly eavesdropped when Louis asked Bryce why he thought Cee had not yet awakened. "Seventy-two hours is an estimate, not an exact time frame," Bryce had said soothingly. "Every patient is different. I know Cee is strong and a fighter, but she's almost forty years old, without the strength and resilience of younger patients. She may need a little more time."

Louis had scowled, obviously finding the answer unsatisfactory, and Bryce soon found a reason to leave. Katie's eyes followed him, and she was alarmed by the thin gauntness of his face and limbs. Why, Bryce looked as though he'd lost ten or fifteen pounds since he'd come to Harwick Memorial and he'd had none to spare then! Still, nothing could lessen his attraction and desirability for Katie. Even the merest, casual glimpse of him made her pulse race and her skin tingle from memories. So she waited, and she worried, and whenever her concern over Cee lessened enough to allow her to think about anything else, her thoughts always flew to Bryce.

Now she stirred, sighing, as a brief burst of spring rain splattered gaily on the windows of the waiting room. The sound still triggered memories of Bryce—so many memories, past and present! Would there be only memories in her future?

Perhaps she owed Bryce an apology, Katie thought

wearily. I know my behavior was beastly the night of Cee's accident—but so was his! And Katie was still not convinced that Bryce's assessment of Dr. Ash Blakely had been correct. She had heard from her father of so many, many patients who simply never awoke but slept on and on, finally slipping into death.

"Coffee, Katie?" She looked up to see Louis extending a paper cup to her and she took it with a nod, grateful to stop her flow of morbid thoughts. What a faithful, wonderful man Louis was! Cee would be so lucky if only—

A soft cough spun them both about. Sheila Rigley stood there. Although she was not Cee's private nurse, her gratitude to Katie had led her to check on Celia regularly. Now Katie and Louis stared their questions at her.

"It may not mean anything," Sheila said half-apologetically, "but I have a hunch—"

"What?" said Louis swiftly.

"I think Celia's about ready to wake up," the nurse went on. "I was talking to her a few minutes ago while an aide changed her bed, and . . . well, I think her toes moved a little."

Hope flared immediately in Louis's face, but Katie tried to think more logically. Couldn't Sheila, wrapped in her happy engagement glow, have imagined the small movement?

"What I mean," Sheila went on doggedly, "is that Cee used to be a neuro nurse, right? Well, one of the first things we nurses ask patients to do, if they hear us, is wiggle their toes. So it may be a signal that she's beginning to wake up. Of course, it could also be just a muscle twitching.''

Louis turned to look inquiringly at Katie and now even her tired heart caught hope. In Katie's years as an administrator, she'd known of so many times when medical personnel—nurses, in particular—felt a hunch that later proved true. ''Thank you,'' she said fervently to Sheila.

After the nurse left them, Louis talked excitedly for a while, then he lapsed into a doze. It was a very quiet night, and for Steve Wills's sake Katie was grateful for that. He had been working long, late hours to cover both his shift and the one Katie usually worked.

At five in the morning Katie jerked awake; the well of confusion in which she'd been mired for the last several days had abruptly lifted. Cee was going to awaken and be all right! Katie felt certain of that in her heart, although there had been nothing further to warrant such a belief. The high-speed, fast-paced system of trauma medicine, which had saved so many other patients, had worked for Cee, too. She just *knew* it—and that meant that Bryce had been right.

Katie thought about him as she washed her face and straightened the clothes she'd slept in. She had not seen Bryce all night, yet she sensed that he was somewhere nearby. That invisible cord seemed to tug irresistibly on her heart. Nurses aren't the only ones who have hunches, Katie thought to herself as she went back into the waiting room.

Now she felt obsessed by the need to set matters right between the two of them. Also, Bryce would know what significance, if any, to attach to Cee's moving her toes. I'll find him and ask him, Katie decided. I'll ask him what's gone wrong between us, too. It's more than just those angry words we said. We love each other! We can forget the words. Oh, I guess I've been waiting for Bryce to come to *me* . . . but he came once. On that last night we spent together, Bryce came to me! Isn't it my turn now to go to him?

Before she could take any action, Steve Wills entered the waiting room. "Good, you're awake," he whispered to Katie and unclipped his beeper from his belt. "Cover me for the next thirty minutes, will you? If I don't get my last paycheck to the bank, my wife's checks will start bouncing all over Dallas!"

"You're going to the bank at this hour?" Katie said incredulously.

"Night depository," Steve said swiftly and was gone.

Katie took the beeper and clipped it to the waistband of her slacks. Across the room from her, Louis was still deep in sleep. A few rumbling noises escaped him as he breathed. Should I warn Cee that he snores? Katie wondered with a little smile. Oh, I'm glad Bryce doesn't!

Her thoughts returning to him, she walked to the wall phone and dialed. She asked her eager question of the night nurse who answered, and heard with disappointment the reply. Dr. Emerson had left at about ten the previous night. The nurse thought he was going away for the weekend.

"Oh," said Katie in deflated chagrin.

Before she could sit down again, Cee's private nurse

appeared, her face aglow. She gave Katie such a triumphant nod that Katie had to bite her lip to stop her sudden tears of joy and relief. Then she flew across the room and shook the sleeping man sprawled on the sofa.

"Louis, wake up!" Katie cried in delight. "Cee has!"

"Wh-what?" he said disbelievingly and stumbled up.

"Celia opened her eyes about five minutes ago," the nurse exclaimed. "She asked about you right away, Mr. Halley. She wanted to be sure you knew why she hadn't kept her date! Just give us a few minutes to get her prettied up and I'll let you see her."

"It's a miracle!" Louis said hoarsely and dashed for the phone.

Katie allowed him the pleasure of calling Cee's house, of arousing Eric, Cee's parents and Wade and Janet. Let Louis do the talking, the laughing and exclaiming. Let him be Cee's first visitor. Katie had an urgent matter of her own to attend to! Oh, damn, how long did it take Steve to drive to the bank?

Fifteen minutes later Steve returned—an eternity to the impatiently waiting Katie. "Everything's nice and quiet," she called over her shoulder as she ran toward the nearest exit.

"Hey!" Steve yelled after her, but Katie had already pushed through the door. She flew down a flight of stairs and plunged out into the grayish dawn. She saw a security guard, Elliot Wainwright, strolling along on the sidewalk below her and asked him to escort her to the garage.

Katie had another request as well, which she made hastily of Elliot as they rode up in the garage elevator.

"Get Dr. Emerson's answering service on the phone. Tell them to beep him. Tell him that Celia is awake and talking. And tell him to call Katie at home STAT! Got that?"

Elliot repeated the message back to be sure he had it, then Katie ran toward her car. She leaped inside and backed out swiftly.

She had driven only two blocks when she realized that she still wore the administrator's beeper clipped to her slacks. No wonder Steve had shouted after her!

Well, she wasn't about to drive back and return it. The hospital was still as a church and Steve could be reached either by phone or voice-paged over the hospital's loudspeaker system. Long before beepers were invented, administrators had managed to answer calls.

Katie drove home and noted with satisfaction that it had taken her only thirteen minutes. Had Bryce gotten her message yet? Or was he—heaven forbid!—out of the city or even the state?

Dawn was streaking the sky with pink and gold fingers when Katie parked her car and jumped out. Then she stopped, dumbfounded and delighted. Bryce sat on the outside stairs leading up to her apartment, his long legs stretched out in front of him.

Katie felt her lips forming an instinctive smile, but there was no answering smile on Bryce's grave face. Hadn't he gotten her message about Cee?

Katie climbed the stairs toward him on legs that felt weak, and her heart was busy doing its somersault act again. Bryce wore jeans and a white pullover shirt. Beard stubble darkened his cheeks, and his eyes looked

weary. Still, he was the most attractive man Katie had
ever seen. Of course love might have prejudiced her
opinion.

She stopped in front of him. "How in the world did
you get over here so fast?" she said, amazed.

"You said STAT." Slowly, Bryce stood up and
stretched. "I'm glad you didn't have George Parker
fired. He let me in."

"Oh," Katie murmured, leading the way to her
apartment. At the door she stopped and spun around.
"Bryce, you *did* get my message about Cee?"

He stood so close to her that his white-clad chest was
only inches away. Katie ached to reach up and touch
him. She looked into his deepset eyes and saw them
soften to their bluest. "Yes." He nodded. "Best news
I've had in a long time!"

"Same here!" Katie unlocked the door with hands
made unsteady by nervousness. Now that Bryce was
actually here, alone with her, what was she to say?

He provided no help. His face was so expressionless
that he might as well have worn his surgical mask. He
followed Katie inside, closed her door and leaned back
against it. "So what is STAT?" he asked quietly.

Katie set down her purse and looked back at him,
gripped by a sudden and uncharacteristic shyness. She
wished Bryce would step further inside the room,
coming closer to her. Instead he leaned against the door
as if it offered him a ready escape.

Katie drew an unsteady breath. "What's wrong,
Bryce?" she asked, realizing that nothing but the direct
approach would do.

"Wrong?" he repeated tonelessly. "Wrong with what?"

"Wrong between us." Katie heard the agonizing uncertainty in her voice and felt her hands clutch together for support.

"I don't know what you mean," Bryce said, but in his eyes gray storm clouds churned. "We've both been so worried about Cee—"

"You know what I mean! I thought what we shared was very, very special." Katie caught her trembling lower lip between her teeth. In a moment, she knew, her voice would tremble, too.

"Oh. That. Yes, it was special." Bryce might have been discussing the weather except that Katie saw his hands spread and flatten against the door behind him. "Well, Katie, I decided I'd better do the mature and sensible thing and stop trying to put roadblocks in your way."

"Why? I'm not going anywhere, you know," she said, and her voice did tremble now. Her hands shook as well and even the muscles of her abdomen began to quake with fear, the terrible grinding fear of having broached all of this too late.

"I know. I got your letter. But I think you ought to reconsider your decision to stay in Texas," Bryce said.

"Why?" Katie said fiercely.

She saw Bryce's eyes light momentarily with surprise, then that light faded and went out. "Why, because of Cee, of course." His voice took on a calm, professional tone. "Now that she's conscious, her recovery will be rapid. You needn't alter your plans on her behalf."

"I didn't change my plans because of Cee!" Katie cried, but her words elicited no response from him. Why, Bryce doesn't believe me, she thought dismally, and nothing—*nothing* about this scene is going the way I thought it would!

"Katie, you're a fine administrator," Bryce said coolly. "You shouldn't discard a splendid opportunity to further your career, especially since that's what you want so badly—"

"Stop it!" she cried agonizedly. "It's *not* what I want anymore! Didn't you happen to notice when my letter was dated?"

He frowned. "Yes. The day of Cee's accident—"

"I wrote it before I ever heard about Cee's accident! I certainly haven't had any time for letter writing since!" Katie said wildly.

"I hadn't thought about that." Again she saw a light flicker momentarily in his eyes. Again it disappeared too quickly, leaving them a chill silver gray.

"Oh, Bryce . . ." Katie felt as though she were strangling. "What about *us?*" Around her heart an awful, terrible pain began to throb.

"I'm trying to forget about us," he said evenly.

With whom? she wondered, jealousy surging through her. With Dr. Gloria Ashton, pediatrician and femme fatale?

She didn't say it aloud because she couldn't, not when Bryce was acting like such a polite, distant stranger.

"I see," Katie managed to gasp.

"Well, if that's settled to your satisfaction, I'll continue on my way to the lake. That's where I was headed when I got your message." Bryce's voice, in dismissal, was pleasant and courteous.

Let him go! Katie's pride cried. He doesn't want you! He doesn't need you at all! He couldn't make it more evident.

But her love for Bryce wouldn't allow him to leave her that easily. "Our last night meant nothing to you?" she demanded.

"Oh, yes. It meant something." His hands clenched into fists. "Later, I realized that it had meant good-bye."

Katie was so stunned that she couldn't utter another word. It must be *me*, she thought sickly. He doesn't like what he's seen of me lately. The lady administrator who questioned his decisions and obviously didn't trust him. Max Brentwood's headstrong, outspoken, iron-willed daughter!

Through eyes filling rapidly with hot, burning tears, she saw Bryce turn back to the door. In another moment he would go through it and out of her life forever.

Apparently, Katie wasn't struck dumb, after all, for she heard herself say suddenly, "Oh, Bryce, I'm so desperately sorry you feel like that!"

"*You're* sorry?" His hands dropped from the door-knob as he swung around to face her, and Katie realized that she had, at last, struck a nerve. Bryce's face paled and his eyes held such a tired, defeated look that the sight wrung her heart.

"You're sorry? I'm the one who's sorry, Katie! I did every damn thing wrong a man could do and I know it! I rushed you, scared you, tried to get a commitment from you too fast, even shouted at you and insulted you! I've done every single thing I said I wasn't going to do . . . because . . . because from that very first moment I had you in my arms again, I just couldn't seem to let you go!"

"Bryce!" Katie whispered, stunned again, this time by the despair in his eyes and voice.

"You want an explanation? I woke up early the other morning, here at your place, and realized that I've changed into a man I don't even recognize! I used to be nice and considerate and easy-going. Nurses enjoyed working with me. Now most of them would like to cut my throat! Did you know I was insanely jealous of Doug Sears? He was younger and so very good-looking! I didn't know, of course, that he was engaged. I thought he might be here, with you, that last night and if he had been I think I would have killed him! I acted like a barbarian, charging in here, grabbing you and carrying you off to bed—"

"I *loved* your grabbing me and carrying me off to bed!" Katie protested, her voice a strangled mixture of laughter and sobs. "Couldn't you tell?"

If Bryce even heard her words they didn't register. Beads of perspiration dotted his forehead and his own inner pain was so obvious and acute that Katie couldn't think of her own unhappiness but only of his.

"I haven't done a thing right," he muttered, his face grim and bleak.

"What on earth are you talking about?" Katie said in astonishment. "Why, Bryce, you've done any number of things right!"

''Name one,'' he said bitterly.

''You were certainly right about Dr. Blakely—and for that you have my apology and my grateful thanks! And—and what about when you rescued me from the garage?'' Katie went on persuasively. ''I probably owe you my life for that.''

''Yes, I'm glad about Cee—and you,'' Bryce admitted with a sigh. He gave his head a shake. ''I've been so torn up, I guess I haven't been thinking straight.''

Katie could understand that. Under the emotional impact of the past few days her own thoughts had been wildly erratic.

''Oh, Bryce, you must have done a few other things right as well,'' Katie went on, daring now to be brave. ''You've made me fall madly in love with you all over again!''

His dark head jerked up; his eyes searched her face. ''When you look at me like *that* . . .'' he said huskily.

''That's how much I love you,'' Katie said clearly and distinctly. ''I thought you saw it before.''

''I did . . . in your beautiful bedroom eyes. But my confidence has been shot to hell! I just couldn't believe . . .'' Words failed him for a moment. ''But, Katie, you *wanted* to go back to Washington! You wanted to look after crippled kids! To walk through the rain forest and sit by the Pacific Ocean—''

''It was a fine dream for a single lady,'' she agreed. ''But how could I possibly enjoy it now? Oh, Bryce, you wouldn't be with me! I'd look at that lovely forest and want you by my side. I'd sit by the sea and long for the sound of your voice. I'd see the children rehabilitated and sent home to their parents, but I wouldn't have my own children, yours and mine! I love you! I've never loved any man but you and I know now I never will!"

Katie stopped, on the verge of tears again. She saw that Bryce looked just as stunned as she'd been earlier. "I *belong* with you," she said, her voice quivering. "I always did. It just took me a little while to wake up and know it. Oh, Bryce, do you still love *me?*"

The sight of his face gave her the answer she sought. His eyes filled with a yearning tenderness. "God, yes!" At last Bryce stepped away from the door and came toward her slowly. "Haven't you noticed? I love you so much I'm not even rational on the subject! I can't shake the feeling that we were absolutely meant to be together." Huskiness roughened his voice. "Oh, yes, I love you, Katie Brentwood. If you'll let me, I'll give you the world!"

With that, Katie's tears began to fall. "Bryce, if I can just have you, I'll have the whole world!"

He reached her side and his hand came up to touch her face gently, warmly. One large, trembling thumb brushed away Katie's tears.

She turned her head and her lips met the palm of his hand. A soft exclamation escaped him. Then, as if Bryce could restrain himself no longer, his arms clasped her to him. His mouth, warm and hungry for her tenderness, captured her lips and pressed them to his own again and again. Joy surged through Katie like a life-giving flame. Bryce kissed her as though he would never stop, deep and searching kisses that demanded all her love, and Katie knew she was kissing him back in exactly the same way. Their kisses lingered—reassuring, pledging, promising—and neither seemed able to tear away from the other. Bryce's hands stroked Katie's hair and her own sought to ease the tense muscles she felt in his neck and back. Gradually, under her touch, she could feel him begin to respond.

Bryce had told her before that he needed her, but not until this moment, when Katie felt the effect of her loving, healing touch, had she fully appreciated just how deep his need was. She was the chink in his armor, too. Without her he was vulnerable, miserable, lacking the confidence he required both as a surgeon and as a man.

Bryce had told her the truth about himself when he had said that he was just a man, "normal and human, smart and stupid, kind and thoughtless." He had been describing the human condition, hers no less than his. Kathryn Brentwood had learned that at last.

Slowly, Bryce's body shifted. He cradled Katie against him in a way that held the promise of desire yet was even stronger than passion. Their greatest need now, at this moment, was simply for the comfort of each other's love.

All at once the beeper clipped to Katie's waist began to shrill.

"Duty calls," Bryce murmured against her lips as the beeper continued its insistent, pulsing demand.

"Oh, for—" Breathlessly, Katie smothered her irritation at the beeper and switched it on reluctantly.

"Administrator on call!" shouted a panicky male voice. "There's a woman in the doctors' locker room! She's in the shower . . . stark naked!"

Firmly, Katie switched off the beeper. She unclipped it and set it down beside her purse. "First things first," she said with a shaky little smile and reached again for Bryce with eager arms.

"But the doctors' locker room!" he said, his face astounded. Then his expression gave way to laughter. "Imagine a naked woman *there!*"

"They're big boys. Let them work it out. I'm more interested in working this out," Katie said and went up on tiptoes to meet Bryce's warm receptive lips with her own.

He smiled at her then, that radiant, curving, flashing smile that she loved to see. He caught her close and kissed her again, his lips as ardent as hers.

Katie was scarcely aware of their moving toward the sofa until they were lying down with Bryce stretched out on his back, molding her against him. Katie's cheek rested over the strong, steady beat of his heart and her body nestled in the haven of his arms. They still clutched each other tightly, shaken by the realization of how close they had come to losing one another once again. She had almost let him go; he had almost given her up. Bryce drew her closer for another kiss.

"Marry me?" he whispered when he could finally wrench his lips from Katie's.

"Yes! When?"

"Next weekend OK?"

"I don't have another thing planned!" She stopped to bestow another kiss. "Oh, Bryce, could we get married in the hospital chapel like Sheila and Doug are doing?"

"Fine!" His lips caressed her eyebrows, her eyelids and the tip of her nose.

Katie burrowed her arms beneath the warmth of his,

hugging him fiercely. "And you'll be yourself once again? That nice, considerate, easy-going man . . ."

"Absolutely—as long as you're not running off to distant places without me or dangling a handsome flyboy in my face!" he said with a mock growl.

"No more of that," Katie promised.

She saw his face grow serious. "You're sure you don't mind my being a doctor?" Bryce asked.

"No. I think I've made peace with the memory of Max Brentwood. You're not like him—you never were." Ruefully, Katie added, "But I'm a lot like him, aren't I?"

"Oh, just a bit," Bryce said kindly. "You have his strength, his daring and bravery. You excel at what you do. Those are the only resemblances I see, Katie."

"You'll have to help me find another job," Katie warned. "Trauma medicine really is fantastic, but I still want to work at a hospital that helps kids."

"I already have a job in mind for you," Bryce confided. "It's the new rehab hospital for young patients with spinal injuries. I'll tell you all about it"—he stopped as Katie's mouth moved toward his—"later!"

"Later," she agreed, and their lips came together again.

A few short days and counting . . .

Genuine Silhouette sterling silver bookmark for only $15.95!

What a beautiful way to hold your place in your current romance! This genuine sterling silver bookmark, with the distinctive Silhouette symbol in elegant black, measures 1½" long and 1" wide. It makes a beautiful gift for yourself, and for every romantic you know! And, at only $15.95 each, including all postage and handling charges, you'll want to order several now, while supplies last.

Send your name and address with check or money order for $15.95 per bookmark ordered to
Simon & Schuster Enterprises
120 Brighton Rd., P.O. Box 5020
Clifton, N.J. 07012
Attn: Bookmark

Bookmarks can be ordered pre-paid only. No charges will be accepted. Please allow 4-6 weeks for delivery.

Silhouette Special Edition

MORE ROMANCE FOR
A SPECIAL WAY TO RELAX
$1.95 each

2 ☐ Hastings	21 ☐ Hastings	41 ☐ Halston	60 ☐ Thorne
3 ☐ Dixon	22 ☐ Howard	42 ☐ Drummond	61 ☐ Beckman
4 ☐ Vitek	23 ☐ Charles	43 ☐ Shaw	62 ☐ Bright
5 ☐ Converse	24 ☐ Dixon	44 ☐ Eden	63 ☐ Wallace
6 ☐ Douglass	25 ☐ Hardy	45 ☐ Charles	64 ☐ Converse
7 ☐ Stanford	26 ☐ Scott	46 ☐ Howard	65 ☐ Cates
8 ☐ Halston	27 ☐ Wisdom	47 ☐ Stephens	66 ☐ Mikels
9 ☐ Baxter	28 ☐ Ripy	48 ☐ Ferrell	67 ☐ Shaw
10 ☐ Thiels	29 ☐ Bergen	49 ☐ Hastings	68 ☐ Sinclair
11 ☐ Thornton	30 ☐ Stephens	50 ☐ Browning	69 ☐ Dalton
12 ☐ Sinclair	31 ☐ Baxter	51 ☐ Trent	70 ☐ Clare
13 ☐ Beckman	32 ☐ Douglass	52 ☐ Sinclair	71 ☐ Skillern
14 ☐ Keene	33 ☐ Palmer	53 ☐ Thomas	72 ☐ Belmont
15 ☐ James	35 ☐ James	54 ☐ Hohl	73 ☐ Taylor
16 ☐ Carr	36 ☐ Dailey	55 ☐ Stanford	74 ☐ Wisdom
17 ☐ John	37 ☐ Stanford	56 ☐ Wallace	75 ☐ John
18 ☐ Hamilton	38 ☐ John	57 ☐ Thornton	76 ☐ Ripy
19 ☐ Shaw	39 ☐ Milan	58 ☐ Douglass	77 ☐ Bergen
20 ☐ Musgrave	40 ☐ Converse	59 ☐ Roberts	78 ☐ Gladstone

$2.25 each

79 ☐ Hastings	87 ☐ Dixon	95 ☐ Doyle	103 ☐ Taylor
80 ☐ Douglass	88 ☐ Saxon	96 ☐ Baxter	104 ☐ Wallace
81 ☐ Thornton	89 ☐ Meriwether	97 ☐ Shaw	105 ☐ Sinclair
82 ☐ McKenna	90 ☐ Justin	98 ☐ Hurley	106 ☐ John
83 ☐ Major	91 ☐ Stanford	99 ☐ Dixon	107 ☐ Ross
84 ☐ Stephens	92 ☐ Hamilton	100 ☐ Roberts	108 ☐ Stephens
85 ☐ Beckman	93 ☐ Lacey	101 ☐ Bergen	109 ☐ Beckman
86 ☐ Halston	94 ☐ Barrie	102 ☐ Wallace	110 ☐ Browning

Silhouette Special Edition

$2.25 each

111 ☐ Thorne	133 ☐ Douglass	155 ☐ Lacey	177 ☐ Howard
112 ☐ Belmont	134 ☐ Ripy	156 ☐ Hastings	178 ☐ Bishop
113 ☐ Camp	135 ☐ Seger	157 ☐ Taylor	179 ☐ Meriwether
114 ☐ Ripy	136 ☐ Scott	158 ☐ Charles	180 ☐ Jackson
115 ☐ Halston	137 ☐ Parker	159 ☐ Camp	181 ☐ Browning
116 ☐ Roberts	138 ☐ Thornton	160 ☐ Wisdom	182 ☐ Thornton
117 ☐ Converse	139 ☐ Halston	161 ☐ Stanford	183 ☐ Sinclair
118 ☐ Jackson	140 ☐ Sinclair	162 ☐ Roberts	184 ☐ Daniels
119 ☐ Langan	141 ☐ Saxon	163 ☐ Halston	185 ☐ Gordon
120 ☐ Dixon	142 ☐ Bergen	164 ☐ Ripy	186 ☐ Scott
121 ☐ Shaw	143 ☐ Bright	165 ☐ Lee	187 ☐ Stanford
122 ☐ Walker	144 ☐ Meriwether	166 ☐ John	188 ☐ Lacey
123 ☐ Douglass	145 ☐ Wallace	167 ☐ Hurley	189 ☐ Ripy
124 ☐ Mikels	146 ☐ Thornton	168 ☐ Thornton	190 ☐ Wisdom
125 ☐ Cates	147 ☐ Dalton	169 ☐ Beckman	191 ☐ Hardy
126 ☐ Wildman	148 ☐ Gordon	170 ☐ Paige	192 ☐ Taylor
127 ☐ Taylor	149 ☐ Claire	171 ☐ Gray	
128 ☐ Macomber	150 ☐ Dailey	172 ☐ Hamilton	
129 ☐ Rowe	151 ☐ Shaw	173 ☐ Belmont	
130 ☐ Carr	152 ☐ Adams	174 ☐ Dixon	
131 ☐ Lee	153 ☐ Sinclair	175 ☐ Roberts	
132 ☐ Dailey	154 ☐ Malek	176 ☐ Walker	

SILHOUETTE SPECIAL EDITION, Department SE/2
1230 Avenue of the Americas
New York, NY 10020

Please send me the books I have checked above. I am enclosing $_____
(please add 75¢ to cover postage and handling. NYS and NYC residents please
add appropriate sales tax). Send check or money order—no cash or C.O.D.'s
please. Allow six weeks for delivery.

NAME _____

ADDRESS _____

CITY _____ STATE/ZIP _____